REALM OF DRAGONS

A DIRGE FOR PRINCES (Book #4)
A JEWEL FOR ROYALS (BOOK #5)
A KISS FOR QUEENS (BOOK #6)
A CROWN FOR ASSASSINS (Book #7)
A CLASP FOR HEIRS (Book #8)

OF CROWNS AND GLORY
SLAVE, WARRIOR, QUEEN (Book #1)
ROGUE, PRISONER, PRINCESS (Book #2)
KNIGHT, HEIR, PRINCE (Book #3)
REBEL, PAWN, KING (Book #4)
SOLDIER, BROTHER, SORCERER (Book #5)
HERO, TRAITOR, DAUGHTER (Book #6)
RULER, RIVAL, EXILE (Book #7)
VICTOR, VANQUISHED, SON (Book #8)

KINGS AND SORCERERS
RISE OF THE DRAGONS (Book #1)
RISE OF THE VALIANT (Book #2)
THE WEIGHT OF HONOR (Book #3)
A FORGE OF VALOR (Book #4)
A REALM OF SHADOWS (Book #5)
NIGHT OF THE BOLD (Book #6)

THE SORCERER'S RING
A QUEST OF HEROES (Book #1)
A MARCH OF KINGS (Book #2)
A FATE OF DRAGONS (Book #3)
A CRY OF HONOR (Book #4)
A VOW OF GLORY (Book #5)
A CHARGE OF VALOR (Book #6)
A RITE OF SWORDS (Book #7)
A GRANT OF ARMS (Book #8)
A SKY OF SPELLS (Book #9)
A SEA OF SHIELDS (Book #10)

REALM OF DRAGONS

(Age of the Sorcerers—Book One)

MORGAN RICE

MORGAN RICE

Morgan Rice is the #1 bestselling and USA Today bestselling author of the epic fantasy series THE SORCERER'S RING, comprising seventeen books; of the #1 bestselling series THE VAMPIRE JOURNALS, comprising twelve books; of the #1 bestselling series THE SURVIVAL TRILOGY, a post-apocalyptic thriller comprising three books; of the epic fantasy series KINGS AND SORCERERS, comprising six books; of the epic fantasy series OF CROWNS AND GLORY, comprising eight books; of the epic fantasy series A THRONE FOR SISTERS, comprising eight books; of the new science fiction series THE INVASION CHRONICLES, comprising four books; of the fantasy series OLIVER BLUE AND THE SCHOOL FOR SEERS, comprising four books; of the fantasy series THE WAY OF STEEL, comprising four books; and of the new fantasy series AGE OF THE SORCERERS. Morgan's books are available in audio and print editions, and translations are available in over 25 languages.

TURNED (Book #1 in the Vampire Journals), ARENA 1 (Book #1 of the Survival Trilogy), A QUEST OF HEROES (Book #1 in the Sorcerer's Ring), RISE OF THE DRAGONS (Kings and Sorcerers—Book #1), A THRONE FOR SISTERS (Book #1), TRANSMISSION (The Invasion Chronicles—Book #1), and THE MAGIC FACTORY (Oliver Blue and the School for Seers—Book One) are each available as a free download on Amazon!

Morgan loves to hear from you, so please feel free to visit www.morganricebooks.com to join the email list, receive a free book, receive free giveaways, download the free app, get the latest exclusive news, connect on Facebook and Twitter, and stay in touch!

SELECT ACCLAIM FOR MORGAN RICE

"If you thought that there was no reason left for living after the end of THE SORCERER'S RING series, you were wrong. In RISE OF THE DRAGONS Morgan Rice has come up with what promises to be another brilliant series, immersing us in a fantasy of trolls and dragons, of valor, honor, courage, magic and faith in your destiny. Morgan has managed again to produce a strong set of characters that make us cheer for them on every page.... Recommended for the permanent library of all readers that love a well-written fantasy."
                    —*Books and Movie Reviews* Roberto Mattos

"An action packed fantasy sure to please fans of Morgan Rice's previous novels, along with fans of works such as THE INHERITANCE CYCLE by Christopher Paolini.... Fans of Young Adult Fiction will devour this latest work by Rice and beg for more."
    —*The Wanderer, A Literary Journal* (regarding *Rise of the Dragons*)

"A spirited fantasy that weaves elements of mystery and intrigue into its story line. *A Quest of Heroes* is all about the making of courage and about realizing a life purpose that leads to growth, maturity, and excellence ....For those seeking meaty fantasy adventures, the protagonists, devices, and action provide a vigorous set of encounters that focus well on Thor's evolution from a dreamy child to a young adult facing impossible odds for survival ....Only the beginning of what promises to be an epic young adult series."
                —*Midwest Book Review* (D. Donovan, eBook Reviewer)

"THE SORCERER'S RING has all the ingredients for an instant success: plots, counterplots, mystery, valiant knights, and blossoming relationships replete with broken hearts, deception and betrayal. It will keep you entertained for hours, and will satisfy all ages. Recommended for the permanent library of all fantasy readers."

—*Books and Movie Reviews*, Roberto Mattos

"In this action-packed first book in the epic fantasy Sorcerer's Ring series (which is currently 14 books strong), Rice introduces readers to 14-year-old Thorgrin "Thor" McLeod, whose dream is to join the Silver Legion, the elite knights who serve the king…. Rice's writing is solid and the premise intriguing."

—*Publishers Weekly*

TABLE OF CONTENTS

CHAPTER ONE

King Godwin III of the Northern Kingdom had seen many things in his time. He'd seen the march of armies and the working of magic, but right now he could only stare at the body of the creature that lay before him, prostrate and unmoving on the grass, its bones and its scales lending a sense of impossibility to the moment in the evening light.

The king dismounted his horse, which was refusing to get any closer, whether because of what the creature was, or simply where they were. They'd ridden more than a day south of Royalsport, so that the roar of the Slate River was just a few dozen yards away, the land of his kingdom dropping away into those roaring, steely, violent waters. Beyond it, there might be watchers staring out from the south, even across its vast width. Godwin hoped not, and not just because he and the others were so far from home, open to any who could get over the bridges between the kingdoms. He didn't want them seeing this.

King Godwin stepped forward, while around him the small crowd that had come with him tried to work out whether they should do the same. There weren't many of them, because this ... this wasn't something he was sure he wanted people to see. His eldest son, Rodry, was there, twenty-three and looking like the man Godwin had once been, tall and powerfully built, with light hair shaved at the temples so it wouldn't obscure his swordsmanship, in the one reminder of his mother. Rodry's brothers, Vars and Greave, were still at home, neither the kind of man to ride out on something like this. Vars would probably complain that Rodry had been chosen for this—not that Vars would ever volunteer for anything with the hint of danger. Greave would be stuck in the library with his books.

His daughters were frankly more likely to have come, or at least two of them were. The youngest, Erin, would have relished the adventure. Nerra would have wanted to see the strangeness of the creature, probably cried over its death in spite of what it was. Godwin smiled at the thought of her kindness, although as always, that smile faded slightly at the thought of her latest coughing fit, and of the sickness that they kept so carefully concealed. Lenore would probably have preferred to stay in the castle, but then, she had a wedding to prepare for.

Instead of any of the others, it was Godwin and Rodry. There were half a dozen Knights of the Spur with him, Lars and Borus, Halfin and Twell, Ursus and Jorin, all men Godwin trusted, who had served him well for decades in some cases, their armor embossed with the symbols they'd chosen, shining slightly in the spray from the river. There were the villagers who had found this thing, and there, on a sickly-looking horse, was the robed figure of his sorcerer.

"Grey," King Godwin said, waving the man forward.

Master Grey stepped forward slowly, leaning on his staff.

In other circumstances, King Godwin would have laughed at the contrast between them. Grey was slender and shaven headed, skin so pale it almost matched his name, with robes of white and gold. Godwin was larger, broad shouldered and frankly broad bellied these days, armored and full bearded, with dark hair down to his shoulders.

"Do you think they're lying about this?" King Godwin said, with a jerk of his head toward the villagers.

Godwin knew the ways men tried, with cow bones and leather plates, but his sorcerer didn't answer his question. Grey merely shook his head and looked him straight in the eye.

A shiver ran up Godwin's spine. There was no doubting the realness of this. This wasn't some joke, to try and gain favor or money or both.

This was a dragon.

Its scales were the red of blood poured over rusted iron. Its teeth were like ivory, as long as a man was tall, and its claws were razor edged. Great wings spread out, ragged and torn through, huge and bat-like, seeming barely enough to hold such a great beast aloft. The creature's body curled on the ground, longer than a dozen horses, large enough that in life it could have lifted Godwin like a toy.

"I've never seen one before," King Godwin admitted, placing a hand against the scaled hide. He half expected it to be warm, but instead, it was only the cold stillness of death.

"Few have," Grey said. Where Godwin's voice was a deep, sonorous thing, Grey's was like the whisper of paper.

The king nodded. Of course the sorcerer wouldn't say all that he knew. It wasn't a thought that comforted him. To see a dragon now, and a dead one…

"What do we know about this one?" the king asked. He walked down the length of it, to the remains of the tail, which stretched out impossibly long behind it.

"A female," the sorcerer said, "and red—with all that implies."

Of course, he didn't explain what it implied. The sorcerer walked around it, looking thoughtful. Occasionally, he glanced back inland, as if calculating something.

"How did it die?" Godwin asked. He'd been in battles in his time, but he couldn't see the wound of axe or sword on the creature, couldn't imagine what weapon could harm such a beast.

"Perhaps…just age."

Godwin stared back.

"I thought they were supposed to live forever," Godwin said. In that moment, he wasn't a king, but the boy who had first gone to Grey all those years ago, seeking help and knowledge. The sorcerer had seemed old even then.

"Not forever. A thousand years, born only on the dragon moon," Grey said, sounding as though he were quoting something.

"A thousand years is still too many for us to find one dead here, now," King Godwin said. "I don't like it. It feels too much like an omen."

3

"Possibly," Grey admitted, and he was rarely a man to admit anything like that. "Death is sometimes a powerful omen. Sometimes it is just death. And sometimes, it is life, too."

He glanced back again toward the kingdom.

King Godwin sighed, despairing of ever truly understanding the man, then kept staring at the beast, trying to determine how something so powerful, so magnificent, could have died. There were no signs of battle upon it, no obvious wounds. He stared into the creature's eyes as if they might provide him with some kind of answers.

"Father?" Rodry called out.

King Godwin turned to his son. He looked much as Godwin had at that age, muscled and powerful, though with a trace of his mother's good looks and lighter hair to remind him of her now she was gone. He sat atop a charger, his armor inlaid with shining blue. He looked impatient at the prospect of being stuck there, doing nothing. Probably, when he'd heard that there was a dragon, he'd been hoping he might get to *fight* one. He was still young enough to think he could win against everything.

The knights around him waited patiently for their king's instructions.

King Godwin knew there was only so much time they should be out. So close to the river, there was a risk of the southerners slipping across one of the bridges, and it was getting dark.

"Take too long and the queen will think we're both trying to get out of the wedding preparations," Rodry pointed out. "It will take us long enough to get back, even riding hard."

There was that. With Lenore's wedding just a week away, Aethe wasn't likely to be forgiving about it, especially not if he was off with Rodry. Despite his efforts, she still thought that he favored his three sons by Illia over the three daughters she'd given him.

"We'll get back soon enough," King Godwin said. "First, though, we need to do something about this." King Godwin glanced over to Grey before he continued. "If people hear about a dragon, let alone a dead dragon, they'll think it's an ill omen, and I'll not have ill omens the week of Lenore's wedding."

"No, of course not," Rodry said, looking ashamed that he hadn't thought of it himself. "So what do we do?"

The king had already thought of that. He walked over to the villagers first, taking out what coin he had.

"You have my thanks for telling me about this," he said, passing them the coins. "Now return to your homes and tell no one what you've seen. You were not here, this did not happen. If I hear otherwise..."

They took the unspoken threat, bowing hastily.

"Yes, my king," one said, before they both hurried off.

"Now," he said, turning to Rodry and the knights. "Ursus, you're the strongest; let's see how much strength you actually have. Fetch ropes, one of you, so we can all drag the beast."

The largest of his knights nodded in approval, and all of them set to work, rooting through saddlebags until one came out with some thick ropes. Trust Twell the planner to have everything needed.

They tied the remains of the dragon, taking longer than King Godwin would have liked. The sheer bulk of the beast seemed to resist attempts to contain it, so that Jorin, ever the nimblest, had to clamber over the creature with a rope over his shoulders to tie it. He leapt down lightly, even in his armor. Eventually though, they got it lashed together. The king went down to them and took hold of the rope.

"Well?" he said to the others. "Do you think I'm going to haul this into the Slate by myself?"

There was a time when he might have, when he'd been as strong as Ursus, aye, or Rodry. Now though, he knew himself well enough to know when he needed help. The men there got the message and took the rope. King Godwin felt the moment when his son started to lend his strength to the effort, pushing at the dragon's corpse from the far side, groaning with the effort.

Slowly, it started to move, leaving tracks in the dirt as they shifted its bulk. Only Grey didn't add his efforts to the rope, and frankly they would have barely counted for much anyway. Step by step, the group of them got the dragon closer to the river.

Finally, they made it to the edge, getting it poised at the point where the ground fell away toward the river that was both the kingdom's border and its defense. It sat there, so perfectly poised that a breath could have taken it over, briefly looking to King Godwin as if it were perched ready to fly out toward the southerners' lands.

He set a boot against its flank and, with a cry of effort, kicked it over the edge.

"It's done," he said as it hit the water with a splash.

It didn't disappear, though. Instead, it bobbed there, the sheer ferocity of the steel-gray waters enough to carry it away downstream, the dragon's body bumping off rocks and twisting in the current. It was a current against which no man could swim, and against which even the dragon's weight was a tiny thing. It was pulled down in the direction of the waiting sea, those dark waters rushing to join up with the greater body of them.

"Let us just hope that it hasn't laid its clutch," Grey murmured.

King Godwin stood there, too tired to question the man, watching the creature's corpse until it was out of sight. He told himself that it was because he wanted to be sure it didn't wash back into his kingdom, didn't come back to cause trouble again. He told himself that he was just catching his breath, because he was hardly a young man anymore.

It wasn't the truth, though. The truth was that he was worried. He'd ruled his kingdom a long time, and he'd never seen the likes of this before. For it to occur now, something was happening.

And King Godwin knew that, whatever it was, it was about to affect the whole kingdom.

CHAPTER TWO

Devin dreamed, finding himself in a place far beyond the forge where he worked, beyond even the city of Royalsport where he and his family lived. He dreamed often, and in his dreams, he could go anywhere, be anything. In his dreams, he could be the knight that he'd always wanted to be.

This dream was a strange one, though. For one thing, he *knew* that he was in a dream, where normally he didn't. It meant that he could walk it, and it seemed to shift as he looked at it, letting him create landscapes around him.

It was as if he were floating over the kingdom. Down below he could see the land spread out beneath him, the north and the south, split by the Slate River, and Leveros, the monks' isle, off to the east. In the far north, on the very fringes of the kingdom, five or six days' ride away, he could see the volcanoes that had lain dormant for years. Far to the west, he could just spot the Third Continent, the one people talked of in whispers, in awe of the things that lived there.

It was a dream, yet it was, he knew, a remarkably accurate view of the kingdom.

Now he wasn't above the world. Now he was in a dark space, and there was something in there with him: a shape that filled that space, the scent of it musty, dry, and reptilian. A flicker of light glimmered off scales, and in the half-dark, he thought he could hear the rustle of movement, along with breathing like bellows. In his dream, Devin could feel his fear rising, his hand closing around the hilt of a sword reflexively, lifting a blade of blue-black metal.

Great golden eyes opened in the dark, and another flicker of light came. By it, he could see a great, dark-scaled body on a scale he had never seen before, wings curled and mouth wide open to reveal a light within. Devin had a moment to realize that it was a flicker of flame coming from the creature's mouth, and then there was nothing *but* flame, surrounding him, filling the world...

The flames gave way, and now he was sitting in a room whose walls formed a circle, like it was at the top of a tower. The place was filled from floor to ceiling with oddments that must have been collected from a dozen times and places; silk screens covered the walls, while there were brass objects on shelves that Devin couldn't begin to guess the purpose of.

There was a man there, sitting cross-legged in a rare patch of open space, in a chalk circle surrounded by candles. He was bald and serious looking, his eyes fixed on Devin. He wore rich robes embroidered with sigils, and jewelry that embodied mystical patterns.

"Do you know me?" Devin asked as he got closer.

A long silence followed, one so long that Devin began to wonder if he had even asked the question.

"The stars said that if I waited here, in dreams, you would come," the voice finally said. "The one who is to be."

Devin realized then who this man was.

"You're Master Grey, the king's sorcerer."

He swallowed at the thought of it. They said that this man had the power to see things that no sane man would want to; that he'd told the king the moment of his first wife's death and everyone had laughed until the fainting fit had struck her, cracking her head on the stone of one of the bridges. They said that he could look into a man's soul and draw out all he saw there.

The one who is to be.

What could that mean?

"You are Master Grey."

"And you are the boy born on the most impossible of days. I have looked and looked, and you should not exist. But you do."

8

Devin's heart raced at the thought that the king's sorcerer knew who he was. Why would a man like this take an interest in him?

And he knew, at that moment, that this was more than just a dream.

This was a meeting.

"What do you want from me?" Devin asked.

"Want?" The question seemed almost to catch the sorcerer by surprise, if anything could. "I merely wanted to see you for myself. To see you on the day that your life will change forever."

Devin burned with questions, but in that moment, Master Grey reached down for one of the candles around him, snuffing it with two long fingers while he murmured something on the edge of hearing.

Devin wanted to step forward, wanted to comprehend what was happening, but instead, he felt a force he couldn't understand dragging him backwards, out of the tower, into the dark...

"Devin!" his mother called. "Wake up, or you'll miss breakfast."

Devin cursed as his eyes snapped open. Already, dawn light was coming in through the window of his family's small home. It meant that if he didn't hurry, he wouldn't be able to get to the House of Weapons early enough, wouldn't have time for anything except plunging straight into work.

He lay in bed, breathing hard, trying to shake off the heaviness, the realness, of the dreams.

But try as he did, he could not. It hung over him like a heavy cloak.

"DEVIN!"

Devin shook his head.

He jumped from bed and hurried to dress. His clothes were simple, plain things, patched in places. Some were hand-me-downs from his father, which didn't fit well since, at sixteen, Devin was still more slender than him, no bigger than average for a boy his age, even if he was a little taller. He brushed dark hair out of his eyes with hands that had their share of the small burn marks and cuts that came from the House of Weapons, knowing that it would be worse when he was older. Old Gund could barely move some of his fingers, the effort of the work had taken so much from him.

Devin dressed and hurried to the kitchen of his family's cottage home. He sat there, eating stew at the kitchen table with his mother and father. He mopped at it with a piece of hard bread, knowing that even though it was simple stuff, he would need it for the hard day of work to come in the House of Weapons. His mother was a small, birdlike woman, who looked so fragile next to him that it seemed as if she might break beneath the weight of the work she did every day, yet she never did.

His father was also shorter than him, but broad and muscled, and hard like teak. Each of his hands was like a hammer, and there were tattoos running along his forearms that hinted of other places, from the Southern Kingdom to the lands on the far side of the sea. There was even a small map there, showing both lands, but also the isle of Leveros and the continent of Sarras, so far across the sea.

"Why are you staring at my arms, boy?" his father asked, his voice rough. He wasn't a man who had ever been good at showing affection. Even when Devin had gotten his position in the House, even when he'd shown himself able to make weapons as fine as the best masters, his father had done little more than nod.

Devin desperately wanted to tell him of his dream. But he knew better not to. His father would belittle him, launch into a jealous rage.

"Just a tattoo I haven't seen," Devin said. Ordinarily, his father wore longer sleeves, and Devin was rarely there long enough to look. "Why does this one have Sarras and Leveros on it? Did you go there when you were a—"

"That's none of your business!" his father snapped, his anger curiously at odds with the simple question. He hurriedly pulled down his sleeves, tying the stays at the wrists so that Devin couldn't see any more. "There are things you don't ask about!"

"I'm sorry," Devin said. There were days when Devin barely knew what to say to his father; days when he barely even felt like his son. "I should get to work."

"So early? You're going to practice the sword again, aren't you?" his father demanded. "You're still trying to be a knight."

He seemed genuinely angry, and Devin couldn't begin to work out why.

"Would that be such a terrible thing?" Devin asked tentatively.

"Know your place, boy," his father spat. "You're no knight. Just a commoner—like the rest of us."

Devin bit back an angry response. He didn't have to go to work for at least an hour yet, but he knew that to stay was to risk an argument, like all the arguments that had come before it.

He stood, not even bothering to finish his meal, and walked out.

A muted sunlight hit him. Around him, most of the city was still asleep, quiet in the earliest part of the morning, even those who worked by night having returned home. It meant that Devin had most of the streets to himself as he made his way to the House of Weapons, running over the cobbles, working hard. The sooner he made it there, the more time he would have, and in any case, he'd heard the sword masters there tell their students that this sort of exercise was vital if they were to have stamina in combat. Devin wasn't sure if any of them did it, but *he* did. He would need every skill he could gain if he was going to become a knight.

Devin continued making his way through the city, running faster, harder, still trying to shake off the remnants of the dream. Had it truly been a meeting?

The one who is to be.

What could that mean?

The day your life will change forever.

Devin looked about, as if looking for some sign, some indication of something that would change him on this day.

Yet he saw nothing other than the ordinary goings-on of the city.

Had it just been a foolish dream? A wish?

Royalsport was a place of bridges and of alleys, dark corners and strange smells. At low tide, when the river between the islands that formed it was low enough, people would walk across the river-beds, although guards would try to manage it and make sure that none of them went to districts where they weren't wanted.

The waterways between the islands formed a series of concentric circles, the wealthier parts toward its heart, protected by the layers of river beyond. There were entertainment districts and noble districts beyond that, then merchant ones, and poorer areas where anyone walking had to be careful to keep an eye on his money pouch.

The Houses stood out on the skyline, their buildings given over to ancient institutions as old as the kingdom; older, since they were relics of the days when the dragon kings were said to have ruled, back before the wars that had driven them out. The House of Weapons stood belching smoke despite the early hour, while the House of Knowledge stood as two entwined spires, the House of Merchants was gilded until it shone, and the House of Sighs stood at the heart of the entertainment district. Devin wove his way forward through the streets, avoiding the few other figures rising as early as him as he ran his way to the House of Weapons.

When he arrived, the House of Weapons was almost as still as the rest of the city. There was a watchman on the door, but he knew Devin by sight, and was used to him coming in at strange hours. Devin passed him with a nod and then headed inside. He took the sword he'd been working on most recently, solid and dependable, fit for a real soldier's hand. He finished the wrapping on the hilt and then took it upstairs.

This space did not have the stink of the forge, or the dirt. It was a place of clean wood and sawdust to catch any stray blood, where arms and armor stood on stands and a twelve-sided practice space stood in the middle, surrounded by a small number of benches where those waiting for lessons might sit. There were posts there and cutting bundles, all set so that noble students could practice.

Devin went to an armsman's quintain, a post taller than him on a base, set with metal poles that served as weapons and free to swing in response to the blows of a swordsman. The skill with it was to strike and then move or parry, to bind to it without getting a weapon caught, and to hit without being hit. Devin took up a high guard, and then struck out.

His first few blows were steady, moving into his work and testing the sword that he held. He caught the first few return swings of the posts, then swayed aside from the next few, slowly getting a feel for the sword he held. He started to increase the pace, adjusting his footwork, moving from one guard to another with his blows: ox, to wraith, to long, and back again.

Somewhere in the flurry of it, he stopped thinking about the individual moves, the strokes and the parries and the binds flowing together into one whole where steel rang on steel and his blade flickered out to cut and thrust. He worked until he was sweating, the post moving at speeds now that could bruise or injure if he misjudged things even once.

Finally, he stepped back, saluting the post as he had seen swordsmen salute an opponent, before checking the blade he held for damage. There were no nicks on it or cracks. That was good.

"Your technique is good," a voice said, and Devin spun, finding himself facing a man of perhaps thirty, dressed in breeches and a shirt that had been tied tighter to his body to avoid cloth tangling with a passing blade. He had long dark hair, tied back in braids that would not come undone in a fight, and aquiline features leading up to eyes of piecing gray. He walked with a slight limp, as if from an old injury. "But you should keep your weight off your heels as you turn; it makes it hard for you to adjust until you complete the movement."

"You…you're Swordmaster Wendros," Devin said. The House had many sword masters, but Wendros was the one nobles paid most to learn from, some waiting years to do it.

"Am I?" He took a moment to stare at his reflection in a suit of plate armor. "Why, so I am. Hmm, I'd listen to what I said then, if

I were you. They tell me I know all there is to know about a sword, as if that's much.

"Now listen to another piece of advice," Swordmaster Wendros added. "Give it up."

"What?" Devin said, shocked.

"Give up your attempt to become a swordsman," he said. "Soldiers just need to know how to stand in a line. There is more to being a warrior." He leaned in close. "*Much* more."

Devin didn't know what to say. He knew he was alluding to something greater, something beyond his wisdom; yet he had no idea what it could be.

Devin wanted to say something, but he couldn't think of the words.

And just like that, Wendros turned and marched off into the sunrise.

Devin found himself thinking about the dream he'd had. He couldn't help feeling as if they were connected.

He couldn't help feeling as if today was the day that would change everything.

CHAPTER THREE

Princess Lenore could barely believe the beauty of the castle as servants transformed it in preparation for her wedding. It went from a thing of gray stone to something sheathed in blue silk and elegant tapestries, chains of woven promises and dangling trinkets. Around her, a dozen maidservants busied themselves with elements of dresses and decorations, buzzing around her like a swarm of worker bees.

They did it for her, and Lenore was truly grateful for that, even if she knew that as a princess she should expect it. Lenore had always found it amazing that others were prepared to do so much for her, simply because of who she was. She appreciated beauty almost more than anything else, and here they were, doing so much with silk and lace to make the castle wondrous ...

"You look perfect," her mother said. Queen Aethe was giving commands at the heart of all of it, looking resplendent as she did so in dark velvet and shining jewels.

"Do you think so?" Lenore asked.

Her mother led her to stand in front of the great mirror that her maids had arranged. In it, Lenore could see the similarities between them, from the near black hair to the tall, slender frame. Except for Greave, all her other siblings had taken after their father but Lenore was definitely her mother's daughter.

Thanks to her maids' efforts, she shone in silks and diamonds, her hair braided with blue thread, her dress embroidered with silver. Her mother made the smallest of adjustments, then kissed her cheek.

"You look perfect, exactly as a princess should."

From her mother, that was about the greatest compliment that she could have. She'd always told Lenore that as the eldest sister, her duty was to be the princess that the realm needed, to look it and to act it in every moment. Lenore did her best, hoping it would be enough. It never felt like it, but still Lenore tried to live up to everything she ought to be.

Of course, that also allowed her little sisters to be...other things. Lenore wished that Nerra and Erin were there too. Oh, Erin would complain about being fitted for a dress, and Nerra would probably have to stop partway through because she felt unwell, but Lenore couldn't think of anyone she wanted there more.

Well, there was one person.

"When will he be here?" Lenore asked her mother.

"They say that Duke Viris's retinue arrived in the city this morning," her mother said. "His son should be with it."

"It did?" Instantly, Lenore ran over to the window and the balcony there, leaning out over it as if being that fraction closer to the city would let her see her betrothed as he arrived. She looked out over the bridge-linked islands that made up Royalsport, but from this height it wasn't possible to make out individuals, only the concentric rings of the water between the islands, and the buildings that stood between. She could see the guard barracks that spilled out men when it was low tide to manage traffic across the rivers, the Houses—of Weapons and Sighs, Knowledge and Merchants—each standing at the heart of their district. There were the houses of the poorer folk on the islands toward the edges of the city, and the great homes of the wealthy closer to, some even on their own small islands. The castle towered over all of it, of course, but that didn't mean that Lenore could spot the man to whom she was going to be married.

"He'll be here," her mother promised. "Your father has arranged a hunt on the morrow, as part of the celebrations, and the duke will not risk missing it."

"His son will come for Father's hunt, but not to see me?" Lenore asked. For a moment, she felt as nervous as a girl, not a woman of eighteen full summers. It was only too easy to imagine him not wanting her, not loving her, in a marriage arranged like this.

"He will see you, and he will love you," her mother promised. "How could anyone not?"

"I don't know, Mother... he hasn't even met me," Lenore said, feeling the nerves that threatened to overwhelm her.

"He will soon, and..." Her mother paused as a knock came at the door to the chamber. "Come in."

Another maidservant entered, this one less richly dressed than then others; a servant for the castle, rather than directly for the princess.

"Your majesty, your highness," she began, with a curtsey. "I've been sent to tell you that Duke Viris's son Finnal has arrived, and is waiting in the greater antechamber, if you have time to meet him before the feasting."

Ah, the feasting. Her father had declared a week of it and more, filled with entertainments, open to all.

"If I have time?" Lenore said, and then remembered how things were done at court. She was a princess, after all. "Of course. Please tell Finnal that I will be down directly."

She turned to her mother. "Can Father afford to be so generous with the feasting?" she asked. "I'm not... I don't *deserve* a whole week and more of it, and it must be eating into both our coin and our food stocks."

"Your father *wants* to be generous," Lenore's mother said. "He says that the hunt tomorrow would bring enough quarry to make up for it." She laughed. "My husband thinks himself the grand hunter still."

"And it's a good chance to organize things while people are busy feasting," Lenore guessed.

"That too," her mother said. "Well, if there's to be a feast, we should make sure that you look fit for it, Lenore."

She fussed around Lenore for a few moments longer, and Lenore hoped she looked good enough.

"Now, shall we go and see your husband-to-be?"

Lenore nodded, not able to quiet the excitement practically bursting from her chest. She walked with her mother and her coterie of maids down through the castle, heading to the antechamber that backed onto the great hall.

There were so many people in the castle, all working on the preparations for the wedding, many of them also heading down in the direction of the great hall. The castle was a place of winding corners and rooms that led into one another, the whole layout spiraling much like the arrangement of the city, so that any attacker would have to face layer upon layer of defenses. Her ancestors had made it more than a thing of gray stone defenses though, each room painted in colors so bright they seemed to bring the outside world in. Well, maybe not the world of the city; much of that was made far too drab by rain, mud, smoke, and choking vapors.

Lenore made her way down through a promenading gallery, which had paintings of her ancestors along one wall, each looking stronger and more refined than the last. From there, she took winding stairs that led through a series of receiving rooms, down to a space where an antechamber stood before the great hall. She stood with her mother outside the door, waiting until the servants opened it, announcing her.

"Princess Lenore of the Northern Kingdom, and her mother, Queen Aethe."

They stepped inside, and there he was.

He was…perfect. There was no other word for it as he turned toward Lenore, sweeping the most graceful bow that she had seen in a long time. He had dark hair in gloriously short curls, features that were refined, almost beautiful, and a form that seemed both slender and athletic, encased in a red slashed doublet and gray hosen. He seemed perhaps a year or two older than Lenore, but that was exciting rather than frightening.

"Your majesty," he said with a look to Lenore's mother. "Princess Lenore. I am Finnal of House Viris. I can only tell you how long I have looked forward to this moment. You are even more lovely than I had thought."

Lenore blushed, and she *didn't* blush. Her mother had always told her that it was unbecoming. When Finnal held out his hand, she took it as gracefully as she could, feeling the strength in those hands, imagining what it would be like for them to pull her close so that they could kiss, or more than kiss...

"Next to you, I hardly feel like the lovely one," she said.

"If I shine, it is only with your reflected light," he replied. So handsome, and he could manage a compliment so poetic too?

"It's hard to believe that in just a week we will be married," Lenore said.

"I think that might be because we aren't the ones who had to put in long months of work negotiating the marriage," Finnal replied. He smiled a beautiful smile. "But I am glad that our parents did." He looked around the room, at her mother and the maids there. "It is almost a pity that I cannot have you here to myself, Princess, but perhaps it is as well. I fear that I might get lost staring into your eyes, and then your father would be annoyed with me for missing so much of his feasting."

"Do you always manage such pretty compliments?" Lenore asked.

"Only when they are warranted," he replied.

Lenore felt herself almost swept away with her thoughts of him as she stood beside him at the door leading from the antechamber to the great hall. When servants opened it, she could see the feast in full flow; could hear the music of minstrels and see the tumblers providing entertainment further down the hall where the common folk sat.

"We should go in," her mother said. "Your father will no doubt wish to show his approval of this marriage, and I am sure that he will want to see how happy you are. You are happy, Lenore?"

Lenore looked into the eyes of her fiancé, and could only nod.

"Yes," she said.

"And I shall strive to see that you stay that way," Finnal said. Taking her hand, he lifted it to his lips, and the heat of that contact shot through Lenore. She found herself imagining all the other places that he might kiss, and Finnal smiled again, as if knowing the effect he was having. "Soon, my love."

His love? Did Lenore love him, so soon after meeting him? Could she love him, when there had been only this brief moment of contact? Lenore knew it was nonsense to think that she could, the stuff of a bard's songs, but in that moment she did. Oh, how she did.

Smiling, she stepped forward in perfect step with Finnal, knowing that together they must look like something out of legend to those who watched, moving like one thing, joined together. Soon they would be, and that thought was more than enough for Lenore as they went to join the feast.

Nothing, she thought, could possibly ruin this moment.

Chapter Four

Prince Vars downed a flagon of ale, making sure he had a good view of Lyril as he did. She lay, still undressed in his bed, sitting up and watching him with just as much obvious interest, the bruises of the night before showing only a little.

As well she should, Vars thought. He was a prince of the blood after all, maybe not as muscled as his older brother, but at twenty-one he was still young, still handsome. She should watch him with interest, and deference, and maybe fear if she could tell all the things he thought about doing to her in that moment.

No, better to leave that for now. Being rough with her was one thing, but she was just noble enough for it to matter. Better to leave the fullness of it for those who wouldn't be missed.

Lyril was rather beautiful herself, of course, because Vars wouldn't be sleeping with her if she weren't: flame-haired and creamy-skinned, full-bodied and green-eyed. She was the eldest daughter of a nobleman who fancied himself a merchant, or a merchant who'd bought nobility, Vars couldn't remember which, and didn't particularly care. She was less than him, so she did as he commanded. What else was there?

"Seen enough, my prince?" she asked. She stood and moved across to him. Vars liked the way she did that. Liked the way she did a lot of things.

"My father wants me to join him on a hunt tomorrow," Vars said.

"I could ride out with you," Lyril said. "Watch you and offer you my favors as you ride."

Vars laughed, and if that caused a flash of hurt to her, who cared? Besides, Lyril would be used to it by now. Ordinarily, he didn't sleep with women for long before he grew bored with them, or they drifted off elsewhere, or he hurt them too much and they ran. Lyril had lasted longer than most. Years now, although obviously there had been others in that time.

"Embarrassed to be seen with me?" she asked.

Vars stepped close to her, stopping her with a look. In that moment of fear, she was as beautiful as anyone he had seen.

"I will do as I wish," Vars said.

"Yes, my prince," she replied, with another shiver that set its answer trembling along Vars's arms with desire.

"You are as lovely as any woman alive, and noble born, and perfect," he said.

"Then why is it that you're taking so long to marry me?" Lyril asked. It was an old argument. She'd been asking, and hinting, and commenting for as long as Vars could remember.

He stepped in, quick and sharp, grabbing her by the hair. "Marry you? Why should I marry you? Do you think you're special?"

"I must be," she countered. "Or a prince like you would never want me."

She had him there.

"Soon," Vars said, pushing down his flash of anger. "When things are right for it."

"And when will things be right?" Lyril demanded. She started to dress, and just the sight of her doing it was enough to make Vars want to undress her again. He moved over to her, kissing her deeply.

"Soon," Vars promised, because promising was easy. "For now though ..."

"For now, we're meant to be at your father's feast, celebrating the arrival of your sister's fiancé," Lyril said. She looked thoughtful for a moment. "I wonder if he's handsome."

Vars spun her to him, his arms grasping hard enough that she gasped. "Am I not enough for you?"

"Enough, and more than enough."

Vars groaned at the trap in that, then went and dressed, finding a flask of wine and sipping it as he went. He offered it to Lyril, who also took some. They headed out into the castle, making their way through its twists and turns, down toward the great hall.

"Your highness, my lady," a servant said as they passed, "the feasting has already begun."

Vars rounded on the man. "Do you think I need you to tell me that? Do you think I'm stupid, or that I have no idea of the time?"

"No, my prince, but your father—"

"My father will be busy with the politics of it all, or he will be listening to Rodry boast about whatever my brother has done now," Vars said.

"As you say, your highness," the man said. He made to go.

"Wait," Lyril said. "Do you think that you just get to go? You should apologize to the prince, and to me, for interrupting us."

"Yes, of course," the servant said. "I am most—"

"A proper apology," Lyril said. "On your knees."

The man hesitated for a moment, and Vars leapt in. "Do it."

The servant sank to his knees. "I apologize for interrupting you, your highness, my lady. I should not have done it."

Vars saw Lyril smile at that.

"No," she said. "Now go, get out of our sight."

The servant all but ran off at her command, like a greyhound after a rabbit. Vars laughed as he went.

"You can be deliciously cruel sometimes," he said. He liked that in her.

"Only when it is amusing," Lyril replied.

They kept going, down to the feast. Of course, by the time they entered, it was in full swing, with everyone drinking and dancing, eating and enjoying themselves. Vars could see his half-sister up at the front, the center of attention along with her husband-to-be. Why the child of a king's second wife should warrant such attention was beyond him.

It was bad enough that Rodry was there with a cluster of noble youths in one corner, receiving their admiration as he told and retold stories of his exploits. Why had fate seen fit to make him the oldest? It made no sense to Vars when it was obvious that Rodry was about as suited to the future role of king as he was to flying by flapping his over-muscled arms.

"Of course, a wedding like this provides possibilities," Lyril said. "It brings together so many lords and ladies..."

"Who can then be made into our friends," Vars said. He understood how the game worked. "Of course, it helps if one knows their weaknesses. Did you know that Earl Durris over there has a weakness for smoking blood amber?"

"I did not," Lyril said.

"Nor will anyone else, if he remembers that I am his friend," Vars said. He and Lyril continued through the crowd, slowly drifting in their separate directions. He could see her eyeing up the women, trying to decide all the ways that they were less pretty than her, or weaker, or just not of her level. Probably trying to decide all of the advantages she could gain with them, too. There was a hardness to that assessment that Vars liked. Maybe that was a part of why he'd been with her so long.

"Of course, that's another reason not to join the hunt tomorrow," he said. "With all the idiots away, I can do what I want, maybe set things up to my advantage."

"Did I hear some mention of the hunt?"

His brother's voice was as booming and as bluff as ever. Vars turned to Rodry, forcing the smile he'd learned to force through so much of his childhood.

"Rodry, brother," he said. "I hadn't realized that you were back from ... where was it you and Father went again?"

Rodry shrugged. "You could have gone and found out."

"Ah, but you went running," Vars said, "and you're the one who matters to him."

If Rodry caught the sharpness of it, he didn't show it.

"Come on," Rodry said, clapping him on the back. "Join me and my friends."

He made joining the bunch of young fools who all but worshipped him as a hero sound like some great gift, rather than a horror Vars would have paid solid gold to avoid. They played at being like his father's Knights of the Spur, but not one of them had made a name for himself yet. His smile became more strained as he walked into the heart of them, and he grabbed a goblet of wine as a welcome distraction. In just a brief space, it was gone, so he grabbed another.

"We're talking about all the hunts we've been on," Rodry said. "Berwick says that he once took down a boar with a dagger."

One of the young men there gave a bow that made Vars want to kick him in the face. "I was gored twice."

"Then perhaps you should have used a spear," Vars said.

"I broke my spear on the training grounds of the House of Weapons," Berwick said.

"When were you last on the training grounds, brother?" Rodry asked, obviously knowing the answer. "When will you be joining the knights, as I have?"

"I train with the sword," Vars said, probably a little more defensively than he should have. "I just think that there are more useful things to do than spending every waking moment doing so."

"Or maybe you just don't like the thought of facing up to an enemy ready to cut you down, eh, brother?" Rodry said, clapping Vars on the shoulder. "The same way you don't like going on the hunt, in case something happens to you."

He laughed, and the cruelest thing was that his brother probably didn't even see it as hurtful. Rodry wasn't a man who went through the world with any care, after all.

"Are you calling me a coward, Rodry?" Vars said.

"Oh no," Rodry said. "There are some men who are meant to be out in the world fighting, and others who are better off staying at home, right?"

"I could hunt if I wanted to," Vars said.

"Ah, the brave knight!" Rodry said, and that got another of those laughs that no one there would see as cruel except Vars. "Well then, you should come with us! We're going down into the city to make sure we have the weapons we need for the morrow."

"And leave the feast?" Vars retorted.

"The feasting will last days yet," Rodry shot back. "Come on, we can pick you out a fine spear so you can show us how to hunt boar."

Vars wished he could simply walk away, or better yet, smash his brother's face into the nearest table. Maybe keep smashing it until it was a pulp, and he was left as the heir he should always have been. Instead, he knew he was going to have to go down into the city, across the bridges, but at least down there, he might find someone on whom to take his anger out. Yes, Vars was looking forward to that, and to more beyond it. Maybe even to being king one day.

For now, though, the part of him that screamed to stay safe to avoid danger was telling him not to confront his brother. No, he would wait for that.

But whoever got in his way down in the city was going to pay.

CHAPTER FIVE

Devin swung his hammer, bashing it down on the lump of metal that was due to become a blade. The muscles on his back ached as he did it, the heat of the forge making sweat run through his clothes. In the House of Weapons, it was always hot, and this close to one of the forges, it was almost unbearable.

"You're doing well, boy," Old Gund said.

"I'm sixteen, I'm not a boy," Devin said.

"Aye, but you're still the size of one. Besides, to an old man like me, you're all boys."

Devin shrugged at that. He knew that, to anyone looking, he must not have looked like a smith, but he thought; the metal *demanded* thinking to truly understand it. The subtle gradations of heat and patterns of steel that could change a weapon from flawed to perfect were almost magical, and Devin was determined to know them all, to truly *understand*.

"Careful, or it will cool too much," Gund said.

Quickly, Devin got the metal back into the heat, watching the shade of it until it was exactly right, then pulling it out to work on it. It was close, but it still wasn't quite right, something about the edge not quite perfect. Devin knew it as surely as he knew his right from his left.

He was still young, but he knew weapons. He knew the best ways to craft them and to sharpen them... he even knew how to wield them, although both his father and Master Wendros seemed determined that he should not. The training the House of Weapons offered was for nobles, young men coming in to learn from the finest sword masters, including the impossibly skilled Wendros. Devin had to do it alone, practicing with everything from swords to axes, spears to knives, cutting at posts and hoping it was right.

A clamor from near the front of the House briefly caught Devin's attention. The great metal doors at the front stood open, perfectly balanced to swing at the slightest touch. The young men who'd come in through it were clearly noble, and just as clearly slightly drunk. Drunk was dangerous in the House of Weapons. A man who showed up drunk to work here was sent home, and if he did it more than once, he was dismissed.

Even clients were generally shown the door if they were not sober enough. A man with a blade who was drunk was a dangerous man, even if he didn't mean to be. These, though ... they wore royal colors, and to be anything less than courteous was to risk more than a job.

"We are in need of weapons," the one at the front said. Devin recognized Prince Rodry at once, from the stories about him if not in person. "There is a hunt tomorrow, and there will probably be a tournament following the wedding."

Gund went to meet them, because he was one of the master blacksmiths there. Devin kept his attention on the blade he was forging, because the least slip or mistake could introduce air bubbles that would form cracks. He made it a point of pride that the weapons he forged didn't break or shatter when struck.

Despite the metal's need for his attention, Devin wasn't able to take his eyes off the young nobles who had come there. They seemed around his age; boys trying to be the prince's friend rather than the Knights of the Spur who served his father. Gund began by showing them spears and blades that might have suited the king's armies, but they quickly waved them away.

"These are the sons of the king!" one of the men said, gesturing first to Prince Rodry and then to another man Devin guessed to be Prince Vars, if only because he didn't look slender, gloomy, or girlish enough for Prince Greave. "They deserve finer stuff than this."

Gund started to show them finer things, the ones with gilt handles or decoration worked into the heads of spears. He even showed them some of the ones that were master made, with layer upon layer of the finest steel, wavy patterns built into them through clay heat treating, and edges that could serve as razors if need be.

"Too fine for them," Devin murmured to himself. He took the blade he was forging and considered it. It was ready. He heated it up once more, ready to quench it in the long bath of dark oil that stood waiting for it.

He could see from the way they were picking up the weapons and waving them that most of those there had no real idea what they were doing. Perhaps Prince Rodry did, but he was away on the far side of the House's main floor by now, trying a great spear with a leaf-bladed head, spinning it with the expertise that came from long practice. In contrast, those with him looked more like they were playing at being knights than actually knights. Devin could see the clumsiness in some of their movements, and the ways that their grips on the weapons were subtly wrong.

"A man should know the weapons he makes, and uses," Devin said, as he plunged the blade he'd made into the quenching trough. It flared and flamed for a moment, then hissed as the weapon slowly cooled.

He practiced with blades so he could know when they were perfect for a trained warrior. He worked at his balance and his flexibility as well as his strength, because it seemed right that a man should forge himself as well as any weapon. He found both difficult; the knowing of things was easier for him, the making of perfect tools, understanding the moment when—

A crash from over where the nobles were toying with the weapons caught his attention, and Devin's gaze snapped over in time to see Prince Vars standing in the midst of a pile of armor collapsed from its stand. He was glaring at Nem, another of the boys who worked at the House of Weapons. Nem had been Devin's friend as long as he could remember, large and frankly too well fed, maybe not the fastest of wit, but with hands that could shape the finest of metalwork. Prince Vars quickly shoved him the way Devin might have pushed a stuck door.

"Stupid boy!" Prince Vars snapped. "Can't you watch where you're going?"

"Sorry, my lord," Nem said, "but you were the one who walked into me."

Devin's breath caught at that, because he knew how dangerous it was to talk back to any noble, let alone a drunk one. Prince Vars drew himself up to his full height and then struck Nem across the ear, hard enough to send him tumbling down among the steel. He cried out and came up with blood on his arm from where something sharp had caught it.

"How dare you talk back to me?" the prince said. "I say that you walked into me, and you're calling me a liar?"

Perhaps someone else there might have come up angry, come up ready to fight, but despite his size, Nem had always been gentle. He just looked hurt and perplexed.

For a moment, Devin hesitated, looking around to see if any of the others would intervene in this. None of the ones with Prince Rodry seemed as though they were going to intervene though, probably too worried about insulting someone who outranked them so greatly even as nobles, and maybe some of them thinking that maybe his friend *did* deserve a beating for whatever they thought he'd done.

As for Prince Rodry, he was still over on the other side of the House's floor, working with the spear. If he'd heard the commotion above the din of working hammers and rushing forge bellows, he didn't show it. Gund wouldn't interfere, because the old man hadn't survived as long as he had in the environment of the forge by causing trouble for his betters.

Devin knew he should stand by too, even when he saw the prince raise his hand again.

"Are you going to apologize?" Vars demanded.

"I didn't do anything!" Nem insisted, probably too stunned to remember how the world worked yet, and truth be told, he wasn't all that bright when it came to things like this. He still thought the world was fair, still thought that not doing anything wrong was enough of an excuse.

"No one talks to me like that," Prince Vars said, and hit Nem again. "I'm going to beat some manners into you, and when I'm done you'll thank me for the lesson. And if you get my title wrong while you do it, I'll beat that into you too. Or, no, let's give you a real lesson."

Devin knew he should do nothing, because he wasn't as young as Nem, and he *did* know the way the world worked. If a prince of the blood stood on your toes, you apologized to him, or thanked him for the privilege. If he wanted your best work, you sold him it, even though it looked as though he couldn't swing it right. You didn't interfere, didn't intervene, because that meant consequences, for you and your family.

Devin had a family, out beyond the walls of the House of Weapons. He didn't want to see them hurt just because he'd been hot-tempered and not minded his manners. He didn't want to stand by and see a boy beaten senseless for a drunken prince's whim either, though. His grip tightened on his hammer, and Devin set it down, trying to tell himself to stand back.

Then Prince Vars grabbed Nem's hand. He forced it down onto one of the anvils.

"Let's see how good a smith you are with a broken hand," he said. He took a hammer and lifted it, and in that moment Devin knew what would happen if he did nothing. His heart raced.

Without thinking, Devin lunged forward and grabbed for the prince's arm. He didn't deflect the blow by much, but it was enough that it missed Nem's hand and struck the iron of the anvil.

Devin held the grip, just in case the prince tried to smash him with it next.

"What?" Prince Vars said. "Take your hands off me."

Devin struggled, pinning down his hand; this close to him, Devin could smell the alcohol on his breath.

"Not if you're going to keep striking my friend," Devin said.

He knew that just by grabbing the prince, he'd created trouble for himself, but it was too late now.

"Nem doesn't understand, and he wasn't the reason you knocked over half the armor in here. That would be the drink."

"Take your hand off me, I said," the prince repeated, and his other hand strayed toward the eating knife at his belt.

Devin pushed him backward as gently as he could manage. A part of him still hoped this could be peaceful, even as he knew exactly what was going to happen next.

"You don't want to do that, your highness."

Vars glared at him, breathing hard, with a look of pure hatred.

"I'm not the one who's made the mistake here, traitor," Prince Vars growled, death in his voice.

Vars set down his hammer and picked up an arming sword from one of the benches, although it was obvious to Devin that he was no expert with it.

"That's right—you're a traitor. Attacking a royal person is treason, and traitors die for it."

He swung the sword at Devin, and instinctively, Devin grabbed for whatever he could find. It turned out to be a forge hammer of his own, and he brought it up to block the blow, hearing the ring of iron on iron as he stopped the sword from connecting with his head. The impact jarred at his hands, and there was no time to think now. Catching the blade against the hammer's head, he wrenched it from the prince's grip with all his strength, sending it clattering across the floor to join the pile of discarded armor.

He made himself stop then. He was angry that the prince could come in and strike at him like that, but Devin was all patience. Metal required it. A man who was impatient at the forge was a man who got hurt.

"You see?" Prince Vars called out, pointing a finger that was trembling in either anger or fear. "He strikes at me! Seize him. I want him dragged to the deepest cell the castle possesses, and his head on a pike by morning."

The young men around him looked reluctant to react, but it was just as obvious that they weren't going to stand by while someone as low-born as Devin fought with a prince. Most were still holding swords or spears that they'd been trying out inexpertly, and now Devin found himself in the middle of a ring of such weapons, all pointed straight at his heart.

"I don't want any trouble," Devin said, not knowing what else to do. He let the hammer thud to the floor, because it was useless to him there. What could he do, try to fight his way out against so many? Even though he suspected he was better with a blade than the men there, there were too many to even try it, and if he did, what then? Where would he be able to run, and what would it mean for his family if he did?

"Maybe there's no need for a cell," Prince Vars said. "Maybe I'll take his head off here, where people can see. Put him on his knees. On his knees, I said!" he repeated when the others didn't do it quickly enough.

Four of them came forward and pushed Devin down, while the others kept their weapons trained on him. Prince Vars, meanwhile, had picked up the sword again. He lifted it, obviously testing the weight, and in that moment Devin knew that he was going to die. Fear filled him, because he couldn't see a way out. No matter how much he thought, no matter how strong he was, it wouldn't change things. The others there might not agree with what the prince was about to do, but they would stand by anyway. They would stand there and watch while the prince swung that sword and ...

... and the world seemed to stretch out in that moment, one heartbeat fading into the next. In that instant, it was as if he could see every muscle in the prince's frame, see the sparks of thought that powered it. It was easy in that moment to reach out, and to change just one of them.

"Ow! My arm!" Prince Vars yelled, his sword clattering to the ground.

Devin stared back, stunned. He tried to make some sense of what he'd just done.

And he was terrified by himself.

The prince stood there, clutching at his arm and trying to rub some feeling back into the fingers.

Devin could only stare at him. Had he really done that somehow? How? How could anyone make someone's arm cramp just by thinking about it?

He thought back to the dream once more...

"That's enough," a voice called out, interrupting. "Let him go."

Prince Rodry stepped into the circle of weapons, and the young men there lowered them in response to his presence, almost breathing a sigh of relief that he was there.

Devin definitely did, yet he kept his eyes on Prince Vars, and the weapon he now held in his off hand.

"That's enough, Vars," Rodry said. He stepped between Devin and the prince, and Prince Vars hesitated for a moment. Devin thought he might even swing the sword anyway, regardless of his brother's presence.

Then he threw the blade aside.

"I didn't want to come here anyway," he said, and stalked out.

Prince Rodry turned to Devin, and it didn't even take another word for him to be released by the men who held him.

"You were brave to stand up for the boy," he said. He lifted the spear he held. "And you do good work. I'm told this is one of yours."

"Yes, your highness," Devin said. He didn't know what to think. In a matter of seconds, he'd gone from being sure he would die to being released, from being thought a traitor to being complimented on his work. It made no sense, but then, why should things have to make sense in a world where he'd somehow just done ... magic?

Prince Rodry nodded and then turned to leave. "Be more careful in the future. I might not be here to save you next time."

It took several more seconds before Devin could bring himself to stand, breaths coming in short bursts. He looked over to Nem, who was trying to hold the wound on his arm closed. He looked scared and shaken by what had happened.

Old Gund was there then, taking Nem's arm and wrapping a strip of cloth around it. He looked over to Devin.

"You had to interfere?" he asked.

"I couldn't let him hurt Nem," Devin said. That was one thing he would do again, a hundred times if he had to.

"The worst he'd have gotten was a beating," Gund said. "We've all had worse. Now … you need to go."

"Go?" Devin said. "For today?"

"For today, and all the days that follow, you fool," Gund said. "Do you think we can let a man who fights a prince stay in the House of Weapons?"

Devin felt the breath leave his chest. Leave the House of Weapons? The only real home he'd ever known?

"But I didn't—" Devin began, and stopped himself.

He wasn't Nem, to believe that the world would turn out the way he wanted just because it was the right thing. Of course Gund would want him gone; Devin had known before he interfered what this might cost him.

Devin stared back and nodded, all he could do in response. He turned and began to walk.

"Wait," Nem called out. He ran to his workbench and then ran back with something wrapped in cloth. "I … I don't have much else. You saved me. You should have this."

"I did it because I'm your friend," Devin said. "You don't have to give me anything."

"I want to," Nem replied. "If he'd hit my hand, I couldn't make anything else, so I want you to have something I made."

He passed it to Devin, and Devin took it carefully. Unwrapping it, he could see that it was … well, not a sword, exactly. A long knife, a messer, sat there, too long to be a true knife, not quite long enough to be a sword. It was single edged, with a hilt that stuck out only on one side, and a wedge-shaped point. It was a peasant's weapon, far removed from the longswords and arming swords of the knights. But it was light. Deadly. And beautiful. Devin could see at a glance, as he turned it and as it gleamed in the light, that it could be far more nimble and deadly than any proper sword. It was a weapon of stealth, cunning, and speed. One perfect for Devin's light frame and young age.

"It's not finished," Nem said, "but I know you can finish it better than I could, and the steel's good, I promise."

Devin gave it an experimental swing, feeling the blade cut the air. He wanted to say that it was too much, that he couldn't take it, but he could see how much Nem wanted him to have this.

"Thank you, Nem," he said.

"You two done?" Gund said. He looked over to Devin. "I won't say I'm not sorry to see you go. You're a good worker, and a finer smith than most here. But you can't be here when this comes back on us. You need to go, boy. Now."

Devin wanted to argue even then. But he knew it was futile, and he realized that he no longer wanted to be there. He didn't want to be somewhere he wasn't wanted. This had never been his dream. This had been a way to survive. His dream had always been to be a knight, and now...

Now it seemed that his dreams held far stranger things. He needed to work out what they were.

The day your life will change forever.

Could this be what the sorcerer meant?

Devin had no choice. He couldn't turn around now, couldn't go back to his forge to set everything back where it should be.

Instead, he walked out into the city. Into his destiny.

And into the waiting day before him.

CHAPTER SIX

Nerra walked the woods alone, slipping between the trees, enjoying the feeling of sunlight on her face. She imagined that everyone back in the castle would have noticed that she had slipped out by now, but she also suspected that they wouldn't care that much. She would only complicate the wedding preparations by being there.

Here in the wild, she fit. She wound flowers into her dark hair, letting them join the braids. She took off her boots, tying them together over her shoulder so she could feel the earth beneath her feet. Her slender form wove in and out of the trees, almost wisp-like in a dress of fall colors. The sleeves were long, of course. Her mother had drummed the need for that into her long ago. Her family might know about her infirmity, but no one else was to.

She loved the outdoors. She loved seeing the plants and picking out their names, bluebell and hogweed, oak and elm, lavender and mushroom. She knew more than their names, too, because each had its own properties, things it could help with or harm it could do. A part of her wished she could spend all her life out here, free and at peace. Maybe she could; maybe she could persuade her father to let her build a home out in the forest, and put what she knew of it to good use, healing the sick and the injured.

Nerra smiled sadly at that, because even though she knew it was a good dream, her father would never go along with it, and in any case … Nerra held back from the thought for a moment, but couldn't forever. In any case, she probably wouldn't live long enough to build any kind of life. The sickness killed, or transformed, too quickly for that.

Nerra picked at a strand of willow bark that would be good for aches, putting strips into her belt pouch.

I'll probably need it soon enough, she guessed. There were no aches today, but if not her, then maybe Widow Merril's boy, down in the town. She'd heard that he had a fever, and Nerra knew as much about dealing with the sick as anyone.

I want one day without having to think about it, Nerra thought to herself.

Almost as if thinking about it brought it to her, Nerra felt herself growing faint, and had to reach out for one of the trees for support. She clung to it, waiting for the dizziness to pass, feeling her breathing come harder as she did it. She could also feel the pulsing on her right arm, itching and throbbing, as if something were striving to get loose under the skin.

Nerra sat down, and here, in the privacy of the forest, she did what she would never do back at the castle: she rolled up her sleeve, hoping that the coolness of the forest air would do some good where nothing else ever had.

The tracery of marks on her arm was familiar by now, black and vein like, standing out against the almost translucent paleness of her skin. Had the marks grown anymore since she'd last looked at them? It was hard to tell, because Nerra avoided looking if she could, and didn't dare show them to anyone else. Even her brothers and sisters didn't know the full truth of it, only knew about the fainting fits, not about the rest of it. That was for her, her parents, Master Grey, and the lone physician her father had trusted with it.

Nerra knew why. Those with the scale-mark were banished, or worse, for fear of the condition spreading, and for fear of what it might mean. Those with the scale sickness, the stories said, eventually transformed into things that were anything but human, and deadly to those who remained.

"And so I must be alone," she said aloud, pulling her sleeve down again because she could no longer stand the sight of what was there.

The thought of being alone bothered her almost as much. As much as she liked the forest, the lack of people hurt. Even as a child, she hadn't been able to have close friends, hadn't had the collection of maidservants and young noblewomen Lenore had, because one of them might have seen. She hadn't even had the promise of lovers, and suitors for a girl who was obviously sick were even less likely. A part of Nerra wished she could have had all that, imagining a life where she had been normal, been well, been safe. Her parents could have found some young nobleman to marry her, as they had with Lenore. They could have had a home and a family. Nerra could have had friends, and been able to help people. Instead … there was only this.

Now I've made even the forest sad, Nerra thought with another wan smile.

She stood and kept walking, determined to let herself enjoy the fineness of the day at least. There would be a hunt tomorrow, but that was too many people to ever really enjoy the outdoors. She would be expected to remember how to chatter to those who saw prowess in killing woodland creatures as a virtue, and the noise of the hunting horns would be deafening.

Nerra heard something else then; it wasn't a hunting horn, but it was still the sound of someone close by. She thought she caught a glimpse of someone in the trees, a young boy, perhaps, although it was hard to tell for sure. She found herself worrying then. How much had he seen?

Maybe it was nothing. Nerra knew there had to be people somewhere else in the woods. Maybe they were charcoal burners or foresters; maybe they were poachers. Whoever they were, if she kept going, Nerra would probably run into them again. She didn't like that idea, didn't like the risk of them seeing more than they should, so she threw herself off in a new direction, almost at random. She could find her way through the woods, so she wasn't worried about getting lost. She just kept going, spotting holly now and birch, celandine, and wild roses.

And something else.

Nerra paused as she caught sight of a clearing that looked as though something large had been in it, branches broken, ground trampled. Had it been a boar, or maybe a pack of them? Was there a bear about somewhere, large enough that maybe the hunt was needed after all? Nerra couldn't see any bear prints among the trees though, or indeed anything at all that suggested something had come through on foot.

She could see an egg though, sitting in the middle of the clearing, rolled onto one side on the grass.

She froze, wondering.

It can't be.

There were stories, of course, and the castle's galleries had some petrified versions, devoid of any life.

But this... it couldn't really be...

She made her way closer to it, and now she could start to take in the sheer size of the egg. It was huge, big enough that Nerra's arms would barely have fit around it if she had tried to embrace it. Big enough that no bird could have laid it.

It was a rich, deep blue that was almost black, with golden veins running through it like streaks of lightning across a night sky. When Nerra reached out, ever so tentatively, to touch it, she felt that the surface of it was strangely warm in a way that no egg should have been. That, as much as any of the rest of it, confirmed what she had found.

A dragon's egg.

That was impossible. How long had it been since someone had seen a dragon? Even those stories were of great winged beasts flying the skies, not of eggs. Dragons were never helpless, small things. They were huge and terrifying and impossible. But Nerra couldn't think what else this could be.

And now the choice is mine.

She knew she couldn't just walk away now that she'd seen the egg here, abandoned with no sign of a nest the way a bird would lay its clutch. If she did that, the odds were that something would simply come and eat the egg, destroying the creature within. That, or there would be people, and she had no doubt that they would sell it. Or crush it out of fear. People could be cruel sometimes.

She couldn't take it home with her either. Imagine that, walking through the gates of the castle with a dragon's egg in her hands. Her father would have it taken from her in a heartbeat, probably for Master Grey to study. At best, the creature within would find itself caged and poked at. At worst... Nerra shuddered at the thought of the egg being dissected by scholars of the House of Knowledge. Even Physicker Jarran would probably want to take it apart to study it.

Where then?

Nerra tried to think.

She knew the woods as well as she knew the path to her chambers. There had to be somewhere that would be better than simply leaving the egg in the open...

Yes, she knew just the place.

She wrapped her arms around the egg, the heat of it strange against her body as she lifted it. It was heavy, and for a moment Nerra was worried she might drop it, but she managed to clasp her hands together and start off through the woods.

It took a while to find the spot that she was looking for, looking out for the aspen trees that signaled the small space where the old cave was, marked out by stones that were long since mossed over. It opened in the side of a small hill in the midst of the wood, and Nerra could see from the ground around it that nothing had decided to use it as a resting place. That was good; she didn't want to take her prize somewhere it would be in fresh danger.

The clearing suggested that dragons didn't make nests, but Nerra made one for the egg anyway, collecting twigs and branches, brush and grass, then weaving all of it slowly into a rough oval on which she was able to rest the egg. She pushed the whole thing back into the dark half of the cave, confident that nothing would be able to see it from outside.

"There," she said to it. "You'll be safe now, at least until I work out what to do with you."

She found tree branches and foliage, deliberately covering the entrance. She took rocks and rolled them into place, each so big she could barely move it. She hoped it would be enough to keep away all the things that might try to get inside.

She was just finishing when she heard a sound and turned with a start. There among the trees was the boy she had glimpsed before. He stood there staring at her as if trying to work out what he'd seen.

"Wait," Nerra called out to him, but the very shout was enough to startle him. He turned and ran off, leaving Nerra wondering exactly what he had seen, and who he would tell.

She had a sinking feeling that it was too late.

CHAPTER SEVEN

Princess Erin knew she shouldn't be here, riding through the forest on the way north to the Spur. She should be back at the castle, being fitted for a dress for her older sister's wedding, but just the thought of it was enough to make her wince.

It brought too many thoughts of what might be waiting for her next, and why she'd left. At the very least, she would rather be riding here in tunic, doublet, and breeches than standing there playing dress-up while Rodry made fun of her with his friends, and Greave moped about, and Vars... Erin shuddered. No, better to be out here, doing something useful, something that would *prove* she was more than just some daughter to marry off.

She rode through the forest, taking in the plants along the side of the path as she passed, even though those were more Nerra's fascination than hers. She rode past broad oak and silver birch, seeing the shadows they cast and trying not to think about all the spaces those shadows gave for someone to hide.

Her father would probably be angry with her for coming out without an escort. Princesses needed to be protected, he would tell her. They didn't wander off alone into places like this, places where the trees seemed to close in and the path was little more than a suggestion. He would be angry at her for more than that, of course. He probably thought she hadn't heard the conversation with her mother, the one that had sent her off practically running for the stables.

"We need to find a husband for Erin," her mother had said.

"A husband? She's as likely to ask for more sword lessons," her father had replied.

"And that's the point. A girl shouldn't be doing such things, putting herself in that kind of danger. We need to find a husband for her."

"After the wedding," her father had said. *"There will be plenty of nobles there for the feasting and the hunting. Maybe we can find a young man who will make a suitable husband for her."*

"We might need to offer a dowry for her."

"Then we will. Gold, a dukedom, whatever is most suitable for my daughter."

The betrayal had been instant, and absolute. Erin had strode to her room to gather her things: her staff and her clothes, a pack full of supplies. She had sworn to herself then that she wouldn't be coming back.

"Besides," she said to her horse, "I'm old enough to do what I want."

She might be the youngest of all her siblings, but she was still sixteen. She might not be everything her mother wanted—too boyish with her dark hair cut at shoulder level where it wouldn't get in the way, never inclined to sew or curtsey or play the harp—but she was still more than capable of looking after herself.

At least, she thought she was.

She would have to be, if she wanted to join the Knights of the Spur. Just the name of their order made Erin's heart leap. They were the finest warriors of the realm, every name among them a hero. They served her father, but also rode out righting wrongs and fighting foes that no others could. Erin would give anything to join them.

That was why she was riding north, to the Spur. That was also why she was taking this route, through parts of the forest long thought dangerous.

She rode on, taking in the place. Any other time, it would have been beautiful, but then, any other time, she wouldn't have been here. Instead, she looked around, eyes darting, all too aware of the shadows on each side of the path, the way the branches brushed at her as she rode. It was a place where she could imagine someone disappearing, never to return.

Even so, it was the route she had to take if she was going to reach the Knights of the Spur. Especially if she wanted to be able to impress them when she got there. Set beside that, her fear didn't matter.

"Why don't you stop there?" a voice from further along the forest path called.

There. Erin felt a brief thrill of fear at the words, the flutter running up through her belly. She drew her horse to a halt, then swung down from the saddle smoothly. Almost as an afterthought, she took down her short staff, gloved hands carrying it lightly.

"Now, what do you think you're going to do with that stick?" the man from further down the forest path said. He stepped out, dressed in rough-spun clothes and holding a hatchet. Two more men stepped out from the trees behind Erin, one holding a long knife, the other an arming sword that suggested he might once have fought on behalf of a nobleman.

"Back in a village I passed through," Erin said, "they told me about bandits in the forest."

They didn't seem to think it was odd that she'd come here anyway. Erin could feel the fear inside her. Should she have come here? She'd had plenty of training bouts, but this ... this was different.

"Looks as though we're famous, boys," the leader called out with a laugh.

Famous was one word for it. In the village, she'd spoken to a young woman who was traveling with her husband. She had said that even when they gave these men everything they had, they still wanted more, and they took it. She had detailed all of it to Erin, and Erin had wished she'd had Lenore's way with people, or Nerra's compassion. Erin didn't have either; all she had was this.

"They say you kill those who fight," Erin said.

"Well then," the leader said. "You'll know not to fight."

"Barely worth it," one of the others said. "Hardly a girl at all."

"You're complaining?" the leader shot back. "The things you've done with boys as well?"

Erin stood there, waiting. The fear was still there, and it had grown into a monstrous thing, a bear-sized thing that threatened to crush her into immobility. She shouldn't have come here. This wasn't a training bout, and she had never truly fought anyone before. She was just a young woman who was about to be killed, or worse…

No. Erin thought about that, thought about the woman from the village, and she forced the fear down, under the anger.

"If you want to make this easy on yourself, you'll hand over everything you have. The horse, your valuables, everything."

"And take off those clothes," the other who'd spoken said. "It will save us getting blood on them."

Erin swallowed, thinking about what that might mean. "No."

"Well then," the leader said. "Looks like we do this the hard way."

The one with the long knife came at Erin first, grabbing for her and slashing with it at her body. Erin broke the grip, but the blade slid through her clothing as easily as it might have through a milk-maid's butter. The man's leer of triumph quickly turned to shock as the blade stopped, caught with the sound of metal on metal.

"Taking off a coat of mail is hard work," Erin said.

She struck out with her staff, smashing the man in the face with the haft, causing him to stagger back. The leader came at her with his hatchet and, bringing her weapon across, she knocked it to one side. She struck out with the end, jabbing it into the man's throat so that he gurgled and stumbled away.

"Bitch!" the knifeman said.

Now Erin twisted the staff, drawing off the end to reveal the long blade beneath that ran almost half its length. The dappled light of the forest shone darkly from it. In the weird, calm space that followed, she spoke. No point in disguising anything now.

"When I was young, my mother made me take sewing lessons, but the woman who taught us was nearly blind, and Nerra, my sister, used to cover for me while I ran out and fought the boys with sticks. When my mother found out, she was angry, but my father said that I might as well learn properly, and he was the king, so …"

"Your father's the king?" the leader said. Fear crossed his face, closely followed by greed. "If they catch us, they'll kill us, but they would have done that anyway, and the ransom we'll get for someone like you..."

Probably they would pay it. Although, given what Erin had overheard and the amount they'd been prepared to pay to get rid of her...

The bandit lunged forward for Erin again, interrupting her train of thought by swinging his hatchet and then kicking out at her. Erin swept the hatchet blow aside one-handed, pushed at the man's elbow, and then kicked him in the knee as he tried to kick her, sending him stumbling to the ground. Her teacher would probably be angry that she hadn't followed up.

Keep moving, end it quickly, take no chances. Erin could almost hear the words of her teacher, Swordmaster Wendros. He had been the one to tell her to use the short spear, a weapon that could make up for her lack of height and power with its speed and reach. Erin had been a little disappointed by the choice at the time, but she wasn't now.

Taking a two-handed grip on her weapon, she spun, covering as the one with a sword came at her. She set blows aside one after another, then aimed a cut of her own at him. A spear can cut as well as thrust. He went to deflect the strike, his sword rising up to meet it, and Erin rolled her wrists to send her blade dancing under the block, the spear's point lancing forward to thrust through his neck. Even as he died, the man flailed another blow at her, and Erin struck it aside, already moving on.

Do not stop. Keep moving until the fight is done.

"She's killed him!" the knifeman shouted. "She's killed Ferris!"

He lunged at her with the long knife, obviously trying to kill, not capture. He rushed in, trying to get in close where the greater length of Erin's weapon wouldn't count. Erin made to step back, then moved in even closer than he expected, wheeling him over her hip so he landed with a whoosh of escaping air...

Or he would have if he hadn't dragged her down with him.

Showy, girl. Just do what's needed.

It was too late for that now, because she was on the floor with the knifeman, caught there while he stabbed at her, only her coat of mail keeping her from death. She'd been overconfident, and now she was in a space where the man's greater strength was starting to tell. He was on top of her now, pushing the knife down toward her throat…

Somehow, Erin managed to get close enough to bite him, and that gave her enough room to scramble free, no art or skill to it now, only desperation. The leader was back on his feet by now, swinging his weapon again. Erin parried the first blow, barely, on her knees, took a kick to the midsection, and spat blood as she came up.

"You picked the wrong people to mess with, bitch," the leader said and went for an overhand stroke, aimed at her head.

There was no time to dodge, no time to parry. All Erin could do was duck down and thrust up with her spear. She felt the crunch as it went through flesh, expected to feel the impact of her foe's weapon in her own body, but for a moment, things just froze. She dared to look up, and he was there, transfixed on the end of her spear, so busy staring down at the weapon that he hadn't finished his own attack.

It is a fine thing to be lucky, and a stupid thing to rely on it, Swordmaster Wendros's voice sounded in her mind.

The knifeman was still down, struggling to rise.

"Mercy, please," the knifeman said.

"Mercy?" Erin said. "How much mercy did you show to the people you robbed, and killed, and raped? When they begged you, did you laugh at them? Did you run them down when they fled? How much mercy would you have shown *me*?"

"Please," the man said, standing. He turned to run, probably hoping he could outpace Erin in the trees.

She almost let him go, but what would he do then? How many more people would die when he thought he could get away with it again? She reversed her blade, hefted it, and flung it.

Over a long distance, it wouldn't have worked, because the spear was shorter than a true javelin, but over the short space between them it sailed through the air perfectly, plunging through the bandit point first and bringing him to the ground. Erin stepped over to him, set a foot on his back, and dragged it out. Lifting it, she brought it down sharply on his neck.

"That's as much mercy as I have today," she said.

She stood there, then moved to the side of the track, suddenly nauseous. It had felt so right and so easy when she'd been fighting, but now…

She threw up. She'd never killed anyone before, and now the horror and the stench of it were almost overwhelming. She knelt there for what felt like hours before her mind insisted that she should move. Swordmaster Wendros's voice came to her again…

When it is done, it is done. You focus on the practical, and you don't regret any of it.

That was easier said than done, but Erin forced herself to her feet. She cleaned her sword on their clothes, then dragged the bodies to the side of the track. That was the hardest part of all of it, because they were all bigger than she was, and a corpse felt heavier than a living thing too. By the time she was done, there was more blood on her clothes than there had been from the fight, not to mention the cut where the knifeman had struck. She had the strange, sudden thought that she was going to have to make sure they got to a servant to mend before her mother saw them. She laughed at that, and for several moments, she couldn't stop laughing.

Battle nerves. The greatest threat to a swordsman, and the greatest drug the world has ever known.

Erin stood there a moment or two longer, letting the excitement of the fight run through her veins. She'd killed men, and she'd done more than that. She'd proved herself. The Knights of the Spur would have to take her now.

CHAPTER EIGHT

Renard kept coming to the Inn of the Broken Scale for three main reasons, and none of them had to do with the frankly terrible beer. The first was the barmaid Yselle, who seemed to have a thing for burly men with red hair like him, and who seemed to alternate between accusing him of cheating on her and demanding that he come by more often.

The second reason was that, on the days when he was inclined to try to make an honest living, they didn't mind him taking out his lute and playing a few of the old ballads. Mostly, Renard didn't feel like doing it, but sometimes his fingers itched for the performance.

The third reason was that his fingers more often itched for other things, and the inn was a good place to hear rumors.

"It sounds too much like a story," he said to the man opposite him, carefully using the distraction to switch a card for one of those he had hidden in his sleeve.

"Ye can call it a story if you like, but I saw it with my own eyes," the man insisted. He was dressed in rough sailor's clothes, and claimed that he worked on the ships that sailed the long route out, away from the crippling rapids of the river and across the sea. That alone made Renard suspicious. Sailors were madmen; had to be, when it was far easier to trade via the bridges between the Northern and Southern Kingdoms than to stray into the dangers of deep water.

"So tell me again," Renard said, laying down his cards.

"Ha, I win!" the sailor said. "I never normally have this luck."

That's because you're so awful at cards, Renard didn't say. He wasn't sure he agreed with having to cheat to lose, as it seemed to defeat the whole point of cheating, frankly, but hopefully the payoff would be better than the losses.

"Tell me again," Renard insisted.

"Ah, eager to get a new song out of it?" the sailor said.

"Maybe."

"Well, this is probably not for songs," the sailor said. "Lord Carrick wouldn't like it."

Renard shrugged. "Tell me anyway. Maybe I'll change a few things. You know what liars singers get to be."

"Aye," the sailor said. He took another swig of the beer Renard had bought him. "Gods, this is awful stuff. Now, where was I?"

"The story."

"Oh, yes. Well, I was crewing on a treasure ship, wasn't I, going out the long way because King Ravin has to be paid by his colonies out west, out on Sarras."

The mention of the Southern king was enough to keep Renard's interest. "And then what?"

"Caught the edge of one of the tides, didn't we?" the sailor said. "Went too close to the mouth of the river's estuary in the wrong tide, and got ourselves sucked onto the rocks." The look of horror on his face as he thought about it was enough to make Renard believe him. Why anyone would chance going near the powerful pull of the Slate, he didn't know.

"I barely got off," the man said. "Me and a few of the others. Obviously, the captain's dead by that point, and some of the lads are stupid enough to go to the local lord, say what we have, say that they'll show him where, for a price."

"And you know that how?" Renard said.

"Because one of them came to me after, looking frightened, like he'd done the stupidest thing in his life. Maybe he had, because I've not seen him since. From what he said, they took Lord Carrick down to the spot where we washed up, and he had his men pick it clean; took the treasure back to his grand house in the city. Then he had those who knew about it killed. My friend barely got away."

He was probably dead now, Renard mused. So, probably, would the sailor be in a few days. Lord Carrick was not rumored to be a kind or gentle lord. The inn sat on his lands, and there were plenty who came through who had their complaints about him. Quietly, if they had sense. Of course, that was what made this prospect so appealing.

"What kind of treasure was on this ship?" Renard asked.

"Why? Planning to go and ask his lordship for some of it?"

Renard forced a laugh at that. "Ha, maybe, or maybe I just need the details for my song. What was it? Statues? Art? Gold bars?"

"Coin," the sailor said, and Renard heaved a silent sigh of relief. If it had been any of the things he'd mentioned, they would have been far too heavy to carry. "Southern pieces mostly, but a few things stamped with the colonies' marks. My friend said they had a clerk count every piece into a book when they took it." He shook his head. "Probably killed him too."

Renard could see why the man was drinking so much. Probably he knew what was coming for him. Probably he thought he might as well see out his last days blind drunk.

"Well," he said, "as stories go, it needs a little work. For a better ending, we really need a cunning but handsome thief to sweep in and take it all from under his lordship's nose."

"Ah, now that would be a thing," the sailor said. "But that don't happen in real life. Thieves mostly rob other poor folk, who can't fight back, not rich bastards who can hire guards."

"True enough," Renard said. "Still, it's a nice thought. Same again?"

"Sure," the sailor said.

Renard found himself wondering if he should keep going with this. Was this something he wanted to push forward with? Did he want to risk annoying Yselle more than usual with this? His purse gave him the answer to that. He needed the coin.

Renard stood and went toward the bar. Yselle was there, and Renard couldn't decide if she was in one of the moods where she cared about his existence or not.

"You're doing a lot of talking to that sailor," she observed.

"Well, I'm a very friendly person," Renard pointed out, with his most charming smile.

"Oh, stop that, you think I don't know when you're lying to me?" Yselle said.

"Would I lie to one so beautiful?" Renard asked.

"Almost constantly," the barmaid retorted. "It's just as well you're pretty, or I'd have thrown you out on your ear months ago."

"Pretty?" Renard affected wounded pride. "I am dashing, and handsome, but not—"

"Pretty," Yselle said firmly. "Pretty as a maiden, though we both know you're not that. Now, did you want something?"

"Tell me about Lord Carrick," Renard said.

Yselle shrugged. "What's to tell? You know all the stories, probably better than I do with that lute of yours. You know that he's hard on the peasants, takes his share and more of their crops, and hangs any who complain. You know he has more serfs than most, and treats them worse. What else do you want?"

Renard considered. "Someone who knows the layout of his home would be useful."

Yselle frowned at that. "No, Renard. That would be stupid."

"*Not* knowing the layout would be stupid," Renard countered. "This is just being prepared."

"You know what I mean," Yselle said. "Doing what you're thinking of doing would be a special kind of stupid, even by your standards."

"Well, a man should always try for self-betterment," Renard said. He slid a few more coins across the bar and raised an eyebrow. "Who, Yselle?"

She hesitated for a long moment and then sighed. "There's one of his former guards lives not far from here. Didn't leave on good terms. He comes in sometimes, and since Lord Carrick doesn't look after those who no longer work for him, he's probably poor enough to bribe."

"He'll do," Renard said.

"Seriously though, you should think again about this. This is a dangerous man."

Renard shrugged. "That's what makes it fun."

He said that because Yselle probably wouldn't understand the real reasons. She wouldn't get that fun didn't come into it, only the thought of everything a man like Lord Carrick could get away with, just because he'd been a big enough thug to amass a fortune. Steal a gold piece, and you could have your fingers cut off. Steal a whole chunk of land, and you got to be the one doing the cutting.

If men like Renard didn't bring lords like this Carrick down to size, who would? If they got to treat those on their lands like dirt with no comeback, what was to stop them from doing it for all time? If they could just kill men and take treasure, how did that make them any better than ...

... well, than *him*? That was always the problem with that kind of philosophizing: sooner or later it showed you head on what kind of man you were. Still, Renard thought, at least there was the gold, and it was an awful, *awful* lot of gold.

Probably even enough to be worth all the risks.

Chapter Nine

King Godwin stretched as he arrived in the great hall, shift-ing the weight of the deer he carried. The noonday light was too bright for his eyes as he strode forward, because there'd been enough drinking on this hunt, and in the feasting before. He threw the creature down onto a table, hearing the wood creak as it landed. Across the hall, his wife looked up from working with Lenore and her maids on their dresses for the coming festivities.

"There, Aethe, my love!" he called out. "I told you that I would make up for yesterday's feasting. We've bagged this, and boar, and pheasant!"

"And what good is it lying on our hall's tables, making a mess?" Aethe asked with a tolerant sigh. She gestured to a couple of ser-vants, who quickly went to take the deer away to the kitchens.

"Ah, you've no heart," King Godwin said. He went to her, sweep-ing her up in his arms and kissing her. To him, she was still as beau-tiful as she had been when they'd first met; not the all-consuming passion that it had been with his first wife, but something pure, and simple, and needed.

"And you've no head, sometimes," Aethe replied. She took him across to the spot where their thrones waited, carved in the basalt of the volcanoes that littered the land, most thankfully long dormant.

"How go the preparations?" King Godwin asked. "Is everything in order?"

"Everything is in chaos, thanks to you. An extra feast wasn't just food, it was time as well, so now we're trying to deal with everything at once. Then there's the fact that half your children aren't doing any of the things they should be to help, your sorcerer is wandering around doing strange things no one can fathom, and Finnal's family is making things more complicated."

King Godwin heaved a sigh. This was why he liked being out on the hunt: things were simpler there, with only the chase and the prey.

"Well, Rodry's with me, along with those lads who follow him around so closely." He raised his voice. "Rodry, come forward so that we can see you."

Rodry strode forward and swept a bow in his father's direction. He was dressed in loose hunting clothes, a sword at his hip.

"What do you need of me, Father?"

"What are you doing to aid in the wedding preparations, my son?" he asked.

"Aside from spearing the largest of the boars this morning?" his son countered with a confident look. His followers had cheered when he'd done that, clearly impressed. All the king had been able to think of was what might have happened if the boar's tusks had gored his son, his heir.

"There's still a lot to do," Aethe said.

Rodry nodded. "Then I and my friends will do all that we can to help. Just tell us where we are needed, and we will do it. I have something special planned for a wedding gift, as well."

"What?" King Godwin asked.

Of course, his eldest son shook his head, before he rushed off to do whatever it was he was set on doing.

"You realize that his would-be knights trying to help will create more chaos?" Aethe said. "You let the boy get away with being too rash."

Godwin spread his hands. "You can't have it both ways, my love." He looked over to a servant. "Find my other children and bring them. Find my soon-to-be son's family and ask them to meet with me too. I would know what the problem is."

Aethe laughed at that. "You're making it sound like all they need is a good talking to."

Godwin shrugged. "Maybe they do. I'm going to start by talking to the daughter who is actually getting married."

He stood and went to Lenore, who looked as perfect as she always did. She was standing there elegantly while her maids were working on her dress. At the same time, she was going through lists and notes while one of the maids read them out.

"Lord Forster and his son will be at the second table. Remember that they have a hatred of music, because the son finds it painful to hear..."

"Trying to remember everything about our guests?" King Godwin asked. "We're the ones who are meant to be making the day perfect for you."

"I still have plenty to do though," Lenore said. "I will be meeting so many people, and I want to acquit myself well; I wouldn't want to embarrass you."

"You could never do that," King Godwin promised her.

"Then there's the tour of the kingdom," Lenore said. "It takes a lot of preparation."

King Godwin smiled at that, remembering when he'd toured it with Illia. People had come out to see them, and had given gifts, and more importantly, had pledged their loyalty.

"I'm sure it will be fine," he said. He looked around at the sight of the doors to the Great Hall opening. "And here are your brothers and sisters."

The brothers, at least, which caught the king a little by surprise. Vars and Greave walked in together, Vars looking like he was nursing a hangover, his shirt and doublet disheveled as if he'd thrown them on in a hurry. Greave was dressed in gray and black, a book of some sort in his hand, his expression downcast. Honestly, Godwin didn't know what it would take to ever make his youngest son smile, and he wasn't sure he had the energy to care. His presence always put Godwin a little on edge, simply because he resembled his mother so much, from his shoulder-length blond hair and blue eyes down to the almost feminine lines of his face.

"Where are your sisters?" he demanded.

Greave shrugged, and somehow managed to do even that mournfully. "I have not seen Erin. Nerra is in her rooms, unwell, I believe."

Godwin flinched at the thought of Nerra unwell again. He would have to see her and make sure she was all right. As for Erin…

He turned to a couple of his knights, Jolin and Borus. Both had served him for many years now. Both were utterly loyal. "Find my youngest daughter, wherever she has gone, and bring her back."

"Yes, your majesty," they chorused, heading for the door together.

King Godwin returned his attention to his sons. "What about you two? Why have you not been doing what you should to help with the wedding? Vars? You were not on the hunt."

"I found more useful things to do," he said. "I will of course aid in any way I can."

"Then you won't mind being Lenore's guard and champion on her wedding procession?" the king said. It was the sort of job Rodry would have volunteered for, but his other sons needed some hardening up. Let Vars learn what being a warrior *meant*.

"Of course," Vars said, although his voice was tight. That only told Godwin just how much his son needed to be made to take responsibility.

"And you, Greave?" the king asked, but cut his son off before he could reply. "No, don't tell me, you were lost in some foolish book of poetry, or you felt the world too bleak to rise from your bed, or… what is that you're carrying?"

"A refutation of Serek's arguments regarding the autonomy of the spirit," Greave said in that too serious voice of his.

"So nothing useful?" King Godwin said. If he'd spoken that way to one of his daughters, Aethe would probably have intervened, but she didn't interfere when it came to Illia's sons.

"If you wish me to help with the wedding, then perhaps I could assist the players with composing—"

"No," King Godwin said. "You'll do work that befits a king's son, and a nobleman."

"Such as what?" Greave demanded, with that edge to his voice that always made Godwin angry with him. "Maybe I could beat some peasants like one of my brothers, or stab some animals like the other?"

The king opened his mouth to reprimand his son, knowing full well that it would only go downhill from there. It was almost a relief when a trumpet blared and Finnal's family walked in. Almost.

The young man himself was a handsome thing, who matched his daughter well, but Godwin could have lived without the whole parade of others who came with him: cousins and uncles, with his father, Duke Viris, at their fore. The duke had gray running through his formerly dark hair, and was dressed as severely as always, in clothes as suited to war or hunting as to the court.

"Your majesty, may I congratulate you on your success in the hunt?"

"You're kind," the king said. "At the same time, I understand that not everything is to your liking here?"

"Oh, it is just a few small matters," Duke Viris said. "The order of arrival at the wedding, for example."

"That is decided by rules of precedence," Aethe said, "as I have already explained to you."

"And I have pointed out that the order you have chosen is not the one that is universal. Typically, dukes process before princes."

"Maybe we can discuss it further," King Godwin said. "I'll not have it said that I was a stickler for rules when they got in the way. What else?"

"There is the small matter of when and how your daughter's dowry will be paid," the duke said.

King Godwin sighed and settled back in his throne. Whoever had said that kings were able to just do what they wished had clearly not spent any time as one. This was going to be a long day; there were a thousand details to discuss now, and if he messed up any one of them, he suspected that his daughter might not be getting married after all.

Chapter Ten

Vars could feel the shame rising up in him, slowly bubbling and turning to anger, as he went through the things he was required to do for the day. The wine was keeping it at bay, but only barely. He lifted a goblet to his lips again.

"Please remain perfectly still, your highness," the tailor with him said, and it was all Vars could do to keep from striking the man. It was so foolish that people like that could talk back to him and expect no punishment in response.

That brought thoughts of the boy in the House of Weapons, the one who had humiliated him. Vars still hadn't worked out the best way to have vengeance on him, and that was just fueling his bad mood. Why hadn't Rodry just let him execute the idiot and be done with it?

He drew his attention back to the fitting, the tailor still about his work.

"Are we nearly done?" Vars asked. He took another, very deliberate, sip of his wine.

"Very nearly, your highness, but we want your newest doublet and breeches to be perfect for the wedding."

The wedding, always the wedding. It seemed as though everything in the castle at the moment was about Lenore's wedding, when Vars couldn't see how his half-sister deserved so much fuss.

"Ah, looking wonderful as always," Lyril said as she came into the chambers unannounced. "More wedding preparations?"

"Do not start about the wedding," Vars said. "My half-sister sits as far removed from the succession as you could imagine, yet she gets a wedding worthy of a queen." He remembered the presence of the tailor. "You, out."

"Your highness..."

"Out!"

The man scurried out, taking his tools with him.

"Well, he'll be around the castle, telling the story of how the prince is jealous of the attention his sister is getting," Lyril said.

"Are you criticizing me?" Vars demanded.

She raised an eyebrow in response. If she was afraid, she didn't show it. "Merely pointing out that usually you are more subtle, my prince. It's just one of the things I love about you."

"Love?" Vars said. That always seemed like such a stupid word. Love was a transaction, and the things that came of it definitely were. I give you money and you give me pleasure. I give you myself in marriage and you give me lands or men for my armies, or a secure bloodline. Love didn't come into it.

"You are a remarkable man, Vars," Lyril said, moving close to him.

Vars made a grab for her, but Lyril stepped back, just out of his reach.

"Not today, my darling," she said. "I too have many preparations to make for the wedding."

"You're going to use my sister's wedding as an excuse not to bed me?" Vars demanded. He could feel the anger continuing to rise. "Do you know what I've already had to put up with for the sake of this farce? My father is sending me into danger. He's putting me in charge of escorting my sister's procession around the kingdom."

"I take it that it is not the honor he is trying to paint it?" Lyril guessed.

Vars snorted at the thought that anyone could think it so. "My sister goes around the land looking beautiful and receiving gifts, while I'm stuck there as if I'm somehow less important, just riding along like some...some guardsman."

"That would take you away from Royalsport for a long time," Lyril said, she looked thoughtful for a moment. "Hmm…I might have to find someone else to keep me company…"

"Do you think I will sit back and stand for that?" Vars demanded. "Remember that there are other noblewomen out there."

"Ah, but none so lovely, don't you agree?" Lyril said. She turned slowly, letting him see her, and in that moment Vars wanted nothing more than to tear the dress from her and have her there on the floor, regardless of the consequences.

"None so lovely," Vars admitted. "And you know it."

"Yes, I know it," Lyril agreed. "And I use it, along with anything else that I can. You see that in me, and I think there is a part of you that desires that more than anything to do with my body."

Vars smiled at that. "Perhaps. Well then, what do you see in me? Is it just that I am a handsome prince for you to try to snare?"

"I think you are a man who takes what he wants," Lyril said. "A cunning man and a clever one. And I think that if you were to think, there would be an easy solution for all of the ways your sister's wedding is overshadowing you. One that will make sure that I'm in your bed and your bed only."

Vars thought he could see where this was going. "Lyril, I've told you—"

"Marry me, Vars. Marry me, and it will be the second in line to the throne getting married, not a girl who's back behind all the men of the family in the succession. Marry me."

Vars didn't like it when people put pressure on him. He would never have used the word coward, because that was a word that the likes of Rodry used to make him feel small, but he knew he couldn't stand up to someone truly forceful head on.

"All right," he said. "All right, I'll marry you!"

Lyril threw her arms around him, kissing him. "That's wonderful! Vars, you just made me the happiest woman in Royalsport."

Vars was glad that one of them was so happy. He could feel his anger almost bursting at being pressured like this, and he knew he was going to have to do something to relieve it. Thankfully, he knew just the thing.

The House of Sighs was a discreet establishment in one of the wealthier areas of the city, gilded and painted so that it looked like something between a theater and an inn. The women who could be glimpsed there told its true purpose, though.

A servant took Prince Vars's cloak and sword at the door, while a discreetly placed man who had once been a mercenary sized him up to make sure he was a suitable patron and unlikely to cause trouble; at least of the kind he didn't pay for. The man was large enough that for a moment Prince Vars flinched, and that just fed into everything else he was feeling.

Madam Meredith was there, as she always was, overseeing the parlor where soft music played and conversation flowed between men and women, some nobles, some there for their entertainment. For a few who came here, the music, the wine, the conversation were all they wanted. Vars thought he caught glimpses of several faces he knew, although many wore masks here. There was even one far too handsome male face that Vars definitely knew, but he shrugged. That was the balance in this place: in revealing another's secrets, one revealed one's own.

Meredith herself was as beautiful as any of the men or women who worked for her, probably no older than thirty, with raven hair and rings on each finger of one hand, supposedly denoting the husbands she had outlived.

"Your highness," she said. "What can I get for you today? Wine? Some company?"

Vars looked around until he saw a suitable-looking woman, slender and blonde-haired, blue-eyed and innocent looking in spite of her profession. He pointed.

"Her."

"Your highness, Yasmine is not really suitable for your tastes."

"Her," Vars said, in a dangerous tone. He took out a money pouch, heavy enough that when he put it in Meredith's hand, her hand moved slightly. "Or I could suggest to my father that now is the time to reconsider the way the House of Sighs works."

Meredith hesitated for a minute, then nodded. "Yasmine, come here. The prince has taken a liking to you. The top room."

The woman looked a little frightened, but held out her hand and Vars took it, delicately for now. He went with her up to the room that he normally took when he was here, and he could feel the excitement he usually felt building within him, alongside the anger, one fueling the other.

They reached the space, which was opulent with silks and tapestries, until it seemed like a world of red and gold gossamer. Prince Vars shoved her toward the bed, hard. The young woman turned to him.

"Your highness, please be gentle…"

Vars struck her, hard, with the flat of his hand, sending her tumbling to her knees. "You do not speak to me without being told."

She looked up at him, the fear obvious in her eyes now.

"That's a better start," he said. He lifted his hand again. "As for being gentle, that's not what you're being paid for, whore. Let's see if you can scream as beautifully as you kneel."

CHAPTER ELEVEN

Devin wandered the streets of Royalsport, still in a daze, crossing the bridges, reflecting on all that had happened to him. Right then he should have been at work; he never wandered the streets this time of day, and it didn't feel right. He no longer had any work to go to. He felt purposeless.

Yet at the same time, he felt a tremendous purpose hovering just outside the realms of his fingertips, one he knew was circling him yet one he could not understand.

Magic. Was that what had happened back there? Had he really made the prince's hand move? Or had he imagined it? Did the prince just have a cramp, perhaps?

The memory brought back other, less comfortable memories, from when Devin was a boy. Memories hovering in the outskirts of his brain, foggy; he was not even sure if they were real memories or just fantasies, dreams. But they were there, still. Moments, flashes of a power Devin had wielded. Of others looking at him as if he were different.

Was he?

His father would be so angry, not just at the thought that he'd lost his job, but at the way he had done it. Devin knew he would shout and rage, demand to know what he'd been thinking. The idea that he had been protecting Nem wouldn't be justification enough, because his father would only think about the things that might follow for all of them.

He couldn't go home until he'd worked out what to do next, that much was clear.

Yet what *could* he do next?

Devin didn't know, so he kept walking. He made his way into the marketplace that sat before the House of Merchants, the large, open space essentially just an extension of the commerce that went on within. Inside, merchants would get loans to finance their expeditions or their businesses; outside, they would sell the fruits of those efforts, trying to recoup enough to start the whole thing over again.

There was a festival attitude there today, with jugglers and musicians in the spaces among the stalls, while criers called out in celebration of Princess Lenore's upcoming wedding.

"The king has declared feasting at the castle, the outer yards open to all!" a man called out as Devin passed.

Right then, feasting sounded like a good idea. As he walked among the stalls, Devin could smell the scents of food cooking in a dozen spots, open-air stalls set with fires to allow them to prepare meat or stew for those who passed, but Devin was fairly sure he couldn't afford it right now. There were brightly colored cloths dyed by the weavers and farmers who had set up in the hope of selling their stock.

Devin was still too stunned to take it all in, though he looked around in the vain hope that someone there might need help with their work. Occasionally, there were fairs where the merchants sought out the strong and the willing for whatever tasks they had. Now, one of those seemed like the best chance Devin had of ever finding work again.

The full impact of losing his place in the House of Weapons started to hit home then. Devin had been on the way to being a master smith; everyone knew he understood metal and the way it worked as well as anyone there. And in the House of Weapons, he could have kept training with weapons, could have kept working to be the warrior he wanted to be.

Now he had nothing. He had no job, and probably no chance of getting another. When people learned that he had been dismissed from the House of Weapons, they would never give him another position, except in the lowliest of jobs.

His stomach was rumbling as he passed an inn, but he stopped himself from going in. He didn't have the coin to spare, and he doubted his parents would be generous with more. Already, his father occasionally dropped hints that it was time he was finding a home of his own.

Devin kept walking, past the inn, on into the city. He crossed another of the bridges, the water rushing by beneath, guards looking him over as if trying to decide if he was someone they should stop. This area had larger, wealthier-looking homes that were mostly half-timbered, the shops having actual glass in their windows, the cobbles of the streets in a better state of repair.

Devin's path took him past the entwined towers of the House of Knowledge, and briefly he stopped, staring at the doors there, which stood at the top of a flight of steps, behind wrought iron gates that had clearly been worked on by a multitude of different smiths. An inscription above stated *Let those who seek understanding enter in peace.*

Devin felt the part of this that he'd been avoiding starting to rise up in him. The loss of his job, and the brief fight with a prince had been bad enough, but one part of it seemed to defy understanding. There had been a moment where things had seemed to stretch out, where he had made Prince Vars drop his weapon without even touching him.

He'd done magic.

There was no other explanation for it, yet it made no sense. How could someone like him, low born, just a smith, do *magic?*

Maybe they would have an answer in the House of Knowledge. Then again, maybe they wouldn't; after all, the kingdom seemed to only have one true sorcerer. Inexorably, Devin found his eyes drawn toward the castle, and to the tower that stood over part of it, sticking out over the water around it in a way that looked tenuous, even dangerous. Devin knew that the occupant of that tower would have answers for him, had even come to him once before, in his dreams.

Suddenly, a sense of purpose, of direction, came rushing to him all at once. Of course. His dream. Master Grey. He had to see

Master Grey, had to ask him what was going on. No one else would be able to explain it all.

Yet how was he supposed to get in to see the king's sorcerer?

A crier shouted again, declaring the feasting once more, and Devin knew that it was his best chance. Setting his eyes on the castle, he started to walk, making his way inward through the circles of the city. He crossed more bridges, and now guards started to frown more, half stepping in front of him as he passed.

"I'm on my way to the feasting," Devin said each time, and each time they stepped back, as if it were some password to let even a commoner like him into the most exalted parts of the city. Soon, the outer walls of the castle were rising above him, tall and gray and sheer as a cliff face, even though they were festooned with banners celebrating the noble lines attending the celebrations.

Once more, the guards stepped back for Devin, although this time, one of them called to him as he passed.

"Just remember that there's none but the nobles allowed in the great hall proper. Keep yourself to the outer courtyards with all the others."

"I will," Devin said, and set off in the direction of the sounds of festivities in progress.

Even in the outer courtyards, things were more lavish than he could have imagined. There were people everywhere, although most seemed to be merchants and burghers rather than truly common folk. There were whole roast boars, and trestle tables set with more food than Devin had seen before. He was more than hungry enough to grab a wooden trencher and pile it high with swan and grouse, buttered parsnips and suet dumplings. Picking at it gave him an excuse to wander through the crowd, avoiding the dancing as a trio of minstrels played, trying to work out what he was going to do next.

Right now, Devin was close, but not close enough. If he was going to get to see Master Grey, he would have to access the rest of the castle, and that was impossible while he was stuck outside its inner spaces.

I could just walk up to a guard and tell them who I am, who I want to see, he thought to himself. Devin could guess how that could go, though. They would think he was drunk, or turn him away on principle, or…or worse, it would attract the wrong attention. Devin doubted it would go well if Prince Vars learned that the boy he'd fought with was there, in the castle, right under his nose.

All he could do for the moment was wait. Periodically, the doors leading to the great hall opened, either to let servants through with more food, or let them back carrying empty platters. Each time they opened, Devin looked at the room beyond, searching for any sign of the sorcerer.

Suddenly, he saw him there, standing in the middle of the hall, staring back. Master Grey's eyes locked with his, and Devin was sure there was a moment of acknowledgment, of understanding, of *connection.*

Devin found himself drawn forward by that gaze, walking deeper into the festivities beyond.

In that instant, Devin felt rough hands on him.

He turned, stunned to see guards there, hands grabbing him, detaining him.

"What have I done?" Devin asked.

But they didn't respond.

Instead, they dragged him away, backward, away from Master Grey.

Devin was sure they were escorting him out of the feasting hall for some reason, perhaps back outside the castle walls. Perhaps he wasn't dressed appropriately.

But a jolt of fear ran through him as he realized they were not dragging him out of the castle, but *into* it. They were heading down a dark corridor, toward a steel door.

And what could only be a dungeon.

CHAPTER TWELVE

Greave didn't understand how anyone could have celebrations when there was clearly so much sadness and evil in the world. He sat in the castle's library, away from the need to be involved in any of it, knowing that his presence would only bring down the others there. His father, in particular, seemed to look on him as an intrusion, and had since the day his mother had fainted and fallen and struck her head on a step, the blow sharp, and sudden, and fatal…

"I will not think of it," Greave said. "I will not."

It was hard not to think of his mother, though, when he saw the echo of her features every time he looked in the mirror. His brothers looked more like their father, with Rodry's blond hair the only hint of her, but Greave… well, his features were as soft and delicate as a man's might get, his hair falling in waves, his hands not calloused by swordplay and his body slender at twenty. Every glance at himself brought back memories of the blood, and then Greave had to retreat here, to the only place that seemed safe.

The library was one of the largest outside of the House of Knowledge, with shelf after shelf of tomes stacked high, copied by the finest hands of the scholars, or by the monks of the Isle of Leveros. There were works here that dated back before the division of the kingdoms, and Greave found that it was the only place in which he felt truly at home.

He started to read through Brother Marcus's *Quotations on a Forthright Life*, since the long dead monk was considered an authority, and since Greave had made it his mission to read through the entire contents of the library, but he found that he couldn't get very far before his thoughts raised natural objections.

"'A good man is upright and willing to trust others,'" he read, then shook his head. "But what if the people he trusts are not worthy of it, or betray him? And this... 'a man should strive for hope in all things.' Was he not looking at the world when he wrote this?"

Greave set the book aside and turned to LeNere's *On the Machinations of Government*, long derided by the House of Knowledge as simply a defense of evil actions. Greave could see that, and he could certainly never imagine the destruction of entire families that the man seemed to argue for, but there were passages that simply seemed to speak to him.

"'The world is a bleak, cruel place,'" he read, "'and a man involved at court must recognize the truth of this. To imagine it happier, to trust or to be kind to one's enemies, is not a virtue, but a vice, for one with power must protect the lives of those he serves by any means.'"

Was *serves* the right word? Did LeNere truly conceive of rulers as serving those they ruled? Perhaps Greave would write something on it and send it to the House of Scholars to prove how much he deserved to be there, or perhaps he would write a play where a ruler who truly believed that was taken advantage of by his entire court...

"Greave? Are you going to miss *all* of the celebrations?"

He turned at the sound of Nerra's voice, standing and going to hug his sister. There was always something so delicate and fragile about Nerra that it almost made his heart break.

"I'm hardly the best at them," he said.

"Because you don't get enough practice," she replied. "I'm sure there will be any number of beautiful noblewomen down there. Perhaps you could dance with one."

Greave shook his head. He couldn't imagine them being interested in him. Couldn't imagine *anyone* seeing him as something other than an impediment to their happiness. "What about you?" he asked. "You look like you've been out in the forest again."

"I have," Nerra said. "It's the only place I can be and not worry about people watching me."

"You had your sleeves up?" Greave asked, suddenly worried. He knew about his sister's condition, knew enough to know that people would call for Nerra's death if they found out.

"It's fine," Nerra said. "I'm fine..."

"You don't sound certain," Greave said.

"I... had a fainting fit," Nerra said.

"Another?" Greave shook his head. He was sure they were getting closer together. "You see, that's another reason for me not to go down to the party. I need to stay here and look through more of the books in case there's a cure for you."

"Don't you think someone would have found it if it were here to find?" Nerra countered. "You're just trying to get out of dancing."

"So *you'll* be running straight down to the hall?" Greave countered. They both knew she wouldn't. That many people always raised too many risks of someone seeing the scale sickness on her arms.

"I need to find Physicker Jarran," Nerra said. "I... need to discuss some things with him."

"About your condition?" Of course it was. The healer was one of the only ones outside the family who knew about Nerra's sickness. He was also the only one who had been able to so much as slow it. But even he didn't have a cure.

"Promise me you won't spend *all* your time here?" Nerra said. "Lenore would love to see you down there, I'm sure."

"I'll try," Greave promised, although he knew he wouldn't make it. He had too many books to get through.

It seemed to Greave that a man could read for a lifetime and not find what he needed in the castle's library.

"I will find it, though," Greave promised himself. He knew he had not always been the best brother, but in this, he would not fail his sister.

He plunged into the stacks, hunting for medical tomes the way Rodry might go into a forest after a boar. Greave set aside works on the higher forms of philosophy, on the correct way to cut a canal system, on the supposed foundations of magic, looking only for something that promised the secret workings of the body. Greave half-remembered a text with a green cover by the ancient physician Velius, and set about searching.

Of course, there were many green covers in the library, but Greave worked his way through them, one by one, setting aside a tome showing a sword master's techniques, a work on the design of the bridges so vital for Royalsport.

Come on, he willed himself. Remember the title. Remember.

Then suddenly, as he poured through books, it came to him: *On The Body.*

Greave shouted aloud in delight, thrilled it came back to him. A slim, green volume.

Yet recalling the title was not, he knew, the same as having the book itself. Surely, it must be in here somewhere?

With even greater urgency, Greave poured through stacks of books.

"It has to be here," he said. "It has to be here."

"What has to be?" a woman's voice asked.

Greave looked up and instantly froze. The young woman who stood before him was as close to perfect as he had ever seen. She had to be around his age, slender and red-haired, with green eyes that seemed to be questioning the world around her with every glance. She wore a dress of grays and silvers that she somehow managed to make look anything but ordinary, and her smile … her smile was the most beautiful thing Greave had seen. The jewelry she wore suggested that she was noble born, for who else could afford so many gold and silver rings and chains? She had a ribbon of the same silver twined into her hair, the end of it spilling down over her shoulder.

"I … I'm looking for a book," Greave managed, remembering to breathe. "I'm sorry, who are you? What are you doing here?"

"I'm looking for you," she said. Her voice was as beautiful as the rest of her, seeming to sing with the notes of the country far beyond the city. "My name is Aurelle Hardacre."

Greave recognized the name of a minor noble family at once, but he still couldn't fathom the rest of her presence.

"You're looking for me?" he said. It made no sense.

"Where my family has its estate, they sing songs about the beautiful prince who sits in his library, wrapped in sorrow," Aurelle said. She glanced away for a moment. "You sounded too good to be true, yet here you are."

Too good to be true? Greave didn't know about that. He knew that some people found his features attractive, but he'd never been ruggedly handsome in the same way his brothers were, and anyone who did like him quickly drifted away once they learned about the true him.

"Shall I help you to pick some of those up?" Aurelle asked, moving to assist Greave in lifting the books that he'd scattered so far in his search.

"No, you don't have to, it's all right," he managed. How could the presence of a woman he'd only just met make him feel as if the world were tilting this way and that? It made no sense.

"I want to help," Aurelle said. "Oh look! A copy of Francesca di Vere's love poems! They're so beautiful, aren't they?"

Greave wanted to say that none of them was as beautiful as her, but he didn't have the words for it. "I haven't read them," he managed instead. It occurred to him that this was a chance to learn something about her. "Are you here for the wedding?"

"I am," Aurelle said. "My family is just important enough to be invited. Although I'm quite lost here. The castle is far larger than I expected, and as for the city…"

"Perhaps I could show you around," Greave blurted, even though he hadn't meant to do it. Even though he had so many more important things that he should be doing.

"I'd like that," Aurelle said. She held out her arm. "Now? Since you've finished looking for your book, I mean?"

Greave knew he couldn't tell her that the love poems weren't what he was searching for, that he still had a book to find, without explaining what, and why. Well, he could, but then it would look as though he had no interest in her, and that simply wasn't the truth. Instead, he stood straight, took the book of Francesca di Vere's poems, and took hold of Aurelle's arm.

"I would like that too," he said. After all, how long could this take? Whatever secret was hidden away in the library, it would still be there when they were done.

And he would find it, whatever it was.

CHAPTER THIRTEEN

Nerra went to Physicker Jarran's quarters and knocked, the strange scent of the place striking her as she did it. There was always a mix of rot and brightness about the place, the sharpness of the herbs he worked with mixed in with the decay of those bodies of criminals he kept for dissection.

"Enter, enter!" he called out in a jolly voice. For someone who worked with the dead and the dying so much, he always managed to sound more cheerful than he had a right to.

Nerra pushed open the door and stepped inside, trying to leave it as long as possible before taking another breath there. The quarters were large, on the bottom level of the castle, with window slits above whose light was patterned by fragments of stained glass. Most of the light came from candles kept in jars, carefully just far enough away from whatever the physicker was working on in that moment that they wouldn't set light to it.

The room had probably once been a crypt or a chapel, with slabs that now held bodies in various states of dissection, and one whole end of the room given over to living quarters, a layer of rugs and carpets marking it out as different from the rest. There was a desk there, a large board filled with chalked observations, a bed, and a table with chairs around it.

Physicker Jarran was a large man whose frame was barely contained by the robes of the House of Knowledge. Currently, he wore an apron over them, and was working on cutting up the arm of a body on one of the nearer slabs. Nerra tried not to stare in horror at that sight, even though she'd been down here plenty of times before for lessons.

"Why are you cutting up someone's arm?" Nerra asked, and she was sure some of her disgust at it leaked through.

"The House of Knowledge says that no knowledge is ever wasted," Physicker Jarran said. "In this case, by better understanding the workings of the arm, I might be able to do more to help those who have injured theirs. It is a study that would help you greatly, if you truly wish to heal others."

Most of the herb lore Nerra knew, she'd learned from the physicker. To her parents, it had just been her taking an interest in her treatment, yet the physicker had quickly seen her interest and taught her far more, to the point where Nerra could recognize almost any plant in the forest and its properties. Even so...

"No, thank you," she said. Some things just weren't for her.

"I wasn't expecting you here for a lesson today," Physicker Jarran said.

All of Nerra's brothers and sisters had taken lessons from the physicker, since as a graduate of the House of Knowledge, he could teach reading, writing, history, and philosophy as easily as any scholar of the House of Knowledge. Nerra's lessons had featured increasing amounts of herb lore once he had seen she was interested in it, along with knowledge of other places she knew she would never live long enough to see. The physicker was also one of the few people who knew the truth of her condition, since he'd been the one trying to at least slow it for years now.

"I don't have a lesson today," Nerra said. Suddenly she was nervous, finding herself wondering if she should be there at all. "I... guess I'm supposed to be at all the feasting."

"With so much feasting, who could attend it all? Even me?" Physicker Jarran countered, with a pat of his stomach. "Why are you here, though, Nerra? It's not to join in my research."

"I..." Nerra wasn't sure whether to just come out and tell him what she'd found or not. She thought back to her worries in the forest: that someone would take the dragon's egg and destroy it, or dissect the dragon within. She knew she couldn't take that much of a chance, but she still needed to know more than she did.

"What do you know about dragons?" Nerra asked.

"Dragons?" Physicker Jarran asked, raising an eyebrow. "I'd have thought that was more Master Grey's field than mine."

"You know he won't answer," Nerra said. Master Grey rarely said anything about dragons, even though the rumors said that he'd seen them, fought them…

Physicker Jarran took off his apron and came over to the living area, sitting down in one of the chairs at the table. It creaked under his bulk.

"I may know some things about them, certainly. I have read of them, in the House of Knowledge."

"What can you tell me about them?" Nerra asked. "And about their eggs?"

"Their eggs?" Physicker Jarran said.

"How would I know for sure if one were real, for example?" Nerra asked.

"That is easy," the physicker said. "It wouldn't be. Preserved dragon eggs are so rare these days…" He spread his hands apart. "A real one would be about this big, if I recall the books correctly. It would have veins of red or gold or green running through it. The shell color would reflect the color of the creature within, and… well, the sources say that the egg would be warm of all things."

Nerra's breath caught. Every detail fit with that of the egg she'd found.

"This is a curiously specific thing to ask about, Nerra," Physicker Jarran said. "Has someone offered you a cast of a shell? I know that there is a market for such things, and people think they know what to look for. They see a large egg and assume it must be a dragon's."

"Well, I wanted to know more about dragons generally," Nerra said. The more she could find out, the better. "Where do they come from? How do they grow? What do they eat?"

"Generally, anything they want," Physicker Jarran said, and it took Nerra a moment to realize that it was his idea of a joke. "According to the books, dragons are creatures of power. In both the magical and every other sense. Their very beings are conduits for power, letting them soar, and shape that energy into fire or lightning or mist or shadow. They are long lived, each living a thousand years if they do not die in combat, starting to wane only in the years after the dragon moon. They are said to roost among volcanoes and places of fire, the heat of them warming their eggs when they lay them, just before they die."

"They lay their eggs immediately before they die?" Nerra said.

"There is a kind of sense to it," the physicker explained. "With creatures so long lived, if they birthed their young earlier, they would soon overrun the world. They would be raising their own competitors. Look at people."

"I don't understand," Nerra said.

"Don't you? You have seen how families can be complicated. How many times in human history have sons and daughters risen up against their parents, or brothers and sisters gone to war? It is a story as old as time."

Physicker Jarran's expression turned serious. "You're asking about dragons. Where do they live? If there are any left out there, they live beyond the realms of men, in the fire places. They are powerful, powerful enough that the kingdoms were separated in the war against those who ruled using them. But they are also not a subject you should waste your time on, Nerra."

"Why not?" Nerra countered.

"Because we both know how little time you have. How bad is your sickness now? Are the herbs I recommended slowing it?"

The suddenness of the question caught Nerra by surprise. So did the sharpness of it. "I ..."

"Show me your arms," he insisted.

Nerra rolled up her sleeves, letting him see the scale sickness there. Pulling on gloves, he poked at the flesh, apparently watching the way the dark lines there distorted at the touch.

"In spite of our efforts, the sickness has progressed," he said. "I am sorry, but at this rate of progression, you will either die or be transformed in a matter of weeks."

"Transformed?" Nerra said. She'd heard of the things the scale sickness could do, but she hadn't believed them to be real until now.

Physicker Jarran went back to his chair. "You have heard the stories."

Nerra nodded, buttoning her sleeves once more. "What's the truth, though? I thought that it was all made up, that it was just that people had seen the scale pattern and thought it meant something."

"You thought that people did what they always do, and surrounded the truth with so many stories and half-truths that it became obscured?"

"Yes," Nerra admitted. "I thought… when they sent people away, I thought they just died. I thought that all the fear was because of the way it could spread."

"You thought, or you hoped?"

"I… hoped," Nerra admitted.

Physicker Jarran shook his head. "The scale sickness is a transformation. People die when their bodies are not strong enough to complete it. The results… you have heard of the horrific beasts of legend, the things that populate Sarras."

It wasn't a question, but Nerra nodded her agreement anyway. She had heard of them, the things that were not even close to being human. Yet if what the physicker was saying was true…

"Was everything to the west once human?" she asked. Fear was already running through her at the thought. Would she become something… else? Something not human, not kind, not able to do as she wished?

"That is a question that is better saved for Master Grey," Physicker Jarran said. "He knows more of the truth of these things than I."

Nerra could only admit that he had a point. Master Grey knew as much as anyone alive about the strange and the unseen, yet she didn't want to talk to him about this, couldn't risk it.

"I must ask again," Physicker Jarran said. "Why are you asking about things like dragons, Nerra?"

"I…" Nerra thought about telling him, she honestly did, but she couldn't bring herself to, not yet. "I just wanted to know more about them."

"Ah, I thought that you had heard one of the old stories," the physicker said.

"What old stories?" Nerra asked.

"That of all the attempts to halt the scale sickness, only one cure has proved certain: cracking a dragon's egg and consuming the yolk within."

He watched Nerra as he said it, so Nerra kept her shock off her face. Even so, it ran through her like a jolt of lightning, seeming to spread through every part of her at once.

"A… cure?" she said, afraid to ask.

"A rumor of one, a note in the books," Physicker Jarran said. "But there are no real dragon eggs. It is the only reason I have not told you this before. I would not want you hoping for an impossible thing."

Except that it wasn't impossible.

She could be cured. Cured.

She could live a normal life, not as a freak, but as a regular girl. Instead of counting down the days to her death, she could count the days of her life before her.

She jumped up, knocking over a table, and ran for the door.

A cure lay just beyond the castle walls. And she knew exactly where to find it.

Chapter Fourteen

Erin rode for the Spur, pushing her horse, wanting to get there before her father realized she wasn't coming back and sent men after her. Because she wasn't going back; not after what she'd heard.

"They think they can just sell me like some cheap whore!" Erin complained to her horse.

Well, not cheap. Probably, her parents would want to get a whole dukedom's loyalty for her, the way they'd done with Lenore.

"They'll have to change their minds when I make it into the Spur," she said. She could see the fortress out in the distance, its multiple rings of walls sitting atop an outcrop of glassy rock at odds with the rest of the landscape, forged by the heat of long-forgotten dragon-fire. In the far north of the kingdom, practically the whole land was said to be like that, with volcanoes everywhere one looked. Here, it was an incongruous black mark against the farmland around it.

There was a stone bridge leading up to the fortress that looked almost like a natural thing, rather than anything humans could have constructed. Erin rode her horse up to it, then leapt down to lead him across.

A figure in full armor barred her way.

"Hold," he said. "Who are you, and why have you come to the Spur?"

"I am …" Erin hesitated. If they knew the truth of who she was, then they might send her back. Still, there had to be more than one girl with her name in the kingdom, right? "Erin. I'm Erin. I'm here to join your number. I want to be a knight."

The man stood there for a moment. "You?" he said. "But you're—"

"If you say 'a girl,'" Erin said, "I will push you off this bridge."

"No," the man said. "You will not. And I was going to say that you're young and inexperienced."

"I've fought men," Erin shot back. "I've *killed* men. Bandits who were hurting folk. Isn't that what the Knights of the Spur do? Help people?"

"We serve the king," the knight said. "But yes, we fight the evils of the world. You still cannot enter."

Erin had prepared for this part. She knew the stories, and what to say.

"They say that anyone may seek to join the knights. Anyone, man or woman, high or low born. They say that you turn no one away."

The knight on the bridge stood, if anything, even stiller than he had. "That...is true. Any may ask to join our number, at least, if they can get inside."

"Then step aside and let me pass," Erin said. Was this a test? Was she supposed to fight this man?

He stood there in his armor, blocking her path. He didn't draw a blade, and Erin wasn't sure what to do. She had her stick in her hand, but she couldn't just strike this man down, especially not now she knew what it was like.

"How do I get past you?" Erin asked.

"You convince me that you're sincere," he said. "You tell me why you're here, and you're honest about it. I know there's plenty you're hiding, girl."

"I've told you," Erin said, not understanding. "I want to join the knights."

"Do you?" he asked. "Why?"

"I..."

"Kneel there, on the rock, and wait. When you tell me the truth, I'll decide."

Erin wanted to snap at him, wanted to order him aside in the name of her father, but something told her that it wouldn't work.

She wanted to strike at the man, but she couldn't bring herself to do that, either. So she did the only thing she could think of, and knelt, and waited.

The rock was hard underneath her, cutting into her legs and eventually numbing them. She knelt, and because there was no sign that the watchman wanted to talk, all she could do was stare ahead.

"How long do I have to stay here?" she demanded.

"You can leave any time you want," the guard said. "You can go past any time, too, if you're honest."

"I'm being honest."

"Not to yourself."

Erin waited. She waited until her body ached with the stillness, and her mind ached with it too. All her life, she'd been someone who wanted to move, to do, to act. Her mother had tried to get her to sit still and be ladylike, but Erin had always been ready to run off, to train, and to fight.

"Why do you want to be here?" the knight demanded, after what had to be more than an hour. "Why don't you just get up and go back?"

Erin shook her head and stayed there. Overhead, the sun wore on in its progress, the day sliding closer to evening. The knight stood there too, staying at his post.

"Why are you here?" he repeated.

"You want to know why I'm here?" Erin snapped, her temper finally giving way. "I'm here because all my life, all I've ever wanted to do was fight. I was playing with swords while my sisters were playing with dolls. And all of that counts for nothing, because my parents want to give me away in marriage!" She stood and moved to the knight. "You can get out of my way, or I'll get you out of my way. I've already killed people once today."

Infuriatingly, he didn't step back; didn't even draw his blade. "And what did that feel like?"

Erin wanted to tell him that it had been fine; that it had been easy.

"Awful," she admitted.

"And?"

"Exciting." That was the part she knew she should have been ashamed of, even afraid of. "I told myself that it needed doing, and it did, but it was more than that. I went there because I wanted to prove myself, and because I was angry with my parents. I'm here for the same reasons, and because ... well, I like to fight."

To her surprise, the knight stepped to one side.

"Finally," he said. "We have some truth from you. Not all of it, but enough. Pass in peace."

Erin stood, and her legs hurt now, so that even the path across the bridge became a test. Every step she took required effort, and she leaned on her staff-spear like a beggar in a market. She walked until she reached the fortress gates, which stood invitingly open, the space beyond empty.

Instantly, Erin found herself suspicious. She paused at the edge of the gate, looked up, and saw the openings there. She looked down, and saw the faint glimmer of wires on the floor. Stepping back, she picked up a rock and threw it in amongst the wires.

Darts fell down from the openings, razor sharp and heavy. If they hit her, they would kill her; Erin had no doubt about it. It was another test. That made Erin angry, and strangely, it wasn't the thought of being killed that made her angry; it was the thought that they were trying to trick her, to test her, that they couldn't see that she should be one of them. She'd thought that she was *through* the tests.

She would get through, though. The darts kept falling, and Erin found herself standing there, trying to understand it. It took her a minute to understand the rhythm of it, the pattern. Getting through without hitting any of the remaining wires would take timing and balance, and doing it without the darts striking her would take speed.

"It's a test," Erin told herself, trying to calm herself. "Just a test."

She leapt through the opening, placing her feet with the speed of a dancer as she sped forward. Erin felt something brush by her shoulder, but she kept going, determined now, and knowing that to stop was to die. She flung herself through and rolled, coming up on the far side of the gate with her spear in her hand.

A man was waiting there, armored and carrying a longsword. He was white-haired, with a beard that came down almost to his waist, braided and tied back.

"I am Commander Harr, of the Knights of the Spur," he said. "And you are Princess Erin, the one who wants to fight for us, be one of us."

"You know who I am?" Erin asked, surprised.

A second figure stepped up beside the commander. Erin recognized the knight who had been at the bridge. Irritation flashed in Erin. There was a second entrance; of course there was. She'd rushed in the front way, but of course there would be another way.

"Why are you here, girl?" the commander asked.

"I want to join you," Erin said.

"Are you sure?" he asked. "The third test is deadly. The knights only take the best."

"I can handle it."

"Your father would not be pleased if you were hurt," he said. "I *should* turn you back."

"They say that the knights will test anyone who wants to join," Erin shot back. "Regardless of who they are."

"That much is true," the commander said. "It still does not make what you are doing wise. I will not go easy on you because of who you are."

"I wouldn't expect it," Erin replied. Why would she want them to go easy? She wanted to *prove* herself.

"I didn't go easy on your brother Rodry when *he* joined our number," the commander said. "I think stories of it put off your other brothers."

Erin suspected that it had more to do with who her brothers were. Vars wouldn't risk his hide in an even contest like that, and Greave had no love of violence.

"I'm not my brothers," Erin assured him.

"You've passed two tests." He drew his blade. "I am the third."

"I'm to fight you?" Erin asked.

"If you still wish to join our ranks. There is still time to walk away, to go home. Our life is not for everyone. Perhaps you should—"

"I'm ready," Erin repeated.

In answer to that, the commander swung his blade at her. It was so fast and ferocious that Erin barely leapt back in time from it, and she knew that if she'd still been standing there, the stroke would have taken her head off her shoulders.

That brought fear with it. The old man really wasn't holding back. Even with what her father might say or do if she died, he was still striking with ferocious power.

"All right," she said, unsheathing the bladed head of her spear. Even as she did it, the commander struck again, and again.

Erin gave ground, trying to find an opening to strike back. Her spear darted out and bounced off the commander's armor. She stepped back, half expecting him to acknowledge the blow.

He kicked her hard enough to send her sprawling. Erin cursed, rolled to her feet, and just managed to get her spear in the way of the next blow. Even that was enough to stagger her. She was getting angry now. What kind of test was this? What was the point of a test that was little more than a fight to the death?

It didn't help that fear was building up in her again, because how could she hope to fight a man who was so well armored, who could survive almost any blow she struck?

"If that's what you want," Erin muttered to herself. She flung herself forward, striking again and again and again. The head of her spear was a striking snake, attacking again and again, trying to find the gaps in the commander's armor.

Each time, though, he twisted just enough to let her blows strike solid plate, parried or cut so that Erin had to break off her attack. Then his leg swept around, and Erin found her feet kicked from under her. Her spear clattered from her hand, and now there was a sword coming for her, and she knew there was no way to avoid it.

Erin wanted to cry out, wanted to roll away or beg, but she didn't; she forced herself not to do it. Instead, she lay there and looked up, and waited for the end that was coming. The blade swept down with brutal speed, and Erin found herself thinking about all the things she would miss when she was dead. She found herself thinking of her sisters, even maybe her brothers, and all the moments she wouldn't be there for…

The blade stopped an inch from her neck.

Commander Harr took it away while Erin lay there panting, not understanding, her fear still there. She could push it down now, though. Commander Harr held out a hand and Erin took it, still not understanding even as he pulled her to her feet.

"Being a warrior isn't just about skill," he said. "We can *teach* skill. A Knight of the Spur needs to be honest with themselves and their fellows, needs to act decisively when they must, and needs to be able to face death head on when it comes."

"What are you saying?" Erin asked. "I lost."

"Everyone loses," Commander Harr said. "Even I lost. It's about *how* you lose, sometimes, and the parts of yourself that you show when you do. You showed that you are brave. Reckless, perhaps, but brave."

"So…" Erin didn't dare to hope it.

"I'm saying that you're in, girl. For now. You will be a squire here, serving with the knights. You will learn, and if you learn, you will stay. If you fail, you will be sent back to Royalsport. It is that simple. Do you understand?"

"Yes, Commander Harr."

He nodded, a certain gruff acknowledgment in the movement. "Very well. Welcome to the Spur."

CHAPTER FIFTEEN

In her chambers, Lenore was finally starting to think that everything might be perfect. Oh, she knew that Finnal's father and
hers had had last-minute talks about things to do with her dowry,
but those seemed to have been sorted out now, and her siblings had
been told to play their parts: Erin and Nerra had even sat through a
dress fitting earlier, with Erin glowering hard in case anyone dared
to call her pretty, and Nerra changing behind a screen so that no
one might see her.

The guests were starting to come into the city, the festivities
were in place, and the whole order of the procession around the
kingdom was arranged. Yes, Lenore would rather have had Rodry
than Vars escorting her, but maybe this would be a good chance for
her to build some bridges with her brother.

Lenore looked out from her window over Royalsport. The tide
was in, so that it became a glittering thing of islands surrounded
by the shimmer of water. In moments like this, even the city was
beautiful. Still, Lenore had to turn away from it, because there was
still plenty to do.

"What's the itinerary for the wedding procession?" she asked.

One of her maids, Zia, took out a map of the kingdom. It
showed the south too, but only in vague terms. The river cut them
off from one another so completely that it was almost not worth
mapping it. Idly, Lenore found herself wondering what it might
be like there. Maybe one day, she and her husband would make
the trip over one of the bridges to find out, maybe on a diplomatic mission.

Lenore smiled at that thought. She was already planning out her life with Finnal even though she wasn't married to him yet. Just the thought of him made her heart swell; he was so handsome, so courtly, so perfect.

"We'll head down through the villages along this route," Zia said, "sweeping south until we come to the coast. Then we'll head west, and north."

"And how long will this take?" Lenore asked. "Have we arranged supplies for all of it?"

"Orianne was doing that," Zia said. She looked around. "I'm not sure where she is today. She said that someone had come she needed to talk to."

"I'm sure she has a good reason," Lenore said. Orianne was one of the women who had been by her side the longest, the daughter of a minor noble house whose parents had decided that the best thing to do was to send her to serve beside a princess. Zia was the same, but had only been with Lenore a few months. Orianne would be the one Lenore trusted with most of the details.

"I'm sure she does," Zia agreed, because Lenore refused to allow her maids to backbite or try to play politics within her circle. She dismissed those who did not help one another as well as her.

They kept going with the preparations, and even with most of it in place, it still seemed that there was a mountain of things to do. They would need wagons for the journey and drivers, sufficient clothes for all weather and an idea of the concerns of each village and region so that Lenore would not appear ignorant of them as she rode through. Then for the wedding itself, there were still issues with the precedence of the seating, and the exact details of the feast, the choice of the entertainers' songs, and—

"Your highness!"

Lenore turned at the sound of Orianne's voice. The maid was approaching with another woman beside her, and this one wasn't dressed for the royal court. Oh, her clothes were expensive enough, almost on par with Orianne's, but there was something about the cut and the style that spoke of lasciviousness and sensuality in a way that Lenore would never have permitted among those around her.

The woman herself was older than Lenore, perhaps thirty, with jet-black hair curling past her shoulders and a rouge-tinged smile that seemed to be mocking the world. She offered a curtsey before Lenore, but even the way she did that was a far cry from the innocent elegance of the court.

"Orianne?" Lenore said. "Who is this?"

"Your highness," her maid said, "this is someone to whom I sometimes go for information."

"Meredith, mistress of the House of Sighs," the woman said, straightening up and not waiting to be introduced.

Lenore's breath caught at that. "You've brought a…a whore into my chambers?"

A flicker of irritation crossed the new woman's features. "It is strange that we are a House as old as the scholars or the weapon smiths, or the players or merchants or the builders, and yet people talk of us with such shame. Still, I am used to it, and it is shame that I have come to talk to you about, Princess."

"I have nothing that I need to be ashamed of," Lenore said.

"That is true," Meredith replied, "but perhaps there are things that you need to be protected from."

"I don't know what you have in mind, but—"

"Please hear her out, Lenore," Orianne said. "You might not approve of Meredith, but she has given me plenty of good information before now, and what she's come to me with…well, you need to hear it."

That was enough to make Lenore pause. She knew Orianne would only have her interests at heart, and she'd heard that the House of Sighs was sometimes a place where people said things they shouldn't. As much as Lenore wanted the older woman out of her presence, she knew she should listen.

"Wine?" she said, and one of her maids brought out a glass. Meredith took it and sipped it.

"From the vineyards of Helast in the south," she said. "Not bad."

"You know about wine?" Lenore said.

"About all the luxuries and pleasures," Meredith replied. "But that is not what you want to hear from me, is it?"

"What is it you've come to tell me?" Lenore asked. "And what do you want in return? Coin?"

"Ordinarily, it would be coin," Meredith said. "I can hardly be ashamed about asking for that. Today though…consider it a wedding present."

Lenore didn't trust that. A woman like this wouldn't do anything unless there was a payoff for her.

"What do you have to tell me?" she repeated.

Meredith smiled in a way that said she knew the effect she was having. "Simply this: your pristine, loving, faithful husband-to-be? He was in my establishment last night, surrounded by beautiful girls…and boys."

Lenore froze.

"In that, he was rather loose-lipped," Meredith said. "He spoke about you, dear, about how he wished he didn't need to marry you, but that his father was insisting, for the connection to royal blood. Apparently, they've argued about it."

Lenore shook her head. "No."

"Yes," Meredith said. "Of course, hearing the truth can often be a shock, but—"

"No," Lenore snapped, her body rigid with tension. "No, I don't know why you're doing this, but I will not hear these lies!"

Meredith shrugged and set down her wine glass. "Believe what you want. I have done my part in this. I'm sure you'll see the truth in time."

Lenore went to slap her, her anger getting the better of her, but Meredith caught the blow.

"One of your family has done quite enough of that already. It's part of why I'm here. Now, I'll take my leave. Good luck, your highness."

She turned and walked out, leaving Lenore there not knowing what to think, or do, or say. She turned her attention to Orianne, who was still standing there as if she might comfort Lenore, but Lenore wanted no part of it.

"Get out," she said to her former friend.

"Lenore..."

"That's 'your highness,'" Lenore said, feeling the frost in her voice. "You bring lies like this to me, and you expect me to be happy?"

"Not happy," Orianne said, "but I thought you needed to hear it. When Meredith told me—"

"And where were you to be told anything by her?" Lenore said. "I have a maid who hangs around with whores? What were you doing in the House of Sighs?" She paused. "It's obvious that I cannot have a maid to whom scandal will attach so easily. You need to go now. Go, and do not come back. You are dismissed from my service."

"Please—"

"Do not speak," Lenore snapped. In that moment, Orianne's years of service didn't matter; only what she'd said. "Just leave. If you are still here in the morning, I will have guards escort you from the castle."

Her maid turned and left, and Lenore just stood there, feeling the anger burning inside her. Zia was there looking caught between trying to comfort her and fear of what she might do.

"We will not speak of this, or of her, again," Lenore said. "Ever."

CHAPTER SIXTEEN

As important as his daughter's wedding was, King Godwin III was almost relieved to be able to fit in some of the normal business of the kingdom, receiving petitioners among the feasting in the great hall to hear their concerns. They lined up through the hall, the courtiers and the commoners, each having to wait their turn, while the music of the feast continued in the background.

"Your majesty," a farmer said, bowing so low his forehead almost scraped his knee, "our harvest looks to be a poor one this year, yet our local lord is still insisting on his full share."

"When the harvest comes, I will send men to assess it," Godwin promised. "Your lord will have his tenth as usual, but no more than that, and if there is not enough for your village after that, there will be recompense made to you."

"Thank you, your majesty."

The next was a man from the House of Merchants, who strode forward dressed in velvet to match any noble. He bowed, although it wasn't as low as the farmer's bow had been.

"Your majesty," he said. "If we are talking of recompense, may we talk of the ships I and my fellow investors have lost out on the far routes wide of the Slate River? In recent weeks, several ships have been lost, never to return."

King Godwin looked at the man. "The risks in far sailing are well known. Go beyond sight of land and you rely on the stars and on charts."

"Indeed," the merchant said. "But if a farmer shall be paid for the loss of his harvest, should we not be paid for the loss of ships with so many aboard?"

Godwin suppressed a flash of irritation. "Are you asking the crown to underwrite your profits? You take risks with others' lives in the hope of making a fortune, while a farmer grows what he can to see his family and those around him fed. So no, I will not recompense you for your losses, but my men will be visiting the House of Merchants to make sure that you are compensating the families of the sailors who have been lost in your ventures."

It was not the politic move, of course, and Godwin could see the irritation on the merchant's face, but sometimes such men had to be put in their place. The trick was knowing when to do it and when not to. Godwin had chosen this merchant because the loss of his ships already made him weak. He could afford the man's hatred.

They came then, one after another. There were common folk with grievances about the ways they were being treated by the guard or their lords. Godwin tried to listen seriously to these. There were more merchants, and men from the various Houses, and these always seemed to think too much of their importance. There were, inevitably, more things to prepare for the wedding.

"If we do not have enough wine for so many guests," he declared to one surprised-looking servant, "then go out and find more. This is not a matter that requires the king's authority."

He tried to be a good ruler, to be patient and just with the people who came to him. A part of it was that it was what he had always promised himself he would be, the memory of his own father's reign far too fresh. Godwin II had not been a kind king, and Godwin III found himself determined to make up for it.

Another part of it was that Rodry and his friends were in the hall, "helping" with the feast, but seeming to spend as much time cavorting as doing anything useful. One day, his son would be the king, and that meant that Godwin needed to set an example for him. He needed to show his son that not everything was about charging around the countryside, playing the knight, fighting and hunting.

The problem was that right then, Godwin would rather have been doing any of those things.

Briefly, he thought of the beast that he, his son, and the others had been summoned to look at. There had been no further news of dragons, because why would there be when none had been seen in years? Even so, Godwin couldn't shake the image of the creature's bones and scaled hide. So far, his son and his friends had done as commanded and kept quiet about it, but Godwin knew that such things had a way of finding their way into the light. He needed to know more.

"Grey will find something," he murmured, thinking of the way the sorcerer had warned him that the boy would be rushing into the hall, warning him to speak with him alone, and suggesting what to do with him.

"Your majesty?" The man standing before him was short and dressed in faded noble clothes. He also looked terrified. "I'm sure that the royal magus has better things to do than help with my paltry problems."

Godwin realized too late that he'd spoken loud enough to be heard, and worse, he couldn't even remember what this man's request had been. Something to do with lost ancestral lands? The truth was that he'd been too caught up in his thoughts to listen.

"Would you shun my sorcerer's help?" he asked.

The man paled visibly.

"Oh, very well," Godwin said. "Return tomorrow, and we will find a better solution. For now though, I am tired. This audience session is at an end. Let the feast recommence."

"Wait, your majesty!" a voice from the far end of the hall called. "For King Ravin wishes to give his congratulations on the wedding of your daughter."

The man who came forward was dressed in a style that Godwin assumed was popular in the Southern Kingdom, with slashed sleeves revealing white silk beneath, and pantaloons that billowed as he walked. He had an oiled black beard and a mustache that had been shaped into two hook-like curls. His hat was broad brimmed and feathered, while his boots laced with white ribbons most of the way up his shins. All in all, Godwin thought he looked ridiculous as he pushed past the long line of audience seekers.

"People usually receive their audiences in the order that they arrive," Godwin said.

"Ah," the man replied with a bow, "but it is not usual to receive an ambassador from King Ravin himself. I am Ambassador D'Entre. I have crossed the bridges and ridden hard to be here. Surely you will hear me, your majesty?"

King Godwin sighed. He knew that making the man wait might be seen as an insult to their neighbor, and even though the river prevented any threat of war, he wanted good relations for the little trade that there was across the bridges.

"Very well," he said. "I take it that your king sends his congratulations on my daughter's forthcoming nuptials?"

"Indeed he does," Ambassador D'Entre said. "And he offers you a gift for your daughter in honor of the occasion."

"What gift?" Godwin asked.

"The continued freedom of your kingdom," the ambassador said.

A gasp went around the room at that, but the king held up a hand. "And no doubt King Ravin wishes something in return for this … 'gift.'"

"It is customary for gifts to be met with gifts," the ambassador agreed.

Godwin's attention was fully focused now. "And what gift does my fellow king desire?"

"Merely that the Northern Kingdom recognize the truth: that it is, and has always been, a part of the greater kingdom ruled by the kings of the south."

Godwin heard the renewed gasp that went around the room. Presumably the people there understood what such a thing meant: subservience to the south. Maybe a few had even read enough history to understand the demand; after all, the Northern Kingdom and the Southern had once been one thing, ruled by the ones who joined with the dragons. That had been before the gouge that the Slate ran through had been carved, though, and lay lifetimes in the past.

"And what exactly would that mean?" he asked.

"King Ravin would not interfere in your day-to-day affairs, as he has not to date, in spite of being the ruler of all lands. He would permit you to continue ruling on his behalf. You would, however, pay suitable tribute, in the form of half of all revenues that your royal person receives."

"I see," King Godwin said. In the far corner of the room, he could see Rodry and his friends growing angry. His son was red in the face, as if he wanted to charge forward and cut the man down. King Godwin smiled. "Regretfully, I must decline."

"Then King Ravin has instructed me to inform you of the consequences of such an answer," Ambassador D'Entre said, making it sound as if he genuinely did regret it. "Should you refuse, King Ravin will be forced to march his armies north to retake the lands that rightfully belong to him."

King Godwin stood then, walking down to stand over the man. "There is little room for them across the bridges; bridges that we will destroy the moment we see enemies. Unless your armies are remarkably strong swimmers, I think we have little to fear."

"There is more to fear than you think, King Godwin."

Godwin saw Rodry start forward, but he held up a hand to stop him. This was his court, and this was not a moment for anger.

"I am king in this place," he said, to both his son and the ambassador. "The only king. Go and tell Ravin that. Tell him that his father made threats, and his father before him. They came to nothing, and neither will his."

CHAPTER SEVENTEEN

Rodry stood there while Ambassador D'Entre walked from his father's hall unharmed. He stood there because he couldn't believe it was happening. He was already angry that the boy he recognized from the House of Weapons had just been dragged away. Now, this so-called emissary had come into their kingdom, into their castle, into their home, and made threats, yet he was walking away.

"Father," Rodry began, approaching his father's throne as King Godwin resumed his place there.

To his shock, his father held up a restraining hand. "Not now, Rodry. Do you think there's anything you can say about this situation that I haven't already considered?"

"But you've let him go alive and unharmed!" Rodry said. "The terms he offered were an insult!"

"Keep your voice down, boy," his father snapped back, even though Rodry wasn't a boy but a man, a knight. "I have done the best thing for this kingdom. Now, someone fetch me Master Grey. He's walked out, and we have important matters to discuss."

Important? As if the Southern Kingdom threatening war wasn't important? As if they were simply supposed to let an insult like that go?

Rodry kept from saying that, but only because he knew it wouldn't do any good. His father wasn't going to listen, wasn't going to act. That meant that Rodry had to do it. Rodry had to be the kind of man who would act to defend his kingdom and his sister from these insults.

He stalked from the hall, and a couple of his companions followed, falling into step with him. The ambassador was ahead, with a couple of men who must have been there to guard him on his journey. The southern fighters had curved swords and kite-shaped shields, with deep purple surcoats over chain armor. The ambassador was smiling, and one of them must have made a joke in the southern tongue, because the three of them laughed as they left the castle.

If Rodry's blood hadn't been up enough by then, it was now. He and his companions followed the men out of the castle and down to the stables, where three large, fine southern horses were waiting, ready and saddled as if the ambassador had known he wouldn't be staying. Back in the courtyard, there might have been celebrating people, but here in the stables, there were a few stable hands, but no guards, and no courtiers who might run back to his father.

"You'll apologize before you mount those beasts," Rodry said. His friends took up positions to the side, a little way from the guards.

"Apologize for obeying my instructions from our king?" the ambassador replied.

"Ravin is not king of these lands," Rodry snapped back, "and every word you said in there was an insult to my father, to my sister, to all of us."

"If I were you," Ambassador D'Entre said, "I would concentrate on getting your father to change his mind. King Ravin will not be pleased that his generous offer has been rejected. He will not be happy with the message."

"Do not try to command me," Rodry said. His hand went to his sword.

"If you draw that—" the ambassador began.

Rodry's sword sang from its sheath. This was what these men deserved for the threats they had helped to make.

The two bodyguards moved to intercept him, of course, drawing their curved blades and readying their shields. Rodry waved his companions back as they moved to intercede, because they couldn't

100

be a part of this in the way he could. Besides, he didn't need their help for this. He was a Knight of the Spur, and they were not.

He stepped forward toward the bodyguards, then slammed into the first of them, their swords clashing together. Rodry kicked out, knocking the man back, then turned to hack a blow through the chest of the second even as he raised his blade to strike.

The first came back at him then, attacking with one blow after another. Unarmored as he was, Rodry could only give ground, parrying as he went until the moment came when one of the man's slashes was slightly too extended. He caught the blade on his, binding it in a circle and pushing at the man's elbow with his free hand. He thrust his sword home in the guard's throat, hearing the gurgle of his final cry as he fell at Rodry's feet, still in death.

Rodry turned his attention to the ambassador then, bloody blade still in his hand.

"Pick up a sword," he demanded.

The ambassador shook his head. "If you wish to strike me down, you will do it in cold blood, as a barbarous northerner."

That was almost enough to get Rodry to do it. Instead, he turned to his companions, who were still standing there, obviously unsure what they should be doing.

"Grab him," Rodry ordered. "Hold him still."

Two of them did it, one holding each of the ambassador's arms as they forced him down to his knees.

Very slowly, Rodry cleaned his sword on the ambassador's fancy shirt, leaving a smear of blood behind. He sheathed it and drew a dagger.

"I'll not kill a man in cold blood," he said. "But that doesn't mean I'll stand by while he threatens me and my family. So I'm going to take something from you that I suspect a popinjay like you values more than anything."

He set his blade to the man's face and cut sharply, drawing a shriek that was initially terror, then outrage as he realized that Rodry hadn't cut through his flesh, but through his mustache, the end of it dropping to the ground like a fallen feather.

"Hold still, or I will end up cutting you," Rodry said, and kept going, hacking at the ambassador's beard and hair, scraping it away from him. His dagger was sharp, and several times the man cried out as Rodry nicked him, but he kept going. He deserved this, and more than this.

When he was done, the ambassador was all but bald, with cuts and scratches on his skull from Rodry's work.

"You," he called out to one of the stable hands. "A man like this doesn't deserve a fine horse. Find him a donkey."

"Yes, your highness," the young man said, obviously not daring to argue with the prince in this mood. Rodry didn't care if he was frightening at this point. He was a prince protecting his kingdom.

He pointed to one of his companions. "This fool tried to bring a prisoner's bracelets for my sister, so let's see how he likes it. Find some shackles."

"Where would I—"

"In the dungeon, of course," Rodry said.

The ambassador stared up at him. "You will pay for this. Your actions here will have consequences."

Rodry shook his head. "These are the consequences of your actions. My father was right. What are you going to do? March an army half a dozen at a time across one of the bridges? You came here to do nothing but insult, and I'm going to show you up for the fool you are."

The young man he'd sent for the donkey came back with one soon enough, and the companion he'd sent for shackles arrived shortly after. They were rusted old things, but that was fine by Rodry.

"Stand up," he commanded the ambassador. He fitted the shackles to the man's hands himself, then threw him across the saddle of the donkey, as ungainly as a sack.

"Set the dead men across their horses," Rodry said. "At least they were willing to fight."

"Manhandle a dead body?" one of his friends, Kay, said. He made a face. "We're noblemen, Rodry."

"And you keep saying you want to be knights," Rodry reminded the young man. "You shouldn't be squeamish about a couple of bodies when you're supposed to be ready for battle."

"You'll get all the battles you want and more," the ambassador promised them. Rodry cuffed him around the ear.

"You've talked too much already," he said. "Speak again, and I'll stuff your mouth with straw for the ride back. Kay, these three will need someone to see them to the border."

"And it's to be me?" he said. "But then I'll miss the wedding, and the dancing. One of Princess Lenore's maids has been—"

"If she loves you that much, she'll still be here when you get back," Rodry said. "Think of it as a knightly task, a quest."

"That would impress her..." Kay mused aloud. "May I take the ambassador's horse?"

Rodry shrugged. "It's probably best if you do. I doubt my father will be happy about this."

Happy or not though, it had needed doing. It had taken everything Rodry had to keep from simply killing the ambassador. He had heard the stories of the past, of the conflicts that had shaped the two kingdoms, of knights and dragons and more. Those stories were clear about one thing: when there was a threat to the kingdom, a strong man always rose to fight against those enemies and drive them back. Well, today, Rodry had been that man.

"This is what happens when you threaten those I care about," Rodry said, slapping the rump of the ambassador's donkey to set it in motion. It hurried off with Kay and the two other horses hurrying to keep up.

Insults couldn't go unpunished, whatever his father thought. And the ambassador's threats meant nothing. Let the south play at war. Rodry was strong enough to keep them all safe.

Chapter Eighteen

"Inside," a guard said, and pushed Devin through a set of double doors.

Devin braced himself, afraid he was being thrown into a dungeon.

Yet to his surprise he found himself stepping into a living chamber, or perhaps a reception chamber backing onto other rooms. He froze in place, his heart stopping: there was the *king*.

There he was, seated and crowned. Prince Rodry stood to one side. On a table before the king sat a spear Devin recognized as one the prince had taken with him from the House of Weapons, and the sword Nem had given him. The guards had taken it from him as they'd kept him waiting. Apparently, they'd been waiting for the king.

Devin came forward, remembered himself in time, and bowed.

"This is the same boy?" King Godwin demanded.

"This is Devin of the House of Weapons," Prince Rodry replied. "He made the spear."

Devin frowned as he straightened up, confused as to what was happening.

"And that sword?" King Godwin asked him, gesturing to the messer on the table. "Did you make that, boy?"

Devin shook his head. "No, your majesty. That was my friend Nem."

King Godwin took it and took the spear, staring at them, comparing them.

"I can see the difference," he said, hefting the spear. "Fine work indeed. Are you sure you made this, Devin of the House of

Weapons? If I find that you've lied to me after this, I'll see you in more trouble than you can imagine, even for entering my hall."

"I'm sorry," Devin said. "I needed to speak to Master Grey, and I thought that—"

The king stopped him with a raised hand. "My magus has explained things, as much as he *ever* explains things. The spear; did you make everything?"

"I made everything," Devin assured him. "From forge welding the metal billet to winding the haft to the head."

"Impressive," the king said. "Then it seems that I have a task for you."

"Your majesty?" Devin said.

"Have you heard of star metal?"

"Y-yes, your majesty," Devin said, even though the question caught him by surprise. Star metal was so rare that almost no smith worked with it today. They said it was stronger and sharper than any steel around.

"I know where you can find the ore for it," the king said. "And I want you to make a sword for me."

"For you, your majesty?"

"On my behalf," the king corrected himself. "To give as a gift to my future son-in-law. There is a place on the slopes of the volcano where a lump of star metal ore fell many years ago. You will travel there, with the protection of my son Rodry and his companions."

"We're to go with him?" Rodry said, looking surprised and a little put out by that. "So that Finnal can have a sword? Have you *heard* the rumors spreading about him?"

"I have heard," King Godwin said. "And I choose not to believe mere fishwives' tales. The alliance with the duke and his family is too important. Besides, Devin will need protection. Grey says that the metal is in Clearwater Deep."

"But that's…they say it's a place of magic," Rodry said. "I mentioned it once to Master Grey and he refused to speak of it. The stories…"

"Nevertheless, it is where you will go," King Godwin said. "Devin, you will gather the metal and forge it for me." He placed a pouch on the table. "You will be well compensated for your efforts."

Even if there had been no money, Devin might have said yes. The chance to work with star metal was too great an opportunity to pass up. Besides, he had the feeling that his fight with the king's son was only being forgotten because he could be useful.

"But…" Devin began. "I'm not a smith anymore. They threw me out of the House of Weapons."

"After what happened with my brother?" Rodry asked.

Devin nodded.

"It doesn't matter," the king said. "We will find you a forge. Will you do it?"

"Yes, your majesty," he said. Devin wasn't sure he had much of a choice.

The king passed him back his sword.

"Go with him, Rodry. I want you to set off at once."

"Yes, Father," the prince said, but Devin could see that he wasn't happy. The two of them left the room almost in step with one another. Prince Rodry was silent until they were well clear of the room and the guards.

"I'm sorry for getting you into this," he said. "I thought that by telling my father you were a fine smith I might save you after you ran in like that. Had I known that it was Clearwater Deep, I would not have mentioned you."

"I am glad to serve, your highness," Devin said. For the chance to work with star metal, he would have given far more.

"Then are you willing to serve *me*?" Prince Rodry said, turning to him with an earnest look. "After all, I'm the one who saved your life with my brother. And I spoke for you with my father."

"What is it you need?" Devin asked. He hadn't forgotten all that he owed the prince.

"We'll go there, and you'll forge the blade, but you'll give it to me rather than my father. I will give it to my sister myself."

"To your sister?" Devin said.

"If it's given to her directly, it doesn't form part of her bride price, and it comes back to her should the marriage be annulled," Rodry said. "Finnal might seem perfect to Lenore now, but she'll see what he is soon enough. Then I don't have to suffer the indignity of watching him wander around with such a weapon on his hip. Will you do it, Devin? Will you do what I ask?"

Devin thought about it. He didn't like the idea of getting between the king and his son in whatever conflict this was, didn't like the danger of it, but the truth was that he did owe Rodry, and as far as he could see, the results were the same.

He nodded. "Aye, I'll do it."

"Then we go," Rodry said. "And we just have to hope that whatever's in Clearwater Deep isn't as dangerous as a sorcerer's silence suggests."

CHAPTER NINETEEN

For Brother Odd, the hour of silence was always the hardest part of life on the Isle of Leveros. For that hour, the sounds of the great monastery faded away, and none were permitted to speak. Even those who normally meditated by reciting the hidden names of the gods had to do so silently, not a sound permitted to mar the tranquility there.

It was a moment designed to leave the inhabitants alone with their thoughts, free to delve inward to seek the divine connection, to look for peace. Brother Odd hated it.

Brother Odd; that hadn't always been his name. He suspected it might have been a joke on the part of the abbot. After all, he made such an odd monk. Oh, the shaving of his head had taken away the long mane of shaggy dark locks that had been there, and he deliberately extended that hairlessness to the beard he had once forked and dyed to intimidate his enemies, but he was still larger than most of them, still had to hunch in so that he didn't show his brothers the frame of the knight he had been.

No, he told himself as he sat in his cell, do not think of that. Clear your mind. Think of nothing.

Thinking of nothing should have been easy in a space like this. His monastic cell was bare save for a simple cot to sleep on, with nothing but empty gray stone to fill his mind. It was such a contrast to the chambers he'd once enjoyed. Even on campaign, his tent had featured a feather mattress, and there had always been a golden wine jug close to hand...

Stop it, Brother Odd ordered himself.

These memories were the seductive ones, the ones that seemed innocuous until he started to think about them. Yet if he sat with them, he knew that the others would follow. Knowing that he couldn't keep sitting in his cell, he rose and padded from it, feeling the itch of his rough habit as he walked.

He did even that in silence, because the hour was absolute. Even the abbot made no sound during it. Those who broke the rule were punished through extra work in the scriptorium or even expulsion. Maybe, Brother Odd thought, it would be better to be punished like that. All the gods knew he deserved it.

He couldn't risk leaving, though. Here he was safe, from the man he was, and from the things he'd done. Out in the world, who knew what evil he would visit on it?

Brother Odd wove his way through the monastery in silence, out into the gardens where he would normally work with the others, the backbreaking labor easy to a man with muscles honed through years of warfare. He went past that garden, to a garden of contemplation where stones carved with gods and demons and more stood, and the floor was a tiled thing, worn by so many feet that there were grooves in it.

He sat there among the statues for a moment or two, but could already feel the memories rising, blood and death sitting on the edge of his thoughts as if waiting for the merest slip. A fragment of memory seeped through: a child's body, broken by fallen masonry. Brother Odd shuddered at that image, but the worst part of it was that he couldn't even remember exactly when it had been.

Has there been so much violence that I can't even place it? he wondered.

The answer to that came as more thoughts of his past life flooded in, past the barriers he had so carefully built on the island. He saw a foe swinging a sword, felt the crunch of impact as he stepped to the side and struck back. He saw the brightness of the tournament field, soon giving way to the fire pits used to get rid of the bodies in the aftermath of a battle. Was it Landshane, or Merivel? Not one of the skirmishes, nor even the last foray into the Southern Kingdom, but Brother Odd still couldn't place it all.

He felt his disgust rising with the memories, and his hatred. Not of anything else, for he had sworn to love all things as a monk, but of himself. Of the man he had been. To wipe away that hatred, he stood and started to move his body through the stretches and movements some monks used to try to meditate in motion, forcing his body to twist and turn and even wheel upside down.

He felt the moment when something switched in his movements. A stretch became a lunge at an opponent, a twist turned into a kick that would have knocked a man flat. He turned as if he had a blade in his hand, moving through the movements of the twelve plays of the sword in two hands. By the time that he was done, Brother Odd was sweating, and he hated himself even more.

This can't continue, he told himself. *I can't be that man.*

He set out in search of the abbot, finding him where he always was in the silent hour: kneeling on a ramp that came out from the monastery's walls, looking out over the island in his meditations. Brother Odd approached, and with the silent hour still continuing, could only stand there while the abbot continued to kneel. He stood and waited, knowing that he should be meditating himself, but now all he could see in his mind's eye was death.

It didn't matter that the cause had been noble, that he'd been a knight who had fought on the king's behalf. Brother Odd knew better than anyone that he hadn't cared about that at the time, only about the violence, about the chance to prove he was the greatest, about the thrill of it.

Finally, sonorously, the great bell in the monastery's tower tolled, bringing an end to the hour of silence. Brother Odd made to approach the abbot, but the old man raised a hand to make him pause. It was a good minute later before Abbot Verle rose, turning to face Brother Odd, his face curiously unwrinkled in spite of his advancing age. They said that the old man had possessed the skill to heal wounds as a younger monk, and to see visions of the gods.

"You have come to me because you are troubled, Brother," the abbot said.

"Yes, Father Abbot. I have had … the thoughts and dreams still trouble me in meditation and prayer."

It was such a simple way to put such a wealth of horror; horror that he had inflicted on the world. How many were dead now because of him? What might they have done with their lives?

"The same thoughts?" the abbot asked. "Thoughts of the man you were?"

Brother Odd nodded, hanging his head in shame. "I cannot seem to push them from my mind. It is like the man I was is waiting beneath the surface of me, waiting to fight his way back. How can I put that man away for good?"

"I think you are asking the wrong question," the abbot said. He gestured for Brother Odd to follow as he walked down from the walls, heading back to the body of the monastery.

"Then what question should I be asking?" Brother Odd asked.

The old monk shook his head. "We do not give answers here; we are not fanatics of one of the gods. We are only here to seek them."

"I have sought answers," Brother Odd insisted as he followed. He hunched over so that he would not tower over the old man. "I have meditated, and prayed, and thought for so long. None of it has freed me from the evil of who I was."

"And none of it will," Abbot Verle said. "As I said, it is the wrong thing to seek. The past has happened, Brother; you cannot be rid of it, or of who you are."

"Then what is the point of being here?" Brother Odd snapped, and immediately felt shame coursing through him.

"It is not about who you were, Brother," the abbot said. "It's about who you are, and who you could be. Perhaps you should meditate on that. Now, I believe you are needed in the gardens."

Brother Odd knew that the abbot was right, but even so, it wasn't the answer he had been hoping for.

"Yes, Father Abbot."

"Oh, and Brother Odd? Remember that we are a peaceful order. Practicing old things is no way to become something new."

That caught Brother Odd by surprise. How had the old man known? Just the thought of it added to his shame, but also to his resolve. He would try. He would seek to be the best monk that he could be, try to be the perfect brother, embrace their ways of peace.

Even so, he could feel the violence of his old life bubbling within him, and it scared him.

CHAPTER TWENTY

Devin watched as Rodry checked the saddle on his horse, tying in place the last of his equipment for the journey. He couldn't believe that he was being included in a journey like this; couldn't believe that he was out of the dungeon.

"You need to cinch your saddle tighter," Sir Twell said, showing Devin how it should be done. Devin nodded, even though he'd only rarely had a chance to ride a horse before. He was too busy trying to decide what he would do, now that both the king and Prince Rodry wanted him to make the sword for them. He didn't know what he was going to do. For now, maybe it was better to focus on the act of simply getting the metal.

Three Knights of the Spur were going with them: Lars of the two swords, Twell the planner, Halfin the swift. Given the stories about them, they were probably worth about fifty normal soldiers.

A couple of Rodry's siblings had come down to see them off, and Devin hung back at the sight of Vars. The prince looked disheveled and hung over. Princess Lenore stood tall and almost impossibly beautiful, coming over and hugging Rodry.

"What is so important that you have to leave like this, Rodry?" she asked. "You're not going to miss my wedding, are you?"

Devin saw Rodry flinch. "There shouldn't be a wedding, Lenore. You must have heard what people are saying about Finnal."

"Don't," Lenore said, and there was a hardness to her voice as she said it. Her tone softened then, and Devin felt bad for listening. "Please don't, Rodry. I've heard the things that people are saying, but they aren't true, they can't be. I love Finnal, and I'm going to marry him, and that's an end of it."

"I just want to be sure that when you're marrying for love, he is too," Rodry said.

"He is," Lenore insisted. "I'm sure of it. He is pure, and noble, and good."

Rodry started to reply to that, but Lenore held up a hand.

"Please, Rodry," she said.

"In that case," he said, "I will go and find you a wedding present no one else could get you." He glanced over to Devin, and Devin felt the weight of the prince's expectation on him. "Something for you."

"Thank you," Lenore said.

"What about you, brother?" Rodry joked, turning to Vars. "Come to join us on our dangerous mission?"

"I'm sure you're capable of hitting things stupidly with a sword by yourself," Vars replied.

"At least I'm willing to walk into danger when it's needed," Rodry shot back. "Whereas you just walk to the next wine bottle or woman."

His brother ignored him with a sneer, turning back toward the castle's interior. Lenore caught Rodry's arm.

"Do you have to be cruel to Vars?" she asked. "Maybe if you were kinder to him, he would do better."

Rodry shook his head. "He's…he's a coward, Lenore. If someone poked me like that, I'd be goaded into action. Instead, he slinks away."

"And maybe he wouldn't if you just encouraged him," Lenore suggested. "Stay safe," she added.

"I will," Rodry replied. He glanced to Devin again, and now Devin was starting to understand why the sword was so important to the prince. "And I will bring you back the finest gift that I can."

Devin rode with the others from the castle, feeling very much like the odd one out among the others. Prince Rodry and the knights were all armored in plate and chain, all sitting comfortably on their horses, joking with one another as they rode. Next to them, Devin felt useless, not used to riding long distances, dressed in a blacksmith's leathers and with only the sword he'd forged by his side.

"So, Twell," the knight with two swords rather than a shield called out. "Got the whole trip planned out?"

"We just follow the prince," Twell said. "And I've told you, Lars, I don't plan everything."

"Don't believe him," the last knight said, nudging Devin. "He plans for the possibility of enemies on the way down to dinner."

"I do not!"

"I'm Halfin," the knight said. "Who are you?"

"I'm Devin … my lord," Devin said, overwhelmed for a moment by the sudden friendliness by the knight. He'd heard stories of these men and their deeds: Twell, who could think his way out of anything. Lars, who had once dueled with three brothers at once over the hand of a maiden. Halfin, who had run a hundred miles with no horse over two days to warn of a coming battle ogres.

"Lord," Lars said. "He's no one's lord. Don't go giving him ideas."

They rode on, down through the city and out into the countryside. The sun rose higher, and in its heat, Devin was glad he wasn't wearing the armor that the knights were. Prince Rodry rode at the front, and Devin found himself watching the way the men looked to him with clear respect. Devin could understand that; he'd found the prince to be honorable and just in a way that his brother wasn't.

They rode for hours, and Devin found himself wondering at the fact that he was a part of this, brought along on a journey with a prince and three knights out of stories. He wondered most at how normal they all were, and how willing they were to talk to him like an equal, even when he wasn't.

Slowly, the ground started to drop away, walls of rock rearing up on either side of them to form a canyon. A stream of perfect, clear water ran through it, and Devin saw Halfin drop down, ready to fill his water bottle.

"Don't," Twell said. "The water in Clearwater Deep is contaminated. Drink it and you risk death."

"Then what am I supposed to drink?" Halfin asked.

Twell took a spare water skin out of his pack, tossing it over, as if he'd anticipated this. As if he'd planned for it, Devin thought with a smile.

"There's no time to stop," Rodry said. "I want to get to the spot my father told me about before it gets too late for us to get back."

"I brought a tent, just in case," Twell said.

Lars snorted. "Of course you did."

They kept going, and Devin found himself looking around, taking in the trees and the plants that were starting to grow up around the side of the river. Most of them were misshapen, twisted by the contents of the water. There were trees that were turned in on themselves like snakes biting their tails, and dark flowers that bloomed with nauseating scents. Away from the stream, there were bushes that clung to the walls of the canyon, and because Devin was looking that way, he was the first one to spot the movement there. Creatures sprang forward, mouths open wide, teeth bared as they snarled.

"Wolves!"

They weren't wolves, though, or weren't anything like normal ones. These were huge, muscled things that shambled on their hind legs, leaving the knifelike claws of their front legs free to swipe. There were at least a dozen of them, and one leapt at Devin's horse even as he called out the warning.

The impact knocked him from his saddle while his horse screamed. Devin came up, drawing the sword that he'd forged, and struck at the beast as it lunged at him. It moved back with a wound across its snout, but circled, watching for openings.

Around him, Devin heard the sound of battle, and he could feel the fear of the violence rising in him. He saw Sir Lars striking out with two swords, Twell moving carefully, picking his cuts, Halfin striking out with lightning speed. Rodry was there too, hacking at the wolf-things, showing the skill with a sword that Devin had suspected he possessed.

Devin struck out at another of the things. This was nothing like striking a training post, because the beast didn't come at him in a predictable way, seemed almost to ignore his sword stroke to lash out with wickedly sharp claws. Devin had to throw himself aside to avoid them, rolled up, and managed to thrust his sword through the thing's arm as it came at him again.

Around him, the others seemed to have had similar success, in the face of the initial rush, but Devin could see that Lars was wounded too, blood dripping from his shoulder. Worse, none of the creatures seemed to be down, and they definitely weren't retreating. Instead, they circled, snarling and growling, clearly looking for any opening.

Devin held the sword he'd made in two hands, but he knew it wasn't going to be enough. Twelve of these things against the five of them was too many. If these had been men, it would have been easy, but these were far more dangerous than men, faster and stronger, able to withstand what Devin had felt were clean blows of the sword.

Fear rose in him, along with the urge to run, but there was nowhere to run to, and these creatures would be faster than any man. Better to stand and fight, but they couldn't fight. Devin looked around, hoping that one of the others would have a plan, but even Rodry was standing there in obvious fear. They knew just as well as Devin what was about to happen:

They were going to die.

CHAPTER TWENTY ONE

Nerra crept out of the castle, leaving the doors to her rooms closed so that no one would come looking for her. One advantage of people knowing how often she was ill was that they didn't question her not being there at the heart of things.

She slipped out, picking her route carefully, so that if anyone saw her they would probably assume she was going out into the gardens. She needn't have worried. All the attention was on Lenore, and on the growing array of guests in the castle. Almost no one paid attention to the slender, almost gaunt figure drifting through it all. Maybe if she'd cared about the attention, Nerra might have worried about that, but she was grateful. It made it possible for her to slip out to the forest, taking her horse and making the ride down to the cave that sat there.

She clung to the saddle as she rode, feeling the weakness that came from her illness. Here, away from people, she felt isolated enough to lift her sleeve, checking on the creeping tracery of black lines on her arm. Nerra quickly yanked her sleeve down again. She needed to focus on the cave and what lay within. It wasn't far.

Carefully, Nerra levered away the rocks in front of the entrance, slipping inside. The egg sat there, in the nest that Nerra had made for it. It looked as impossible as ever, blue and gold, as if someone had pieced together a fractured thing with molten metal. Nerra knelt beside it, staring at it and running her hands over the surface to feel the warmth of it.

"All I have to do is break you," she whispered to it. "If I crack you open, I'm cured. I can have a life."

Nerra could barely imagine it. What would it be like to be well; to be the same as everyone else? She could go out into the world and be the healer that she'd always wanted to be. She could help people; she could have a family. There would be no more fainting fits, no more black lines growing darker and darker on her arms, threatening to change her into something she had never wanted to be.

All of it could be done, she could be cured, and all she had to do was break the egg, destroy the burgeoning life within.

Nerra wasn't sure she could do that. She wasn't sure that she could end anything, especially not something so unique, so rare, so special. Dragons were things that almost no one had seen before, and their eggs... Nerra had never even heard of such things until she saw them. Could she really destroy something like this... even to save her life?

She didn't want to die. Carefully, precisely, Nerra took out her eating knife. She held it to the edge of the shell. She stood perfectly still, willing herself to do it, knowing that this was the only choice...

...She tossed the knife to one side.

"I can't do it," she said. "I won't. I won't kill you, even for this."

She set her hand against the shell again, feeling the warmth there. She felt something else too: movement, sharp and sudden against the interior of the shell. Nerra jerked her hand back and saw the shell distend as something pushed at it from the inside. She saw a faint tracery of cracks spread across the surface of the egg, cutting across those golden lines.

A tiny segment of it fell away first, forming a hole, letting a small, scaled snout poke through. The hole widened, and claws followed, a small, reptilian body slinking through the space as the egg continued to fall apart. It split in too, letting the creature's form roll out onto the floor.

Bright yellow eyes blinked up at her, with a forked tongue that flicked out to scent the air and eyes that blinked half closed the way a cat's might have, as if testing out the world. Its scales were the blue of a cloudless sky, with the shine of other colors running through them here and there. It was small, because how else would it fit into an egg like that, but nowhere near as small as Nerra might have thought it was. It looked up at her, the expression strangely intelligent for something that had just been born.

It leapt up, and Nerra flinched, certain that it was attacking. Those claws caught hold of her, clinging to her, and she tumbled to the ground with the dragon, its weight atop her. Then its tongue flicked out to lick her face.

"That tickles," Nerra said with a laugh.

The dragon lay there on her chest, making a rumbling sound that Nerra assumed was one of pleasure. It turned to one side and gave a kind of hiccup. A small burst of flame came forth from its mouth, the heat of it palpable. The dragon looked almost as surprised as Nerra was.

She lay there and looked at it.

"You're beautiful," she said. She couldn't imagine now how she'd been about to break the egg that contained something so wonderful, couldn't imagine even contemplating it. The dragon curled up against her.

Nerra wasn't sure how long she lay there like that with the creature. At some point, she got up and went out into the forest, gathering what plants she could to feed the dragon. It looked at them, blinked, and then leapt out of the cave, wings flapping. Nerra saw it chomp down on something, and it came back to her with what looked like a whole pigeon clamped in its mouth.

"All right," Nerra said.

It chomped down on the pigeon, and while it ate, Nerra went to her horse. She had a little roasted venison, stolen from the feast so that she wouldn't get hungry on her journey. She threw that toward the dragon and its sinuous neck snaked up.

Flame crackled out over the venison, scorching and burning until the meat was almost black. Finally, the baby dragon seemed happy with it, and it chomped down on the meat. When it was done, it sat there, staring at Nerra expectantly.

"I don't have anything else," she said. The best she could do was go to it and hug it tight. The dragon made the rumbling sound that seemed to indicate pleasure. A worrying realization crept over Nerra.

"I have to go back."

The dragon made a sound of protest.

"I have to," Nerra said. "And you have to go back in the cave."

The dragon made a whining sound.

"You have to. I can't take you with me, because people will be scared. They haven't seen dragons."

She could imagine all the ways people might react. None of them were kind. No, the dragon was safest here. Nerra lifted it, putting it back in the cave and moving the rocks back into position even though it broke her heart to do it. The dragon mewled, and Nerra wished she could take it with her.

"Soon," she promised. "I'll be back soon."

She saw the dragon, and now it *wasn't* small. It was the size of a tower, a ship, a hill. It soared through clouds so vast that the world below was lost through them. When it opened its mouth, it didn't just breathe fire; grown like this, it could manipulate its breath to be many more manifestations of the power within it: lightning and frost, shadow and rippling force.

Nerra saw it swoop down, and there was an army below, of men, and things that had never been men. The dragon's breath swept out across the army, scything down creatures there. It landed among them, claws rending, teeth crushing. Its tail whipped around, scattering more foes, then it roared, and the sound seemed to fill the world, shifting and changing, becoming something else, becoming her name ...

"Nerra!" Lenore said, shaking her awake.

Nerra's eyes snapped open, and she stared at her sister. She was breathing hard, sweating with the force of the dream, or maybe with something else.

"You were crying out in your sleep," Lenore said. "I came to see you, but you were ... like this."

"Just a dream," Nerra said, sitting up.

"Obviously a bad one," Lenore said.

Nerra wanted to tell her about the dragon. Her sister was kind, and good, and probably one of the closest things to a friend she had. Yet instinctively, Nerra knew that it was a secret she shouldn't talk about. Dragons were ... well, impossible, but more than that. They were large and dangerous, and if Lenore mentioned hers to anyone, wouldn't it be *in* danger?

"I don't remember it," Nerra lied, hating that she had to. "But my dreams don't matter. I guess that in the middle of your wedding preparations, you didn't just come to see me."

"I do want to see how you are," Lenore said. "I've barely seen you in days."

Of course she did. Her sister had always been there when she was younger, trying to look after her. It was just that they had lived such different lives.

"You've been busy," Nerra said. "That's normal, when you're so close to being married. And I've been ..."

"How have you been?" Lenore asked, looking concerned. "You've been stuck in your room a lot."

"Afraid I won't be able to make the wedding?" Nerra asked. She wasn't sure she liked the idea of so many people around her; people who were noisy, and often cruel; people might see all that was wrong with her.

"I'd like you to be there," Lenore said. "I'd like you to be by my side. Erin is ... well, no one knows where she is, even though Father has men looking. One of my sisters should be there. I know you're sick sometimes, but—"

"Not sometimes," Nerra corrected her. "All the time."

"I know," Lenore said. "But you've been living with the scale mark for a long time now."

The sudden urge to be honest gripped Nerra. She couldn't tell Lenore about the dragon, but at least she could tell her about this.

She would understand then; it would show her why Nerra couldn't be around people, couldn't be a part of her wedding.

"It's not that simple," Nerra said. She rolled up her sleeve to show the dark, spreading lines beneath. She heard her sister's intake of breath. "It's getting worse."

"That's…" Lenore stared at her arms. "I thought it was under control."

"Something like this, you can't control," Nerra said. "I'm dying, Lenore."

Or worse, but she couldn't talk about the worse things.

Lenore threw her arms around Nerra. "Oh, Nerra, I'm so sorry. I didn't know."

"No one can know," Nerra reminded her.

"Does *Father* know about this?" Lenore asked. "I'll talk to him. I'll talk to Master Grey, force them to work harder to find a cure."

"Don't," Nerra said. "There's nothing to be done, Lenore."

She didn't tell her sister about the dragon's egg, and what it could have done for her. She wouldn't be able to explain it. Lenore would assume that she'd done the wrong thing, would want to know why she'd thrown her life away like that.

Nerra wouldn't be able to explain it, but she knew that the world was better with the dragon in it… even if it cost her life.

Chapter Twenty Two

Bern sat with people around him laughing and buying him drinks, the way they always did when he set himself down in the middle of a tavern. It wasn't that they liked him, Bern had no time for such things, but they knew what was good for them. One man who hadn't lay on the floor, several of his teeth spilled out across the dirty straw of it.

His "friends" stood around him, although they weren't really friends, just men who were smaller and less violent than him, but who had worked out that being on his side was safer than not being. To be fair, most men were smaller and less violent than Bern; he was a mountain of a man who could crush a skull in his bare hands if it came to it, and had tattoos across both shoulders that wove their way down his arms as if to pick out the muscles. There were a lot to pick out. He kept his head shaved so there would be nothing for a man to grab onto to head butt him, while his face was pinched and roughened by the blows he had taken over the years.

He sat there at the center of attention, telling whatever stories he felt like, listening to the news that people brought him. People often brought him news, because they'd worked out that it was the one thing that Bern *did* pay for, and paid well. People assumed he didn't think, but he'd found that thinking paid almost as well as hurting people.

He spotted the peasant boy instantly, because this wasn't the kind of place where young boys came in safely. One of Bern's men moved to intercept him, but Bern pushed past, shouldering his man out of the way casually, because it wasn't like he mattered.

"You've something to tell me," he said, his voice rumbling.

The boy nodded. Bern produced a coin, holding it just out of reach.

"Tell me then."

"It's about Princess Nerra," the boy said.

"How would you know a princess when you see one?" Bern shot back. "If you're wasting my time..."

"She goes into the woods a lot," the boy said. "And I've seen her coming out of the castle, it's her."

It might be her or not. Probably the boy didn't know the difference between a princess and a scullery maid.

"What about her?" Bern demanded.

"There's... two things," the boy tried.

Bern grabbed the front of his tunic then. "Trying to weasel a second coin? Tell me, and *then* I'll decide if it's worth it."

"She has the scale-mark!" the boy blurted.

That was enough to make Bern pause. If true, it could cause a lot of trouble for the royals. It could also earn him a lot of coin. There were those who paid even better than him for the right information.

"And I'm to believe that?" he said.

"I saw it," the boy replied. "All over her arm. I promise."

"You know what I'll do if you're lying?" Bern said.

"I'm not!" He could see the fear there. More than enough to say that this was true.

"All right," Bern said. "What's the second thing?"

"It's... what she found out there," the boy said. "You... you won't believe me."

"I'll believe what's true," Bern said.

"She found... she found a dragon's egg!"

For a moment, Bern considered hitting the boy for saying something so stupid. Then he saw the fear in the lad's face. He was serious, and even if it wasn't something Bern had heard about in his lifetime, he believed him.

"A dragon's egg?" one of the men around him said. "Do you think we're..."

Bern hit him without looking, and the man went sprawling to the floor. "Shut up. I'm listening. What makes you think it was a dragon's egg?"

"It was bigger than any egg I've seen," the boy said, holding out his arms to indicate the size. "It had all golden veins over it too, just like in the stories."

Bern hesitated. He'd heard the same stories. He'd even had people offer him petrified eggs before, when they couldn't fence them elsewhere. It *sounded* right, even though it couldn't be.

"Where's this egg?"

Something like that... well, it might not be real, but if it was, then how much would someone pay for it? How much would some rich man give to have the only fresh dragon's egg in living memory?

"It's in the forest," the boy said. "There's a clearing. I can show you."

"You will," Bern said. He snapped his fingers at another of those there. "Run to the castle. Bring the news of the princess's... condition to one of the ones who pays for these things. I expect gold for it, not silver."

"Yes, Bern," the man said.

"You cheat me and I'll know." Bern turned his attention back to the boy. "Now, show me where I can find this egg, and we'll see if you've found an impossible thing. And if you've lied to me..."

"It's not *here!*" Bern shouted, his roar echoing out over the silence of the forest. He struck out at a nearby tree, and his strength was enough to splinter the trunk. "Where is it? Where's that boy?"

He looked around for the peasant boy and found him in the middle of quickly scaling a tree. Smart lad. Bern might have smacked him one otherwise, and a small thing like that would only have broken.

"You, you lied to me!" Bern called out, stalking up to the tree. Half a dozen men came with him, surrounding it. They were the ones out of his crew who had been nearest when he called, hard men, the lot of them. None would think anything of putting this boy in the ground if he'd lied to them.

"Didn't!" the boy called down. He was shaking so hard that the whole tree seemed to tremble with it.

"Then where's the *egg*?" Bern demanded.

"This is where she found it," the boy replied, "I promise this is the spot."

"Then where *is* it?" Bern demanded.

"She spotted me and I had to run. Maybe...she took it somewhere?"

Bern growled to himself. "Do you *think*?"

"So it's probably somewhere in the castle," one of the others said.

Bern shook his head. "If it were, I'd have heard. Think that runt's the only one who tells me things? No, it's hidden somewhere. We'll find it."

"And if we can't?" the man said. Bern silenced him with a look.

"Then we'll wait until this girl comes back for it, and we'll ask her where it is."

"Hurt a princess?"

Bern laughed. "Think she's *actually* a princess?"

The others laughed with him. It was what they were best at.

The truth was that Bern didn't care. A dragon's egg was enough to be worth the risk, and a princess...well, she could go missing as easy as a peasant girl in a forest this size.

CHAPTER TWENTY THREE

The creatures continued to circle and Devin didn't know what to do. How long would it be before they leapt at him and the others again? Halfin, Twell, Lars, and Rodry were all fine fighters, but they would die just as quickly as he would. Devin swallowed at that thought. He was about to die; they were all about to die.

He found himself thinking about the moment in the House of Weapons when he had stopped Vars from killing him. He'd done that accidentally, but could he do it deliberately? Could he actually use magic on purpose?

Devin found himself thinking of all the things he would lose when the creatures tore him apart. It was a shorter list than he wanted. He'd already lost his place in the House of Weapons. His parents... well, his father was angry all the time, and his mother anything but kind. He tried to think of the things he might now have though. He would never go on to have a family of his own, never see any of the world, never...

"No," Devin said, shaking his head. "No."

The creatures' jaws slavered with the prospect of the kills to come. Their eyes focused with hatred, and Devin could see one of the beasts' muscles bunching to leap.

He wasn't sure what happened then. It was like something in the fear, the certainty of his own death, flicked some kind of switch in him, changed something in him in a way that seemed familiar. Devin recognized this feeling, because he'd felt it once before. He tried to reach down into it, tried to remember the sensation of it. In that moment, looking at the world, he could see something close to another world layered on top of it, a place composed of writhing energies, and with things there that moved like shadows on the edge of sight.

Devin understood in that moment how to pull the energy of that other place through himself, knew how to do it the same way that he knew how to breathe. He reached out, and, as easily as if he were pulling aside a curtain, he ripped aside a fragment of the barrier between the two places.

In that instant, power spilled out into the world, in a wave of force that rippled out, sending the wolf-things reeling back. They toppled over one another, and they weren't the only ones, because Rodry and the others were also knocked from their feet. Only Devin seemed to be able to stay standing there, perhaps because he'd been the one to do this.

He looked at his arms, and he could see something that looked like black fire flickering around them, down along his limbs to the tip of the blade he held. The wolf creatures rose and stared at him, then turned as one with a whimper and ran, back away from the stream. Devin couldn't understand it, couldn't begin to guess what was happening, but he watched them run nonetheless, and he knew they wouldn't be back.

As suddenly as the flames had come, they were gone, extinguished with a whoomph of inrushing air. Around him, Devin could see the world as it was, with no sign of that other place, just the thickness of a thought away. All that was there was Rodry and the others, who were finding their feet again after being knocked flat.

"What," Rodry asked, "just happened?"

He and the knights were staring at Devin, Rodry's expression caught somewhere between shock and awe.

"What just happened?" Rodry repeated. "What…did you do that?"

"I…don't know," Devin said, because he wasn't sure that he could explain it all to the prince. "I…maybe."

"Those things were there one moment, and we were all knocked flat with them running the next," Halfin said. "They just ran. Twell?"

The other knight shook his head. "I've no idea." He looked over at Devin. "How did you stay standing? Did you do something?"

"I don't know," Devin said. He realized that they hadn't seen what he'd seen. They hadn't seen him rip through the world to grab power, hadn't seen the black fire around him, only felt the effects of the force he'd called.

He could have tried to explain it, but somehow he knew that it would be a bad idea to say too much. Sorcerers like Master Grey were rare and feared, and men like this might not react well to the idea of suddenly traveling with one who didn't know what he was doing.

Rodry stared at Devin with something like awe. "You did magic."

"I ..." Devin shook his head. "I didn't do anything."

The others stared at him, and in that moment, Devin fully expected them to back away from him; to fear him now that they knew what he could do. Instead, they looked at him with something like awe.

"That was ... impressive," Sir Twell said. "Whatever it was."

"Very," Sir Halfin agreed. "Can you do it again?"

Devin shook his head, even though the feeling of what he'd done was down there in him now, buried away and there to touch. He didn't know enough about what he was doing to risk even trying.

"Then there's no time to keep standing here," Rodry said. "We need to get moving again in case those things come back. We still need to find the star metal. Devin, mount up."

Devin nodded, only too grateful for the distraction, and *more* grateful that Rodry didn't seem to be treating him like some kind of freak. Of all of them, he was the one whose opinion mattered most.

The others seemed grateful for the chance to put some distance between themselves and the things that had tried to kill them. Gathering himself up, Devin found his horse and managed to mount it. The five of them set off again.

They kept riding until they found a space where the ground fell away even more sharply than it had, and as they rode, the landscape around them was curiously quiet. No more animals came out toward them, or even watched them. It was as if everything there had seen what Devin could do, and was staying back.

He still didn't understand it. How could he do something that powerful? He wasn't some trained magus, like Master Grey, or someone who had made a pact for power. He was just a smith, who knew about steel but not about magic.

"There," Rodry said, pointing, and breaking Devin's chain of thought.

Devin saw what he meant at once. A large rock sat in the ground, in a crater obviously caused by its fall from the heavens. It shone with a silvery tint, and the stream washed around it. From where he sat on his horse, Devin could see that the stream was ordinary above it, but had a faint shine to it downstream of the rock. This was where the oddness of the place came from, everything around the rock twisted and changed by its presence, so that there were flowers taller than their heads, and furred things with butterfly and dragonfly wings that flitted around their heads.

"We'll need to gather the metal," Devin said.

"I have a pick," Twell said, taking one from his saddle and passing it across to Devin. By this point, it wasn't even a surprise that he did.

"We'll watch for dangers while you gather what you need," Rodry said.

That seemed fair to Devin, since they were the knights and he was just a peasant boy. Even so, a part of him wanted to point out that he'd been the one to drive off the wolf-things. Then again, Devin was the one who had worked with metal enough to know what he was doing. He got down from his horse and headed to the sky-fallen rock, seeking the spots where he would be able to get the most metal ore for his efforts.

He set to work, striking at the rock. It was hard work, even for someone who had worked in the forges for so long, and before long, Devin was sweating.

"Here," Rodry said after a while, "let me take a turn with that pick."

He did, although Devin would never have thought that a prince would work like that. Rodry chipped away at the stone, and soon, there was enough ore to fill a sack, and more. Devin lifted it onto the back of his horse, feeling the weight of it. Now that he had the ore, he had a sword to make, and then he had to decide who to give it to, and who to anger.

Then there was the question of the magic. Devin could still feel the connection bubbling within him. He'd always wanted to be a swordsman, a knight, but he knew that this power had other ideas. He needed to understand it, needed to learn about it, and for that, he would need to seek out Master Grey.

CHAPTER TWENTY FOUR

The tower that housed King Ravin's throne room had taken a thousand men and women three years to construct, along with the finest minds to come out of the south's schools. He had employed not one, but three architects, so that no one of them would understand the whole picture of it, with its passages and its secrets.

Of course, he'd ensured that everyone involved died shortly thereafter. The servants had been easy, because they were bond slaves and bought things. The architects... well, he'd accused one of treason, ensured another slipped from a high spot in the building, and the third had apparently choked on a fish bone a year after the completion. King Ravin was a thorough man.

It had been worth the effort, towering over any who entered, with the individual symbols of the lands he claimed arranged high above, a map of the known world covering the ceiling. There were galleries for the higher nobles, a vast expanse of mosaic floor for those who were lesser, and guards arranged by every pillar of the hall to ensure that they remembered their place.

Ravin's place was the one he had carved for himself with blood, the throne sitting at the head of it all a thing of pure white and gold that matched the robes he wore. At thirty, he filled that throne with a muscular frame, his crown of platinum sitting atop close-cropped dark hair. A darkly curling beard went down to his chest, his great sword, Heart Splitter, sat in its sheath beside him, while the purple robes of state did little to disguise the fact that he was a warrior, and more than a warrior. He'd had the symbols of the old magic woven into the hem and sleeves as a reminder to all that he'd spent as much time with the scholars as the warriors, that he was not the same barbarous fool his father and his father's father had been.

There was no second throne beside his for a wife. Instead, the latest of his concubines knelt in the finest silks beside his throne, a slender chain from her ankle running to his hand. Before, she had been the daughter of a noble house, given to him as an honor. Maybe he would even keep her for a while.

For now though, there was the business of running the Southern Kingdom and its possessions across the sea.

"Is there any news on the latest expedition to the Western Continent?" he demanded, looking to the spot where the admiral of his fleets stood.

"Not so far, my king," the man said. "But perhaps the messages are just delayed."

"They will be dead like the others," Ravin said. "My seers tell me as much."

That angered him. When he commanded men to do a thing, he expected them to find a way to succeed. With the current ones, he had ordered their families taken as an incentive to go and come back with news. He would have to have them sold now, or just killed.

"What else?" he demanded.

"My king…" A man moved forward, obviously a merchant by the look of him. He fell to his knees. "I beg your aid. A nobleman has taken goods from my carts without payment, claiming that they are his by right, yet I have the papers to show that they are mine."

Ravin quirked an eyebrow. It took bravery to come to him with something like this, given what the penalties could be for wasting his time. Still, let no one say that he was not a fair and even generous ruler.

"You will bring these papers to my chancellor," he ordered. "If all is as you say, your goods will be returned, and the noble will pay on top of that."

"You are the wisest of rulers," the merchant said.

"However," Ravin said, "I will also be sending word to the noble. If your goods fall within his legitimate taxes, the rest of what you own will be taken as an example."

He saw the merchant swallow, and wondered if he would be so foolish as to say something then.

"Of... of course, your majesty," the man said, starting to crawl backward. "Thank you."

Ravin sighed and looked around at the men and women there. He wondered how many of them understood what it was truly like to sit where he was. They all had their schemes and their plans, which was why he had so many guards and spies, his sorcerers and his quiet men, yet did any of them think about what it would be like if they actually succeeded? Did they understand that there was no point where it ended, that every day meant dealing with the problems of a kingdom, trying to gain more, be more, to pay for the rest of it? Of course they didn't.

Instead, they came to him, one by one, with their problems. Guards brought in prisoners and Ravin ordered some sacrificed to the gods, some sent to the arena to fight and die, some sold, some maimed for their crimes. A couple he even let go, teary-eyed and grateful for his justice, because it was important for a king to be just.

Eventually, a figure staggered in. He was so ragged and rough looking that Ravin's guards started toward him, and it took even the king a moment to recognize the form of his emissary to the northern lands.

"Let him through," Ravin said, and although he didn't raise his voice, it still carried over the rest of the sounds of the hall. His dead architects had seen to that as well.

The man came forward, staggered slightly, and then managed to execute a perfect bow in spite of how unsteady he was.

"Your majesty, I bring grave news."

"My generous offer to the north has been rejected, I take it?" Ravin guessed.

"It has, my king," the emissary said. "I also regret to inform you that I was attacked by Rodry, the son of King Godwin of the North.

He slew my guards in cold blood, and then … humiliated me in the way that you see now."

King Ravin stood and went to the man, seeing the fear there in him. Did he truly believe that his king would do him harm?

"You have been through much, my friend," he said, placing a hand on the emissary's shoulder. "Not as much as I had hoped, but perhaps enough."

"My king?" the emissary said.

King Ravin smiled. "It is well known that Godwin's son has no control. I had expected that he would cut you down for the things I offered. Still, he slew your men, and that is something."

He looked around the hall. "From this moment, we are at war with the North. Attacks will be made to bring it to heel."

"Your majesty," the admiral of his fleet said. "How are we to do this when the river …"

King Ravin nodded, and three of his quiet men stepped out of the crowd, their knives flashing. The figures were masked so that none could guess at their true names, or seek to bribe them. The admiral fell with a gurgling sound, while around him, others stepped back, hoping they would not be next.

"I have long felt that you have not been trying your utmost," Ravin said to the dying man. "Again and again, your fleets have failed. I suspect that your successor will be more motivated to succeed."

He returned his attention to the room. "As we speak, soldiers are finding their way across the bridges in small groups, ready to strike. Quiet men will kill their nobles and take those they hold dear. Desperate men from the arena will be given the chance to throw themselves across the bridges and take them. At the same time, my fleets will strike its coast. Will no one ask me how?"

None dared, of course, so Ravin had to answer a question that wasn't asked.

"We will not sail directly north," he said. "We will head east first, where the current will not snatch us."

He heard the murmurs as people started to understand what he meant.

"For too long, we have been held back by thoughts of peace and neutrality, by the idea of places that should be held only by the gods," he said. "The time for such things is over. We will act, and we will reunite the kingdom as it should be."

"But how?" the emissary asked, and King Ravin smiled again, because once more the man had done something useful. It almost made him glad the man wasn't dead.

"That part is simple," he said. "We will take a staging post from which to strike, and attack our foes from there. We will encircle them and overwhelm them, because they believe that no one would dare to do what we will do."

He went back to his throne and tore off the purple robes, revealing scale armor underneath. Ravin drew his sword and pointed up, to the spot on the map that hung to the east of the two kingdoms.

"Prepare ships," he commanded. "For soon, we will take the Isle of Leveros."

CHAPTER TWENTY FIVE

Training with the Knights of the Spur was one of the hardest things Erin had done. Her blade crashed against the shield of her current opponent, a knight named Persh, and he bludgeoned into her with his shoulder. She barely twisted aside from the blow, coming up with her spear ready for the next attack.

That was when Commander Harr hit her from the side, striking her with the flat of his sword. Erin wheeled toward him, anger rising, but he was already sheathing it.

"I don't need to worry about attacks from someone who has already died," he said.

"But that wasn't—"

"If you say 'fair' I'll have you run laps of the walls," the commander warned.

Erin almost said it anyway, just for the sake of the defiance. Somehow though she reined in the urge. She took the cover for her spear, ready to make it a staff once more.

"So I'm supposed to watch out for random old men attacking me," she shot back at him. A part of her was hoping to goad him, just to have the chance to fight with him again. He hadn't sparred with her since she'd arrived, and he was clearly the best of them. It was ... frustrating.

Commander Harr didn't rise to the barbs in her words. Instead, he considered her levelly.

"You should be aware that I have sent a message to your father, explaining that you are here."

"But…" Erin didn't know what to say to that. She should have seen it coming; these were her father's knights, after all.

"I have *also* explained that you have passed our test, and are therefore here to train with us," the commander said. "Frankly, if you wish to stay, you will need to do far better."

"How am I supposed to do better?" Erin demanded.

"Your sword masters have obviously taught you well, but here in the Spur we do not train to fight duels. We train for battle, where anything is fair."

"Like this?" Erin asked, and lunged at the commander. For a moment, she thought that her lunge was fast enough to get through, but Commander Harr twisted aside, letting the blow scrape from his armor. He pushed her, sending Erin stumbling.

"A nice attempt," he said, "but you're still ignoring the obvious. Skill will get you some of the way, but power matters, armor matters, surprise matters. There are a thousand things that go into a real fight, and it doesn't matter if it is fair that you have them or not. All that matters is if you're the one left at the end of it."

"And how am I supposed to be the one with the most size and power?" Erin asked. It seemed like the commander's way of making her feel that she wasn't wanted. Maybe he was trying to convince her that she wasn't meant to be here, that she was supposed to go home and be the princess her parents wanted.

"You're not supposed to," Commander Harr said. "You're supposed to find your own edge. Each of our knights has something they do that is unique. Be faster than the other person, be sneakier, outthink your foes. Oh, and never assume that a battle is done until your foe is down."

Erin saw the blur of movement from the corner of her eye and brought the haft of her spear up in time to parry Persh's blow. She stepped to the side and struck back, kicking his feet from under him and then bringing her short spear down to rest an inch from his throat.

"Better," Commander Harr said. "But the only way you will truly learn is to be in the world. Two of my men are about to ride a patrol. Ride with them, listen, and learn."

"Truly?" Erin asked. She could think of nothing she wanted more. Her father would never have let her ride out into danger, yet the commander was actively sending her. Joy flared in her at the thought.

"Til and Fenir will be by the gate by now," Commander Harr said. "You'll need to hurry to catch them. Your horse is saddled. Tell them I sent you."

"I will," Erin said, turning to run down there. At the last minute, she remembered to turn and salute him. "Thank you!"

She ran to the spot where her horse was waiting, held by a groom. Erin all but leapt into the saddle, riding to the spot where two knights in half plate were waiting atop their chargers. In her chain shirt and leathers, Erin felt surprisingly vulnerable by comparison.

"The commander says that I'm to patrol with you," she said, enjoying how easy it felt to say those words. She felt as though she belonged here in a way that she didn't anywhere else.

"As you say," one of the knights said. "I'm Til. This is Fenir. He doesn't say much."

The other knight nodded in her direction.

"We're to set off along the East Road," Til said. "There are reports of folk going missing out near a cluster of old crofters' huts there."

"Then let's go," Erin said. "I'm ready."

Ready? She was practically bursting with the need to do this. She'd been hoping for something like this all her life, and now... now she had a chance to prove herself.

"Is it always so boring on patrol?" Erin asked. How long had they been riding now? Hours at least, with nothing to show for it except the ache that came from too long in the saddle.

"Seeing nothing is good," Til said. "It means everything's as it should be."

Beside him, Fenir grunted his agreement.

They rode along a path across open ground, between fields as empty as they were beautiful. It was the kind of place Erin was sure Nerra would have liked, and for a brief moment, she missed her sister, but she knew she had to be here, doing this. Their father would never take her seriously otherwise.

They kept riding, and ahead, Erin saw a village, barely more than a hamlet, really, with people wandering the streets. There were scarecrows out in the fields beyond it, although they were poor at their job, because crows were landing on them, pecking on flesh that…

Erin almost gagged as she realized the truth: that those were people who had been tied outside there, their throats cut, their bodies left as some kind of cruel display. She looked around and saw that both Til and Fenir had come to a halt, staring out at the village.

"What's happening here?" Erin asked.

"Hard to say," Til replied. "Except that those aren't villagers in that hamlet."

"Aye," Fenir said. It was almost the first word Erin had heard from him.

She could feel the fear in her, and the uncertainty. "If not villagers, then who?"

"Quiet," Fenir said, and for a moment, Erin thought he was giving her an instruction.

But Til nodded. "The quiet men would be about right."

"Quiet men?" Erin had heard of them. Her brother Vars had tried to tell her stories of them, only stopping when it became obvious to him that he wasn't going to get her to scream in fear by doing it. "What are southerners doing here?"

"Hard to say," Til said. He looked around, then nodded to one of the scarecrows. "We need to leave, before we end up like them."

"Leave?" Erin demanded. She could hardly believe her ears. She could feel her anger rising, pushing down her fear the same way it had with the bandits. "Leave them to get away with what they've done?"

"We need to go and report this to the commander," Til said. "We don't know how many there are, or how they're armed. It's too dangerous to go into that village."

"We're supposed to be knights!" Erin insisted.

"And a part of that is knowing to follow orders," Til shot back. "Our job on patrol is to deal with minor threats and report the rest back. We need to do it now, too. Do you think they aren't watching us? That they wouldn't bring us down if we were in bow range?"

Erin knew that everything the knight was suggesting was sensible. It was probably even the right thing to do, but right then, staring at the scarecrows they'd made of men and women, she knew she couldn't just turn around and walk away. She couldn't do it, any more than she'd been able to walk away when she heard about the bandits who had attacked the villagers before. She was supposed to be royal, and if that didn't mean she was there to protect people, what did it mean?

"Fenir," Til said. "You head back to the Spur with the princess. Bring back at least a dozen. I'll sit and keep watch."

Fenir nodded in response, as if it were the most obvious thing to do.

"You're going to sit here?" Erin said. "You're going to wait? For all we know, they might be about to leave."

"What else would you have me do?" Til demanded, his voice booming from inside his helm.

Erin could still feel the fear pulsing up inside her, urging her to turn back, urging her to do what the knights suggested. She ignored it, gripping her spear tighter. This wasn't the time to give in to fear, or doubt, or caution. She would be the warrior that she knew she was, not a scared little girl, and not a princess.

"I'd have you do this," she said, and heeled her horse forward, heading for the village, whatever the danger it held.

CHAPTER TWENTY SIX

Greave had never met anyone like Aurelle before. She led him down through the castle, into the spaces where the long period of feasting and celebration for the wedding was ongoing. These were spaces open to anyone who wished to come, letting in ordinary folk as easily as nobles to celebrate Lenore's upcoming wedding. Greave tensed as they entered the main feasting hall, then felt Aurelle's touch there, gentle on his arm.

"Is everything all right, my prince?" she asked.

"I normally avoid so many people," he said. "They stare at me as if they know everything that is wrong with me."

Aurelle laughed as though he had made a joke, even though he hadn't. "They look at you because you are the most beautiful man here."

Greave flinched again at that, because his brothers, and even his father, had used his looks like a weapon against him. Vars and Rodry had always said he looked too girlish, while his father... he looked too much like his mother for his father's liking.

"It is not how I feel," Greave said.

Aurelle turned to him. "Greave, I promise you that I find you the handsomest man in this room, and you are more than that, as well. From what I hear, you are learned, and thoughtful, and kind."

Greave didn't know how to answer that. He strove to be all of those things, because he could not bring himself to add to the cruelty or stupidity of the world. With Aurelle's touch on his arm, for a brief moment he felt as though he actually was the things she thought of him.

"Now," Aurelle said, "have you seen the entertainments yet?"

"I've made notes on some of the lutenists' techniques, and listened to the playwrights run through their—"

"No," Aurelle said, "that's not what I mean. Have you been there, been a part of it?"

Greave shook his head. He hadn't wanted to stand there in the middle of a crowd, the only one who still felt alone. He'd also guessed what his father would say if he showed too much of an interest in the players. He would have dismissed it as frivolity or unmanly, or both.

"I have always been more at the sides," Greave said.

"Not today," Aurelle declared. Her touch on his arm turned into a grip on his wrist, pulling him forward into the crowds of people there. Many of them turned to him and bowed. Some even smiled, and that wasn't something that Greave was used to.

She led the way to a table filled with the lightest of pastries and the finest of wine. She held out a pastry to Greave, and he realized as she did it that he was expected to bite down on it. He did so, because the alternative seemed to be getting it smeared on his face. He swallowed, and was about to complain about the indignity of it when the taste hit him. It was bright, sharp, and sweet, and for once, Greave didn't feel as though the food was about to turn to ash in his mouth.

"That's…" Greave didn't know what to say. "Amazing."

"You have been denying yourself too many pleasures," Aurelle guessed. "Or perhaps you just haven't had someone to really appreciate them with you."

She passed him wine, and Greave sipped it delicately. He wasn't going to quaff it the way Vars might, wasn't going to turn into something as debauched as him. Yet maybe, just maybe, there was a middle ground. Didn't the philosopher van Greten write, "We can enjoy the world in moderation, without it becoming something to be avoided"?

It seemed that Aurelle wasn't done with him, because she led the way over to a spot where players were putting on a raucous performance, in which it seemed that an explorer of the southern lands was stumbling into more and more laughable circumstances. Currently, a peasant character seemed to be trying to sell him a donkey, trying to convince him that it was a thoroughbred racehorse.

On another day, Greave might have stood there, examining all the ways that the playwright worked at his craft, all the subtle tricks used to make the language flow and the scenes contrast with one another. He would have felt like a man apart, understanding but not truly enjoying any of it.

Here, now, with Aurelle there, he laughed. He actually laughed, at stupid jokes about a man who couldn't see the truth in front of him.

"And will it jump?" the noble asked the peasant. "I've a mind to race it over hedges and fences."

"Aye, it will get past all those," the peasant said, and then stage whispered to the audience, "if you get off to open the gates for it."

Greave laughed along with the rest of them, and glanced over to find Aurelle looking at him with apparent joy at the sight of him like that. She seemed to be taking as much pleasure in his presence as he was in hers, and that seemed almost like a miracle. Greave was about to say how impossible it seemed that someone so perfect should appear in his life so suddenly, but he got no chance to do so, because Aurelle was already glancing in a different direction.

"Do you hear that?" she asked. "They're starting a dance. Come on."

She pulled at Greave and he went with her, because he didn't want to break contact with her, didn't want to break that slender connection to everything that seemed good, and right, and real. He watched Aurelle as they walked, and she was perfection itself in every movement, so that it was hard to imagine being anywhere but there with her.

Was this what love was like? Greave had no point of comparison except the things that had been written in plays and books. His brothers had always treated him as a kind of failed brother, who didn't do the things they did. His sisters possibly loved him, but

Queen Aethe had always emphasized their separateness and difference to him. His father … no, while his mother's death had robbed Greave of even that love.

This was different. It was sudden and sharp, like lightning across his body.

"Will you dance with me?" Aurelle asked.

"I don't dance," Greave said.

"I find that hard to believe. You must be beauty itself when you move. Please, for me?"

Greave could have countered any other argument. He could have provided a dozen objections to dancing based on everything from the works of sword masters to philosophers, religious writers to poets. But he couldn't simply say no to Aurelle in this, or anything else.

"I don't know what I'm supposed to do," he pointed out.

"That's all right," she said. "I'll show you. Here, you hold me like this."

She moved close to him, so close that there was no space between the two of them, and Greave felt sure he could feel her heartbeat against his. Or maybe it was his heartbeat, thrumming with the excitement of being there like this.

"Now we move together. Feel the music. Move in time to it," she said.

Greave did his best, listening to the music not for the technical components of meter and scale for once, but just for the flow of it. He felt himself falling into that flow, and Aurelle's presence made it easy. He felt as though he could feel every moment she was going to make and respond to it automatically, as if she lent him her grace in some indefinable way.

In the moment when she kissed him, even that felt like the most natural thing in the world to do. Her lips met his, and in that moment, Greave couldn't work out which of them was leading the kiss, which of them was kissing the other.

"I … haven't done that before," Greave breathed when they pulled back from one another.

"You haven't kissed someone?" Aurelle asked.

Greave shook his head.

"Then you're a very fast learner," she said with a smile.

In that moment, there was no doubt left for Greave; he knew he was in love. It made no sense that he should be in love so quickly, but he knew he was.

"It makes me wonder what else I might teach you," Aurelle said. Her finger hooked into Greave's shirt, gently drawing him with her.

"Where are we going?" Greave asked.

"To my rooms," Aurelle said. She hesitated for a moment, looking suddenly as shy as Greave felt. "That is ... if you want to?"

That hint of shyness was the thing that clinched it for Greave. It said to him that this was as strange an experience for her as it was for him, and that some part of her felt all the strange, impossible things that were running through him. Greave stared at her, seeing yet another side to her: this vulnerable, gentle need to be loved as much as he needed it. Slowly, carefully, Greave nodded.

"I want that more than anything," he said.

CHAPTER TWENTY SEVEN

Renard watched Lord Carrick's castle home the way he might have stared at a musical score, or perhaps at Yselle when she was in one of her more unfathomable moods: looking for understanding, for the chink of light that would show the way in. He stared at it from the fields beyond, dressed in peasant garb so that none would think twice about his presence there, memorizing all he could of the movements of the guards and the hidden spots around the walls.

"Patience," he told himself, and in truth, this was the one thing in life where he had patience. Tell him to work a farmer's tasks, and he'd be gone in a day. Leave him to work as a chandler or a merchant's runner... he'd tried it once, and had lasted a full week before the itch got to him, the pressing, weighty feeling that this wasn't all there was, that there had to be more. He'd run off with half the man's takings and drunk most of it the week after to try to forget the sheer boredom of it.

Give him a locked place to look at, though, and he could wait all day. Had been waiting all day, just to make sure that everything he'd gotten from the former guard was right. Renard smiled to himself at that; Lord Carrick should pay his guards better if he didn't want them betraying him. Apparently, he'd spent enough on locks for his doors to make up for it.

Behind him, his horse whinnied where Renard had left it tied to a tree. It was obviously as impatient as he was, but then, it was a flighty horse. After all, the man he'd stolen it from had sworn it was finest southern thoroughbred.

"Now," Renard decided as the light started to fail. Changing quickly in a stand of bushes, he threw on darker clothing, complete with a hood to hide his features, and leathers that might at least do something to protect him if this all went wrong. He hurried forward, in the direction of a spot the guard had told him about, and which seemed obvious now that Renard knew it was there.

In that spot, the wall was crumbling slightly with age and disrepair; apparently, Lord Carrick didn't see the point in spending money on stone when he could spend it on gilt and silver for the inside. That was good, because it meant that a man like Renard could climb without the need to throw a grapnel, trusting to knowing hands and feet to raise him up a little at a time. He would drop a rope on the way back, but for now, it was better not to have the noise.

"No harder than climbing a tree," Renard tried to tell himself, although in truth, it was plenty harder than that. Even with the handholds, the wall was a thing of nearly sheer stone, and Renard had to press himself to it like a lover, one limb and then the next searching for the way up. He was almost at the top when he heard the sound of approaching footsteps.

He froze in place, willing himself to be just another part of the wall, a shadow as natural as any cast in the evening light. His muscles complained at the effort of hanging there like that, but he ordered them to be quiet. What did they want him to do? Drop off and see if he could fly?

The shadow of a guard passed above, standing there for far too long for Renard's liking. Every second spent there felt like an agony of immobility, but Renard forced himself to patience until the man passed. Better not to attract attention just yet.

He hopped onto the battlements, quickly took in the locations of the patrolling guards, and smiled to himself. All was exactly as he'd thought it would be. Of course, if he stood there congratulating himself on his genius, they would probably spot him anyway, so it was best to get moving. Now he just had to remember the timing, as perfect as any song. Had he decided that this worked better to "The Seven Lilies" or "Tinker's Gig"? The notes of "A Harpist's Lament" came into his head. Ah, that was it...

In time to the rhythm of it, Renard dropped down from the wall, rolled, came up, and sprinted in a burst to the wall of the keep. He paused there, counting the beat, waiting while another set of footsteps passed by. Silent as a shadow, Renard climbed again, looking for the window he wanted.

There was an art to getting through a window without making a sound. Quiet as the growing darkness around him, Renard started to remove pieces of glass, depositing them in a small sack he'd brought to catch them. With the glass gone, it was relatively easy to cut through the lead and bend it back, giving enough room for his muscled form to slide through. It didn't matter what kind of locks Lord Carrick put on his doors when there was a window to the room. Renard started to take a step forward, then stopped himself just in time as he saw a tripwire set there.

He lit a thief's lamp, the hood over it providing a small circle of light directed downward so it wouldn't show beyond the room. He bent, looking along the wire and seeing the crossbow it was connected to. Very, very carefully, he disconnected the wire. Even though he was sure he did it right, he still breathed a sigh of relief when the crossbow didn't go off.

Renard looked up and his eyes lit up almost as much as the lamp at what he saw in the room. The sailor he'd talked to at the Broken Scale hadn't been lying about what they'd been carrying. There were chests there that, when opened, gleamed with the shine of gold. There was enough here to last a lifetime, maybe, if he were able to take it all.

"And how would I do that?" he muttered to himself. "Enlist the guards?"

Better to stick with the plan. Taking a bag from his shoulder, Renard opened it, trying to decide what would be the easiest to carry, and to dispose of. Coins, definitely. He knelt by the chests, scooping them into his sack the way a farmer might have gathered potatoes. He kept going, wanting to take as much as he could get away with, because a chance like this only came along once.

That was roughly when everything went wrong.

Renard heard the snick of locks being opened, but there was nowhere to hide in a room this size, and no time to get back out the window. He tied off the end of his sack of stolen coins, but by then, the door was already swinging open.

A pair of guards came in, accompanying a man who might have been a clerk of some kind. The guards took one look at him and reached for their swords, while the clerk opened his mouth and let out a cry that could probably be heard two villages away.

"Thief!"

With no time to run, Renard knew he had to go the other way. He barreled into the first of the guards, smashing him back into the door frame with his shoulder. The second had his sword out by now, but in such close quarters, there was no space to swing the weapon. Renard grabbed the guard's arm and pinned it back as the man tried to find an angle to swing at him. He knew that at any moment, the second guard might be there at his back, ready to kill him. He did the only thing he could do in that moment: he drew his dagger and thrust up, around the side of the man's breastplate and into his lungs.

As the guard collapsed, Renard spun just in time to try to block the swing of a sword. He only partly managed it, and felt the blade cutting through the layers of his leathers, wounding the flesh beneath. Renard cut back, slicing across the man's throat. He paused, trying to make sense of the chaos, and then cursed himself for doing it. You couldn't make sense of chaos like this; you could only ride it and hope for the best.

He grabbed the sack he'd filled, flung it over his shoulder, and leapt through the window he'd come through. Renard rolled as he landed, but even so, it hurt, the clink of the coins against his ribs knocking the wind out of him. He forced himself to his feet, saw people staring, but he was already running.

A crossbow bolt flashed past him and he ducked instinctively, but what good was ducking when the bolt was already past? He wove as he ran, heading for the patch of wall he'd come over.

"No time," he told himself. He ran for the castle stables instead. Another bolt flashed past him, but Renard ducked into cover, hiding behind a door, then scuttling low to duck in behind some hay bales. The guard who had fired at him came in, loading a fresh bolt, and the germs of a plan formed in Renard's mind when no more followed.

"Don't think," he reminded himself. "Ride the chaos."

He waited until the man's back was turned, lunged up, and wrapped a meaty arm around his throat. Renard squeezed, and kept squeezing until the guard went limp. Then he dragged him back behind the hay and started to change.

The disguise that resulted was a long way from perfect. Renard had the man's surcoat with Lord Carrick's insignia, and he had a helm that would disguise some of his features, but they were built too differently for Renard to steal the other man's armor. He would just have to hope that confidence was enough.

Going through the stable, he selected a mount and saddled it, throwing his ill-gotten gains into the saddle bags. Renard mounted up, trying not to think of all the ways that this could go wrong, then, very deliberately, he rode out into the middle of the castle.

Around it, he could see guards milling about, clearly trying to find him. How long would he have now? Minutes? Seconds? In the voice he normally reserved for quieting rowdy crowds when he played, Renard called out to them.

"Quick, he's over the wall! We need to get after him! Open the gate!"

For a second, he thought it wouldn't work. It shouldn't have worked, because he knew just how flimsy this disguise was, and how stupid it was to open a gate when a thief was inside. Yet it seemed that these men were too afraid of losing part of Lord Carrick's spoils to think properly, and the gate swung open.

Renard charged through it, bellowing more nonsense about getting after the thief. Men came out with him on foot, but Renard surged forward, outpacing them with what he hoped looked like his eagerness for the chase. He rode for what must have been half a mile before he grabbed the saddlebags and hopped down from the saddle, striking the horse to send it off in a fresh direction in case the guards had worked out his ruse by now.

Renard went the other way, to the spot where he'd left his own horse. He could feel the pain of the sword blow he'd taken, and the ache in his ribs from the fall, but as he mounted up it seemed worth it. He'd done it; he'd actually robbed Lord Carrick. With the sounds of the hunt for him still in the distance, it would be easy to ride clear.

Now, it was just a question of celebrating.

Chapter Twenty Eight

Brother Odd was working in the gardens when the call went out around the monastery. "Ships!" one of those meditating on the walls called out, echoed seconds later by more of the brothers, and still more. The sheer number of those calling out told him that this wasn't some cluster of merchant ships come to bargain, or a noble aiming to give a grand farewell to a son offered up to the monastic life.

Even so, he had to see it for himself, had to hope that everything he suspected in that moment was wrong. Still clinging to the rake he'd been using to gather leaves, he climbed the stairs to the walls, looking out.

A trio of ships stood there on the horizon, enough to be called a fleet, enough to carry a whole company of men. They were surging forward from the sea, and by now they were already close enough that Brother Odd could make out the banners of the Southern Kingdom.

"What's happening?" one of the brothers asked, even though it must have been obvious.

Another beside him looked hopeful. "Maybe it is a procession, or a royal expedition."

Brother Odd couldn't help laughing bitterly, and caught himself. That was the kind of thing the man he had been did. He gripped the rake tighter. This was the man he was now.

"Those are not trading ships, brothers," he said softly. "That is an attack."

"An attack?" the first brother said. "But why would they attack us? This is a holy place, a place of peace!"

"Perhaps that is why they have sent so few ships," Brother Odd said. "They know that they can take the island easily."

"But why would they?" the second brother demanded.

Brother Odd shook his head. "Because that would give Ravin easy access to the Northern Kingdom? No, don't say anything else. I have no time to explain the evils of the world to you, brother. I need to find the abbot, and you need to get out of the monastery. Tell everyone who will listen that they need to run, now!"

He didn't wait for a reply, but hurried instead down from the walls, seeking out the abbot and hoping he wouldn't be too late. It was too easy to imagine the progress of the ships in toward the shore, the lowering of small boats or the throwing of ropes over to the docks. Brother Odd found himself imagining how he would organize the capture of a place like the monastery, and it was all too easy. Maybe if they'd had a company of soldiers here to defend those solid walls that cut them off from the world, it would have been different, but as it was...

He found the abbot in a cloister near the main gate, other senior figures from the monastery there with him. The precentor and the sacristan were both there, the head of the lay brothers and the librarian. Around them was a ring of other brothers, all waiting for information.

"Brothers, brothers," the abbot said, making a placating gesture. "Calm yourselves. I am sure it is not as bad as you imagine."

"It's as bad and worse," Brother Odd said, stepping forward. "The ships there have Ravin's colors, which means that they're probably the head of a larger invasion force to follow."

The abbot turned to him. "Brother Odd, this is a matter which the senior monks must discuss. You must calm yourself. Seek the equilibrium that our home offers."

"That's going to be hard to do with a blade in me," Brother Odd said. "And have no doubt, there will be blades. You need to evacuate while there's still time, or at least shut the gates so that they can't get in."

"Brother Odd, you overstep your bounds," the abbot said. "This monastery welcomes those who come to it. I and others will go down to the docks to meet our visitors. I will discuss things with them. I am sure they will see that we offer them no threat."

"Men like that like it when the people they attack aren't a threat," Brother Odd snapped back. "They'll cut you down, and—"

"That is enough, Brother," the abbot said. "You are still thinking like the man you were; the man you claim you do not wish to be. I want you to kneel here and contemplate that. In silence, please."

Brother Odd wanted to argue, but he couldn't see a way to do it, not with every other eye there on him. To say anything more would be to defy the abbot openly. A monk did not do that. Seeing no other choice, he knelt, the rake before him, forcing down the waves of frustration and anger that threatened to overwhelm him.

The abbot turned to the others there.

"You will come with me," he said to them. "We will greet our visitors in peace and remind them of the holy neutrality of our isle."

He set off through the monastery's gates, the others trailing in his wake.

Brother Odd continued to kneel, his thoughts racing in a way no monk's should have. Maybe the abbot was right. Maybe he did need to slow himself, contemplate, not react the way the old him would have. Maybe the abbot going to the docks was the best move, peacefully welcoming those who came, trying diplomacy because the island had no swords to offer.

Instinctively, though, Brother Odd knew it was the wrong move. He knew what the men coming to the island would do. He'd been those men, and he knew how they thought. Men like the abbot were normally blessed that they had never known thoughts like that, but here… here it was a curse. They didn't know what it was like to be a man who would see innocent people as an enemy to be crushed, who would kill for the least provocation. They couldn't see the true danger coming for them.

Yet what could he do? The abbot's instructions to him had been clear. Breaking them wasn't something a monk could do, and Brother Odd was a monk, not the man he had been.

I am not that man, he thought.

But are you a man who lets his friends, good men, be slaughtered? another part demanded.

I am Brother Odd, a loyal monk, he insisted.

But that was not always your name.

Brother Odd wrestled with it, fought with it, but he already knew what the answer was. With limbs already cramping from the kneeling, he stood, lifting the rake and considering it.

"It will have to do," he said, and set off in the direction of the docks.

The run down from the monastery to the docks was a short one, but by the time he got there, Brother Odd could feel his breath coming shorter. He was out of condition, not used to this.

You're not supposed to be used to this, he reminded himself.

Ahead, he could see the spot where one of the ships had docked next to the island, a gangplank down to let down a cluster of soldiers who looked like beetles in their steel and leather compared to the monks. There weren't many on the shore yet, but it was already too many, especially when they made no pretense of keeping their weapons sheathed.

As he got closer, Brother Odd could hear the abbot talking with their leader, a man with the design of a leopard on his shield.

"And I say to you that we are a holy place, Captain. We must not be used for war, lest it anger the gods."

"It is King Ravin's anger you need to worry about," the man said, in the thick accent of the southerners.

"Kings swear to uphold Leveros's neutrality when they are crowned," the abbot pointed out. All the time, Brother Odd was making his way forward, hoping he would make it there in time. Hope that he wouldn't be needed at all were long gone by now. "As many of our monks come from the south as from the north."

"Then they will have told you that a king's power is absolute,"
the captain said. "Merely by refusing, you are traitors, and will suffer
a traitor's end." He turned to the others with him. "Kill them all!"

He raised his sword to strike, but Brother Odd was already in
motion. He caught the blow with the head of the rake, twisted, and
sent the weapon spinning from the man's hand. Turning, he swept
his opponent's feet from under him, sending him to the floor in a
clatter of armor.

"No, there will be no violence here!" the abbot shouted, but it
was too late for that. The spark had already fallen in the forest, and
all they could do was hope to survive the conflagration of violence
that followed.

Brother Odd certainly didn't stop. Instead, he charged at the
next of the soldiers there, and maybe the man still hadn't realized
quite what his opponent was, because he brought his sword up lazily.
Brother Odd swept round the parry and slammed the end of the
rake into his throat, hearing the crack and gurgle of it before the
soldier started to topple. Odd dropped his rake, caught the sword,
and turned to the other monks there.

"Run!" he bellowed, in the voice he'd long used to command
men in the field. Some obeyed immediately. Others hesitated, looking to the abbot. Those were the first to die. The soldiers on the
dock were already hacking down with blades, lashing out at any
target they could see without a care over who they hit. They were
expecting pleas and peaceful protestations... Odd gave them violence instead.

He charged a pair of them, slicing out low then high with his
newly captured blade. He was still getting used to the weight of
it, and the first man was able to parry, while the second thrust at
Odd's flank. He twisted away from the blow, but still felt the steel
slicing into his flesh.

That triggered the old fury, bringing out the side of himself that
didn't stop, didn't hold back, didn't care. He roared like a wounded
animal, hacked down on the soldier's arm hard enough to cut it off
at the wrist, kicked the first one back.

"Back, damn you!" he bellowed to the monks, and now even
the slowest of them on the uptake were trying to run. Odd moved
between them and the soldiers, giving ground slowly even though
the battle rage in him wanted to charge at them. He maneuvered
around crates and boxes, lining it up so that the men there could
only come at him one at a time, could only die one at a time.

Oh, how they died.

The first went down in a fountain of blood, charging forward
too carelessly and all but running onto Odd's sword. The second
came in more cautiously, with the mechanical sword work of the
badly trained. Odd parried two blows to get the measure of him,
took a slicing cut on his arm, then took the man's head off in one
sweep of the blade.

He gave ground, step by careful step. There was a problem with
that, of course, because once he got to the open ground beyond the
slender dock, they would be able to surround him. Only one plan
occurred to Odd then: he charged.

He leapt at them like the man he had once been, not Odd,
but Oderick. Sir Oderick. Oderick the Mad, Oderick who would
ride down foes just because he could. Oderick, who had known
the truth of battle: that it wasn't about men's flesh, but their hearts.
The next man gave ground as he charged, and that was all it took
to send the rest of them back toward their ship, waiting for the rest
of their men to unload before they dared to take him on.

That was when Oderick ran, catching the others up as they
made their way up the short path to the monastery.

"Run faster, damn you!" he ordered them, and it worked in a
way that an order from Brother Odd would not have. They all ran
faster, even the librarian, who never moved quicker than he needed
to get from his shelves to the refectory and back. Oderick threw his
arm around a wounded brother, helping him to make the journey,
determined that they would lose no more.

"There!" he said, pointing to the gates. They ran for them, and
behind, he could hear the sounds of pursuit now. Glancing back, he
could see men marching in formation, more disciplined now after

the shock of his attack. He wouldn't catch them like that again. A few men lifted bows, and arrows sang out. One caught the librarian in the back, and he fell, dead before he hit the ground.

"Inside, inside!" Oderick called as he dove through. "Now close the gates!"

It said something for the tone in which he ordered it that they obeyed without question. The gates swung shut ponderously, the thick wood and iron clanging. Only when the bars were in place did Oderick relax, the battle rage fading. That was when the full enormity of everything that had happened struck him.

His sword clattered from bloody hands. He'd saved people today, but he'd also killed, time and again. He'd put aside the calm of the monastery for the fury within. He'd reveled in the violence. Oderick looked down at the blood covering him, only some of it his.

"What have I done?"

There was no time to think about that though, because Oderick knew that men would soon be coming to try to batter those gates down. They needed to prepare for the defense.

CHAPTER TWENTY NINE

All along the ride back to Royalsport, Devin could feel the eyes of Rodry and the others on him. They might not know for sure what he was, but they had seen a glimpse of what he could do now, and there was awe there, maybe even a bit of fear. Devin didn't know whether to be flattered by the hint of respect in those gazes, or worried about people's reactions once more found out about him.

Magic wasn't something for the likes of him, after all. It was something for strange men and women who walked out of the wild places, for herbalists and seers, and for men like Master Grey. None of that sounded like Devin to his ears.

Eventually, the city came into sight. Devin was grateful that it gave him the chance to get back home, or at least to the House of Weapons. He understood steel in a way that he could never understand what had happened out there in Clearwater Deep.

"Do you have any clothes other than those?" Rodry asked, out of nowhere, as they got close to the city.

"Other clothes?" Devin said. "I don't understand."

"Well, you can't come to the feast looking like that, can you?" Rodry said. "Halfin, you're about the same size as him, maybe you could lend him something."

"Wait," Devin said. "You want me to come to the feast? The feast for your sister's wedding?"

"Of course," Rodry said, as if it were the most obvious thing in the world. "You've fought beside me, you've done more to help than either of my brothers could have, and you're going to make the most perfect gift for me to give to my sister. It's only right that you should come. Don't think that I abandon my friends, Devin!"

He seemed to have declared them friends just like that. Devin had to admit that he liked Rodry, admired his bravery and his strength. He felt honored that a prince would think of him as a friend, even if it was as sudden and impulsive a decision as everything else he did.

"I would be honored to attend," Devin said. "The outer feast is—"

"Not the outer feast," Rodry said. "You'd have been able to walk into that anyway. You're coming to the inner feasting, and that's an end to it."

Even having known him such a short time, Devin knew better than to argue. He saw Sir Twell shrug.

"His highness is like that," the knight said, moving his horse closer. "When a man shows courage and honor, he's a true friend to them. Besides, you're worthy enough."

The other two knights nodded. It seemed that it was settled: Devin was going to the feast.

When they arrived at the castle, Rodry headed off to the feasting hall with Sir Lars and his prize of star metal, to show it to his father before he gave it back to Devin for the forging. Devin, meanwhile, found himself taken to the rooms of Sir Halfin, trying to find suitable clothes. The knight was much older than him, but it was true that they were similar sizes, and soon, they were rooting through his clothes, picking out this doublet and that.

"I swear he's more your size, Twell," the knight grumbled, as he went through a chest to drag out hose, shirt, doublet, and boots. "Here, try these, they might fit you."

They did, and they were finer than anything Devin had worn in his life. The shirt was silk, the double dark velvet embroidered with curls and spirals. The boots were soft leather, a far cry from the hard ones Devin wore. Devin washed the worst of the dirt from himself and dragged his fingers through his hair, wondering all the while exactly what was happening to him.

"You get used to Prince Rodry's generosity eventually," Halfin said. "He's a good young man, reminds me of his father in that respect. So long as you don't do anything to pick a fight with him."

"Like being late for the feast when he's invited you," Twell suggested. "They'll forgive us old Knights of the Spur a lot, but not *too* much."

"Especially not when one of us has a reputation for speed," Halfin said.

Sir Twell laughed at him. "Maybe ten years ago."

"Oh, that would be back before the great planner started forgetting things?" Halfin shot back.

It was so strange for Devin, sitting there with two Knights of the Spur, listening to them make fun of one another like two old comrades, rather than the heroes out of stories.

"We need to hurry," Halfin said.

He led the way down through the castle. Even though Devin had been there before, that had been brief, and he'd been in a dungeon for much of it. Now Devin found himself staring at the expanse of the interior. There were tapestries on all the wars, depicting everything from the rise of the Northern kings to the myths of the gods, and the dragons that no one had seen in more than a lifetime. They seemed to shimmer, picked out in metallic thread and shimmering as air caught the tapestries they stood on.

Devin hadn't thought that anywhere could be grander, but when they reached the feasting hall, he knew he was wrong. He'd been in it for brief moment before, but now he got a true look at it. This was a place that was the epitome of opulence, strung with decorations and pennants, gilded and with marble columns supporting arches overhead, with music coming from lutenists and trumpeters. There were people dancing and talking everywhere Devin looked, while at the far end of the hall, the king and his wife sat on thrones next to one another.

"There are so many people," Devin said, and not just people, nobles. Devin could see the difference. Everyone there, even the servants, was dressed in ways that were more expensive than anything Devin owned, and he immediately felt as though he stood out in spite of his borrowed clothes helping him to blend in.

Rodry was there, next to his sister Lenore. Devin had seen her when she had been seeing Rodry off, but now...she was perfect. Her dark hair was lustrous and her body encased expertly in a dress of gold and green. Her features were delicate, and when she laughed at something Rodry said, Devin couldn't have imagined anything more beautiful.

Something caught at his heart then, sharp and almost painful. He felt as if he couldn't look away. Then Rodry did something Devin hadn't expected: he looked around and waved Devin over.

Devin should have felt as though he had no right to set foot on that floor. He should have felt as though he was about to stumble and fall with every step, yet he didn't. The sight of her seemed to pull Devin across the floor, dragging him across just with the need to be near her, so that he glided evenly over to them. He remembered to bow when he got there.

"There's no need for that, Devin," Rodry said. "Devin, I would like you to meet my sister Lenore. Lenore, this is my friend Devin."

His friend? There were so many other things that he could have described Devin as. He could have mentioned the sword Devin was making, or the fact that he was from the House of Weapons. It seemed strange to be introduced just as that.

"It's lovely to meet you, Devin," Lenore said, offering him her hand. Devin took it as delicately as he could, kissing her knuckles. Even that contact was electric.

"And you, your highness," he said, remembering the correct term. For a moment, he found himself wishing he could ask her to dance along with the others, but he knew he had no right to do it.

"I'm told that I have you to thank for bringing my brother back to me, along with Father's knights," she said. She smiled slightly.

"Although he won't tell me exactly what it was that he went out to fetch."

Devin saw Rodry shake his head pointedly.

"Then I shouldn't be the one to give away his secrets," Devin said.

"Ah, loyalty," Lenore said. She didn't seem displeased, though. "I will have to leave you two to talk," Lenore said. "For now, Finnal is waiting for me. It was good to meet you, Devin."

She didn't so much step away as glide, and Devin found that he couldn't take his eyes from her as she did it. She went to stand with a young man who seemed almost as beautiful as she was, who took her hand with perfect grace. They moved out onto the dance floor together, stepping in perfect time to the music. The people around seemed entranced by them, rapt in joy as they watched.

Rodry didn't seem happy, and Devin found that nor was he. *He* wanted to be the one dancing with Lenore, as impossible as that was.

"That man ..." Rodry said, with something close to a snarl.

"You don't like him?" Devin asked with a frown. It seemed strange that someone would seem to have that much loathing for anyone who so obviously made his sister happy.

"Let's just say that I would rather he were marrying a good man," Rodry said. He gestured to Devin. "Like you. *You'd* be a much better match, because at least you have honor."

Devin laughed, because he assumed that Rodry was making a joke. Even so, he couldn't help thinking about it. What would it be like to be the one marrying Princess Lenore? What would it be like to be the one standing there in front of a priest when the time came, declaring their mutual love for one another? Devin could feel his heart swelling at the image, and he turned to Rodry to ask him more about his sister, but before he could do it, trumpets blared, bringing a halt to the dancing.

In the ensuing silence, the king stood.

"Where are my children?" he called out. "Come to me! I would speak with you!"

Devin saw Rodry look around in surprise.

"Looks like I have to go," Rodry said. "Enjoy the rest of the feast, Devin."

Devin nodded, watching his new friend go to his father. He found himself edging forward too, because he wanted to know what this was about. The king's tone had sounded serious. Something was happening, and Devin wanted to know what it was.

CHAPTER THIRTY

"**B**ring my children to me!" King Godwin called out over the controlled chaos of the feasting hall. He could hear the anger in his voice, though it wasn't at any of them—it was at the men who stood in front of him, a collection of nobles who stood there with all the solemnity of men standing at a funeral. He wanted to dismiss them, to tell them all to leave and take their stories with them, yet he couldn't. Duke Viris was among them, and the rest... these men supplied half of the kingdom's armies. The Knights of the Spur might be his men, but the rest were summoned from around the kingdom.

"Where are you?" he demanded again, loud enough that the feast fell silent.

His children came forward; at least, those of them who were there. Erin was still absent, and his men had yet to send word that they'd found her. Rodry was there, looking as though he expected to be sent off on some mission, and Vars was drunk, looking as though he hoped he wouldn't be. Greave was besotted on the arm of some girl, which was a strange look for him, but probably a better one than his usual moping in the library. Lenore was there, elegant and perfect as always...

...and then there was Nerra. Godwin wasn't supposed to have favorites, but he'd always cared for Nerra so much. Looking after her; keeping her secret from the world, had drawn him closer and closer to his daughter. He wanted her to be safe...

...he just couldn't see how he could manage it now.

"There have been ... claims," he said. The word almost stuck in his throat. He looked over to Aethe, knowing how much this would hurt his wife, because it was hurting him at least as much. "Claims about you, Nerra."

Fear filled him then, and as great as his fear for Nerra was, only part of that fear was for his middle daughter. Much of it was for the others there, for all the rest of his family. If people knew that he had kept something like this from them, had not sent away his daughter the moment he knew… they would never forgive him. His whole family might fall and die.

That was the terror that made him say it as if he didn't know all of this, as if he had never heard the words the nobles had said before, rather than hearing them almost the moment his daughter had been born.

"What claims?" Nerra asked, and she sounded genuinely confused, as if there might be more than one thing that this might be about.

King Godwin gestured to one of the nobles there, a minor earl, Earl Fontaine a few paces ahead of Duke Viris. The duke himself wasn't going to say it, because that would have been too much, but he was there, he was part of this.

"We have received information that Princess Nerra has the scale sickness," Earl Fontaine said.

"What?" Rodry demanded from the side. "How *dare* you make such a claim!"

He stepped forward as if he would fight the man, and on another occasion, King Godwin would have let him. Instead, he had to raise a hand to stop his son, because to do anything else would be to go against the most powerful men in the kingdom.

"That's enough, Rodry," Godwin said. He looked to Earl Fontaine. "Do you have evidence of this claim?"

"A boy saw her in the woods," the earl said. "Her arm bears the mark of the illness."

"A boy's word?" Greave said from the side. "Where is this boy? The laws do not permit someone to be condemned on the basis of rumor. I will show you the places in the legal tomes, if it helps."

For a moment Godwin was grateful for his son's time in the library, but he knew it wouldn't be enough.

Sure enough, Earl Fontaine spoke again. "The truth is easy enough to establish, my king. Let us see your daughter's arms. If the mark is not upon them, I will bow down and beg her forgiveness, but if it is... then this is a serious matter; one that has been kept from your nobles."

"You dare to demand that?" Rodry asked. "Should my other sisters strip for your amusement? Should *I*?"

King Godwin wished he could stop this. He stood to do just that, but he could hear the voices speaking up around the hall...

"... trying to hide it..."

"... all helping her..."

"... why won't they check? Does he already know?"

He knew then that he couldn't dismiss this. To do that would be to confirm in the minds of his nobles that he and his other children were all in on the secret of Nerra's illness.

Even so, he tried. "If there is no evidence of this claim, then we must dismiss it as the foolish rumor that it is. I will *not* have my daughter treated like this."

"With respect, your majesty," Earl Fontaine said, "we must insist."

"Insist?" Godwin shot back. He knew he shouldn't. "You wish to *insist*?"

He knew he shouldn't be doing this, that it put the rest of his children in danger. Arguing made it look as if he had been a part of hiding his daughter's illness, which of course he had been, but *showing* that to his nobles risked bringing his whole family down. They might rebel. They might kill all of them. Even so, he was willing to stand there and deny them, for Nerra's sake.

"It's all right, Father," Nerra said, stepping forward. Apparently, she understood what was at stake too. She pulled up her sleeve before Godwin could stop her. "Here, is *this* what you want to see?"

She rolled up her sleeve, revealing the scale mark all over her arm. There was a gasp around the room at the sight of it. King

Godwin knew it was too late now. Some things couldn't be undone, couldn't be unseen, or unsaid. Looking around, he knew he had to act, or his family would die. He knew what he had to do, even though it hurt more than anything to do it.

"She bears the mark of the scale!" Earl Fontaine said. "She has the sickness!"

He stepped back from her, pointing in obvious horror.

"She has to die!" another noble said.

"Take her and behead her!"

Rodry was there with his hand on his sword, ready to fight anyone who came close. Godwin wanted to leap forward with him, but he knew that was how the destruction of his whole family would start. He would leap down and fight, and in moments, his kingdom would be torn apart. Depending on who fought and who did not, his family might even be slain there and then.

He had to find a better way. "There will be no killing here," he said. He made his voice stern, because it was the only barrier stopping them from hearing the heartbreak he felt.

"The law requires it," Earl Fontaine said. Those around him nodded.

"Father," Nerra began.

The next part broke his heart. "I cannot be your father, Nerra."

"What?"

"Those with the scale sickness have no families, have no friends. They are outcasts."

Godwin heard the intake of breath around the hall.

"King Godwin, the law calls for *death*," Earl Fontaine said.

"The laws say that they must no longer be a part of the world, that they may be killed if found," Godwin shot back at him. "Do you wish to argue with me on this, Fontaine? Here, and now? You will *not* call for my daughter's death." Even what he had to do was enough to hurt like his heart was about to leap from his chest.

Aethe moved to him, gripping his arm.

"Husband, you can't—"

"I can," he said, raising his voice to stop her as well. "I *must*. A king must protect his people from this scourge. Nerra, I...I wish there were another way. You must go from this place. You must leave and not come back."

"Father," Rodry said, storming forward. "Nerra is my sister and your daughter. You're going to send her away just like that? She should stay here. She is no danger to anyone here."

"The scale sickness is a danger to *everyone*," a noble called out from further back in the hall.

"Aye, they say those with it herald a time of death!" another called out.

Godwin made a mental note of which people they were. He could not act now, but he would find a way to pay them back for their part in this. How he would ever *begin* to repay his own part in this, he didn't know. Still, those voices confirmed the truth of this: Nerra could not stay.

"You do not get to gainsay me in this," he said to Rodry. He looked around at the others. "None of you do. I take this on myself."

How could Rodry understand that he was already doing all he could for Nerra? That he'd kept her as safe as he could for years? That anyone else would have sought to have his daughter killed out of hand?

"Nerra," he repeated. "You will leave this place. You will be gone from the city by the turn of the next month, and if you are seen again within the kingdom, your life..." He paused as he forced the next words past the wash of emotion that threatened to overwhelm them. "Your life will be forfeit."

"I..." Nerra looked down. There were so many things that King Godwin wished he could say to her, so many ways he wished he could have prevented this. "I love you, Father."

She turned, with more dignity than should have been possible, and started to walk to the door. People stepped aside for her, partly because of the fear of what she was, and partly because Rodry was there, making sure that none came too close. He saw Lenore going with them, obviously not wanting to leave her sister's side.

171

"Call her back," Aethe said by his side. "*Please* call her back."

"I can't," King Godwin said, and he saw his wife turn her face from him. That hurt even more than the rest of it, because she of all people ought to know that he was trying to protect his family.

Then some idiot tried to start the dancing again, the music coming loud and happy and jarring.

"Silence!" King Godwin called out. "Do you think this is a time for joy and feasting?" He couldn't let out all the things he was truly feeling then at the loss of his daughter, but he didn't have to stand there and pretend that all was well. "The feasting is over! The wedding harvest will commence, and we will be done with this!"

Nerra was … broken. Everything in her felt fragmented and splinter sharp right then. She stared at her sleeve. She couldn't even remember how it had come undone. She thought someone had snagged it in the dancing, but that didn't even matter. All that mattered was that people had seen her, seen all that was wrong with her.

"I shouldn't have been there," she said.

Beside her, Rodry reached out to hug her, hesitated, and that was all that was needed to make Nerra cry. He did hug her then, but it was too late.

"I'm sorry," he said.

"It's not you who needs to be sorry, it's me," Lenore said. "I shouldn't have insisted that you come to the feasting. If you hadn't been there, they couldn't have done this."

"I wanted to," Nerra managed. "But this … I don't know what to do."

"We'll get Father to change his mind," Lenore said. "I'll …"

"There's nothing you can do," Nerra insisted.

"There has to be." Lenore held her out at arm's length. "We'll find a way. I'm going to have you there at my wedding, you understand?"

Nerra managed a smile at that. "Anything to get me there."

"Anything," Lenore said. "But also anything to make sure I don't lose my sister."

"We'll find a way to help you," Rodry agreed. "Whatever it takes."

Godwin sat in his chambers, waiting for his children to come to him. To his surprise, Greave was the first of them, rushing in with more anger and energy than he had ever seen in the boy.

"You're going to send Nerra away?" Greave demanded, bringing his hands down on the desk behind which Godwin sat. The king looked up at him, seeing far too much of his mother in him, the pain of that making it impossible to simply *talk* to his son.

"Do not presume to lecture me," Godwin said. "Not on this."

"If not on this, then on what?" Greave demanded. "The law books hold all kinds of loopholes. I could find one—"

"And then what?" Godwin demanded. "What do you think it will look like if we do that?"

"You're concerned about how things *look*?" Greave demanded. "Do you even care about your family at all?"

Godwin stood, towering over his son. "I care more than you could ever understand, locked away in your library, learning nothing about the world!"

"You think I've learned nothing? Well, shall I quote Liviricus? 'A man who loses the love of his family loses everything.'"

"Not as much as a man who *actually* loses his family," Godwin snapped back.

"'The king's authority is absolute in matters relating to the immediate security of the kingdom,'" Greave shot back. "That's from a charter more than three hundred years old."

"It doesn't *matter* what the law says, or what your books say," Godwin replied. His voice was raised now. There was always something about Greave that riled him where Nerra had soothed him. It only made it worse that he was here while Nerra was on the verge of being sent away. "It matters what the nobles will do. Do you not understand what was happening in there? Someone was trying to ferment rebellion. These are men with half the soldiers in the kingdom between them, men who could bring our entire family down if I do not do as they demand."

"So you're just going to throw Nerra out into the wilds?" Greave demanded.

"Do you really believe that?" Godwin shot back. "We have family elsewhere. Your mother had brothers. I will send Nerra to one of them, away from the sight of others. She will be safe there."

"She'll be a prisoner in all but name," Greave insisted.

"It's better than being dead," Godwin said. He felt so old in that moment, so tired. "If you want things to turn out so differently, maybe you should look in those books of yours for a cure to the scale sickness."

Greave stood there for a moment or two longer.

"Maybe I will," he said. "Maybe I will."

CHAPTER THIRTY ONE

Lenore was still trying to think of ways to help her sister the next morning, while her maids were helping her to prepare. They'd brought her traveling clothes, and Lenore frowned at them.

"What are these for?" she asked.

"Your father has declared that the wedding harvest will begin early," one of her maids said.

"Early?" Lenore said. She knew why. He had called an end to the feasting in the wake of her sister's banishment. Just the word was enough to make Lenore want to find Nerra again, want to tell her that they would go to their father now that he had calmed down and force him to reconsider.

"Where is my sister now?" Lenore asked.

"She is … already gone, your highness," the maid said.

"No," Lenore said. She couldn't be. Nerra wouldn't just leave. She had until the end of the month. Without waiting for her maids, she grabbed her traveling clothes and set off through the castle, determined to find Nerra, sure that this was some kind of mistake. Lenore made for her rooms, so tucked away and so private. Now that Lenore knew about her condition, it made sense: she'd been kept there out of the way.

Which meant that her father had known.

Lenore stopped short at that thought, because it brought with it a host of questions: who else had known, and why had they stayed silent. How could their father banish her sister like that for something he had been complicit in? Anger rose in her at the thought of what he'd done. He would have his reasons, of course, but it was playing politics when Nerra was at risk. She would find him and...

"My love, is everything well with you?"

Lenore turned and found herself staring at Finnal, who looked as impossibly handsome as always. Instantly, she was aware that she was only half dressed in front of the man she was due to marry, and her fingers fumbled to make sure that all the stays of her traveling clothes were in place.

"I'm trying to find Nerra," she said. "What Father did, banishing her for having the scale sickness..."

"It's a hard thing," Finnal said, with a note of sympathy. "But I would guess that your sister is gone by now."

"No," Lenore said, shaking her head. "I will not allow this. I will find her and bring her back. I will—"

"Aren't you to go on the wedding harvest?" Finnal said. He sounded surprised that she was even thinking of being anywhere else.

"How can I do that and still find Nerra?" Lenore demanded.

Finnal caught her up in his arms. "Lenore, you aren't thinking," he said, holding her close. "And I understand it; losing a sister must be the hardest thing in the world. If you don't go now though, people will think that you're being disloyal, trying to disobey your father and siding with your sister. If you *truly* wish to help Nerra, the best thing that you can do is to go."

"You really think that?" Lenore asked. It made a kind of sense. Her strength was that her father believed that she was perfect and obedient. Going against him in this would only shatter that belief, wouldn't it?

"He is angry right now," Finnal said. "Believe me, I know what it is to be made to do things by a father. Yet, if you leave it until the wedding harvest is done... until you are wed..."

"He might have calmed down a little by then," Lenore said. That made sense. Maybe time would let her persuade her father. There was only one problem with that. "What will happen to Nerra in the meantime?"

"She will be safe enough," Finnal said. "We have to hope."

"Will you help me find her, Finnal?" Lenore asked. She felt as though Finnal was one of the few people she could truly trust. He was to be her husband, after all.

He paused only briefly before answering. "If that is what you wish, then of course I shall look. I would do anything for you, my love."

Lenore was more grateful for that than she could say. She wanted to kiss him more than anything right then, but he had already taken her hand and was leading her down toward the courtyard.

"You must not be late," Finnal said.

In the courtyard, a carriage awaited her, of gilt wood and drawn by four white horses. A pair of maids were loading it with her things, before getting up into it to accompany her. Half a dozen guards were with it, which seemed like too few for such a journey, although Lenore was pleased to see Rodry there. Finnal seemed less pleased, though, holding back as Lenore went to go closer.

"I will say goodbye to you here, my love," he said.

"I wish you and Rodry weren't at odds," Lenore said.

"We aren't at odds," Finnal replied. "I just...it's clear that he has no liking for me, and I will not fight with my beloved's family." He lifted her hand to his lips. "I will await your return, Lenore. Each heartbeat that you are gone will be an agony."

He always seemed to know the perfect thing to say.

"I love you," Lenore whispered as she pulled back from him.

"I love you too."

It took an effort to go to Rodry and the carriage.

"Are you going with me?" Lenore asked him as she got near. That would be something, to have the finest warrior of the kingdom with her.

But Rodry shook his head. "Father has said that Vars must do it. He's to gather men and meet you by the crossroads at Averton, to the south. From there, you'll ride a circuit of the kingdom together."

"I can't imagine Vars will like that," Lenore said, thinking of how her brother would hate to be away from the inns of Royalsport.

Her expression turned serious after a moment. "Do you know that Nerra is gone?"

Rodry nodded. "It's the only reason I'm not going to push the issue of accompanying you. I'll stay behind and try to find her, then join you when I can."

That was a good thought on his part, and it made Lenore happy that she wasn't the only one trying to keep their sister safe. She hugged her brother.

"Do one more thing for me," she said.

"What?" Rodry asked, then flinched as Lenore glanced over to her betrothed. "Oh, no, anything but that."

"Please, Rodry. Finnal is going to be my husband, and you are my brother. It's important that you should get along."

"How can I, with the things they say about—"

"Lies," Lenore said. "They're lies, Rodry."

"It's not a lie that his father stood there with the nobles who tried to have Nerra banished," Rodry pointed out.

"Then that's all the more reason to make Finnal a good friend," Lenore replied. "Maybe he can persuade his father to talk to the others. He's not responsible for what his father does, Rodry."

"He's responsible for what *he* does," Rodry said.

"And so far, he hasn't done anything to make him your enemy," Lenore said. "He's the man I'm marrying, Rodry. Make a friend of him."

"How?" Rodry asked, as if he weren't the best of all of them at making friends.

"I don't know. Take him hunting or something. Please."

She said it insistently enough that even Rodry had to nod, and Lenore redoubled her hug.

"Thank you. Good luck finding Nerra."

"And good luck out on the road," Rodry said. "Not that you'll need it. People will flock to see you. This wedding harvest will remind them of all of the things our family has done for them, and they'll love you for it."

"I hope so," Lenore said. "I really hope so."

Lenore, her maids, and the few guards with her rode down through the city, and on every side there were people gathered to see her off. Lenore couldn't help smiling at the joy they showed, and she waved, even though there was still so much of her thinking about weightier things.

"They will find Nerra," Lenore said to herself, careful not to say it loud enough that her maids might hear. For now, Finnal and Rodry were right—she had to focus on this duty. It was a duty, even if it was a pleasurable one. She and the others with her would have to visit every corner of the kingdom, and that would mean traveling every day, to reach places she barely knew about. Not the far north, obviously, where the dead lands around the volcanoes lay, but all of the rest of the kingdom, all of the towns, and probably many of the villages.

Looking out at the people waving and throwing flowers, Lenore didn't think it would be that much of a chore.

They gave her more than that, too. At several spots in the city, her carriage drew to a halt and representatives of the Houses gave her chests that when she opened them shone with gold or stones.

"A sign of our loyalty," a young woman from the House of Sighs said as she curtseyed and held out the gift of a necklace strung with the finest pearls.

No wonder they called it a wedding harvest.

As the carriage continued, slowly leaving Royalsport in its wake, Lenore found herself wondering if there shouldn't be more men with it. After all, it already contained as much wealth as she had seen in one place, plus herself and her maids, who were both from noble families.

"That's why we're meeting up with Vars," she reminded herself. Her brother would be there to keep her safe. Besides, the sight of more cheering folk along the side of the road told her how foolish her fears were. The people loved her, so what could go wrong?

CHAPTER THIRTY TWO

Odd walked around the monastery and tried to work out how long it would be able to hold out once the bulk of the Southern forces put their minds to taking it. It wasn't a pleasant calculation. They wouldn't have brought any siege equipment with them on the ships, and that would buy some time, but not much when the monks were mostly untrained in the arts of walls. Really, all they needed were ladders.

"We'll need to evacuate," he said to the others walking with him. For the most part, they were younger monks, because he hadn't seen the older ones since the attack. "That means that some of us will have to slow them down while we get to—"

"Brother Odd?" A young monk ran up to him. "The abbot requires your presence, Brother."

Brother Odd nodded. Of course he must speak to the abbot. They had to discuss what to do next, and work out the best way to save as many of the monks as possible. He followed the young monk through the monastery to the abbot's chambers. The old man sat there in a chair, writing what looked like a series of letters. That wasn't the part that made Brother Odd stop short, though.

There was a chest by the abbot's side that Odd recognized. It was made from dark wood that they said had been charred by the fringes of a dragon's breath, and bound in dull iron. The lock was a simple, solid thing, and Brother Odd was shocked to see that a key sat in it, ready.

"I thought that had been destroyed," he said, without thinking.

"Typically, a brother waits for the abbot to speak," the abbot pointed out. He looked up at Odd. "Although this is not an issue in this case."

"What?" Odd said, incapable of saying more. Already, his thoughts were racing with the possibilities of what might follow. The abbot couldn't mean to—

"When you came to us," the abbot said, "you told me that you wanted to be a different man. You gave away the things that you had come with, renounced who you were. I told you at the time that it does not work like that, and have told you several times since."

Odd could remember the most recent conversation, when he'd been unable to rid himself of the memories of all he'd done.

"Even so," the abbot continued, "I had thought that you might come to terms with who you were, and you were at least a loyal and dutiful brother of our monastery. Until earlier."

"They were going to kill you," Odd said. "I know that the order's rules forbid violence, but—"

"That is just it," the abbot said, with a sad smile. "You are seeking an excuse now, as you have sought excuses since you arrived. I am not the man I was. I did not know what would happen. It was necessary. They were going to kill you. Sometimes you must accept responsibility, Sir Oderick."

"Do not call me that," Odd said. He'd thought of himself that way in the battle, but to hear it from the abbot's lips hurt too much.

"Why should I not?" the abbot asked. "Will you strike me down for doing so? Will you kill me?"

"Of... of course not," Odd said. "I am a brother, and you are my abbot. I could never harm you."

The abbot considered him for several seconds. He stood. There was a power to the old man now that had nothing to do with violence.

"If you were a brother, you would have obeyed my instructions," the abbot said. "I commanded you to kneel in silence and wait. You chose not to do that."

"If I had, you would have died!" Odd said, and there was more force in his tone than he intended.

"I would have," the abbot agreed. "And those with me, but the monastery would have been spared, because the men here would have surrendered. You would not have blood on your hands."

"What kind of man can stand by while good people are killed?" Odd demanded.

"A monk," the abbot said simply. He shook his head. "What do you think will happen now?"

"They'll come at us," Odd said. "Probably a couple of scouting parties at first, then in force. If we can hold them, then that might give us enough time to escape over the sea. There are enough small boats around the island for that."

"No, that is not what will happen," the abbot said. "Because that will result in more death. Instead, I will go out to them."

"They'll kill you," Odd said.

"Yes."

"You...you can't!"

The abbot's look this time was one that had a hard edge to it. "If you truly think that I fear death, then you have learned nothing in your time here, Sir Oderick."

"I am not that man," Odd said.

The abbot shook his head. "You are not a monk. What else you are is up to you."

Not a monk? The words caught Odd by surprise, as brutal as a blow might have been. He reeled from them.

"What are you saying?" he demanded.

"You have done violence here, and wish to do more," the abbot said. "You have ignored my instructions, and worse, some of the other young monks are starting to look to you as if your way is a kind of answer. That cannot be permitted. From this moment, you are no longer a brother of this monastery. You will leave, and not return."

"Just like that?" Odd said. He could feel the old anger rising in him, the one that threatened to drown out the rest of him. No, he wouldn't be that man.

"Turn the key in the lock," the abbot said. "It is time to take what is yours. There is no place for it here, or for you."

"I don't want to," Odd said.

The abbot looked at him evenly. "What we want doesn't come into it. Sometimes there are things we must do."

Odd let out a snarl and knelt before the chest. He turned the key in the lock, forward and then back again, to avoid the dart he'd had placed there by a cunning man of the House of Weapons long ago. He opened the lid carefully, feeling more fear than he'd ever felt in the run up to a battle.

Within, there were a noble's clothes, with the symbol of the blackened flame upon them. There was armor, and a pouch filled with money that Odd had brought in the hope that he could bribe his way into the monastery. There was a second pouch that contained his signet ring and the jewels of his family.

Atop lay a sword. It was long and slender, with a grip designed for two-handed use and an elegantly scrolled hilt of dark metal. Its blade was covered by a sheath of black leather, but Odd's memory supplied the brightness of the steel and the etchings upon it. Odd knew the work that it had taken to produce, because he'd had to wait for it for so long that it had been like waiting for news of a lost lover. Now it seemed to call to him in the same way.

"Take what is yours, Sir Oderick," the abbot said. "Take it and be gone. Take a boat if you will. Maybe the act of my dying will give you time."

Odd fingered the armor, but he let it lie, along with the noble's clothes. He took the sword, though, because there were some bonds too strong to ignore. He took the pouches too, because he would need their contents, along with a length of rope. He stood and stared at the abbot.

"I might no longer be a brother, but I am not Sir Oderick either," he said. "And you ... you are a fool who is about to die for no reason. You could run."

"But then I would not be the man I am," the abbot said, and those words made Odd angrier than ever. He turned before he could act on that anger.

"I'll go," he said. "And if your monks have any sense, they'll go too. King Ravin's men aren't here to be kind or gentle."

He stalked from the abbot's quarters, heading through the monastery. He was aware that the brothers there were staring at him, but right then he didn't care. Let them stare. Let them all see the man he was, the man who had saved their miserable lives. He headed for a patch of wall he hoped he would be able to climb down, seeing brothers turn toward him as he passed. When he reached the part he wanted, he looked down. Good, there were no enemies below this spot, only clustered around the gate.

Odd turned to his home ... his former home, and called out.

"The abbot is going to open the gates. If you think they won't slaughter you, then you're fools. I know what kind of men they are, because I was that kind of man. Run now, while you can."

None of the monks below moved. Fools. Odd sneered at them as he started to clamber down the wall, his sword slung across his shoulder. It was the only thing right then that kept his heart from breaking at the home he'd had and lost, and at the thought of the monk he'd failed to be. He slipped down in silence, moving through the shadows so that any soldiers watching wouldn't be able to spot him.

He set out across the island, keeping to the small paths, heading for the little inlets and coves around the island. From here, he could see the soldiers surrounding the monastery. He hoped his brothers, his *former* brothers, would be safe.

Finally, he came to a cove. There was a small boat there, with a mast and a sail, a pair of oars, and enough room for supplies. Odd settled what he had into it, untying the rope that held it to the shore.

"Where now?" he asked himself.

The truth was that he didn't know. He didn't want to go back to who he'd been, and he couldn't be a monk, so what did that leave? Who did that leave?

He guessed there was only one way to find out.

Chapter Thirty Three

"**A**nother round on me!" Renard called out, and the cheer he got from the other patrons of the Broken Scale was bigger than anything he would have gotten playing the lute. Probably he should have felt worse about that, but how could he feel bad about anything right then?

"You'll have no coin left at this rate," Yselle pointed out to him, as he reached the bar. Renard leaned on it, and if that happened to give him a better view of her, well, he was only human.

"Ah, you know I can never hold onto anything," Renard said. "Coin, women …"

Yselle smacked him playfully on the arm. It felt as though it would leave a bruise.

"I'd better be the only one you're holding onto," she said. She started to pour drinks.

Renard didn't say anything. He thought it probably counted as diplomatic.

"How much do you have left?" Yselle asked, in the tone of someone concerned that he might not be able to afford the round he'd just ordered.

"Aha, I knew you only wanted me for my money," Renard joked. It earned him a matching bruise on his other arm. "How has this turned into the dangerous part of this undertaking?"

"How much?" Yselle asked. "Please tell me you haven't spent it all already. You're not getting any younger, you know. You can't just keep putting yourself in danger and hoping it will turn out right. You need to settle down, put something away."

"Maybe invest in an inn?" Renard suggested. "Maybe settle down with a good woman?"

Yselle laughed at that. "And how would you know the difference?"

Renard definitely knew the difference. He knew how good Yselle was to him, and maybe...but then, thoughts like that were almost as dangerous as a dozen guards; certainly capable of trapping him quicker.

"There's some money left," Renard said. "Obviously, I had to pay off the guard who helped me, and the sailor. Then quite a bit of it..." He hesitated.

"You gave it away, didn't you?" Yselle demanded, in that stern tone she seemed to do so well.

"Well..." Renard began, but the lie he was coming up with wilted under the weight of her stare. "Some of it. A bit. Okay, most of it."

On that note, he could see a group of poor peasant farmers in one corner of the Broken Scale's taproom. Renard wandered over to them, taking a small pouch of the coins he'd liberated from Lord Carrick and placing it on the table.

"What's this?" one of them asked, giving him a suspicious look. He was a broad-faced man of about forty, who had obviously worked for far too long in the sun because it had left him as weather-beaten as old stone.

"I hear times have been hard this year," Renard said. "Taxes, a poor harvest...hard times all round."

"And you're giving us money?" the farmer said.

"Lord Carrick is giving you money," Renard said with a smile. "He just doesn't know it. There should be enough there to pay your next round of taxes, at least."

Another of the men stood up, embracing Renard in a bear hug that stank of sheep.

"Thank you," he said. "My family will eat this winter. Who can I say helped them?"

A humble man would have backed away, pretending that it was nothing. But then, Renard had never pretended to be a humble man. He stepped back and gave the elegant performer's bow he'd perfected for the rare moments when he got applause.

"Renard, at your service."

They did applaud him then. He straightened up with a smile, caught his balance before his drunken feet could trip over themselves, and strode back to the bar. Well, more staggered than strode, but what could you do?

Yselle grabbed him as he got close enough and kissed him. "You," she declared as she pushed another tankard toward him, "are an idiot. A beautiful, wonderful idiot. What kind of man robs the local lord and then gives it away?"

"Well," Renard said. "If I kept the gold, I'd only drink it anyway."

He downed the beer in one, and could see Yselle's eyes still on him. This was shaping up to be a good evening.

There were no words to describe how much Renard's head hurt when he woke. Even opening his eyes hurt. Frankly, he felt as though having his head split open with an axe would be a blessed relief.

As if in some sick answer to that prayer, Renard's eyes started to focus, letting him see the swords just inches from his throat.

"Up," a voice barked, "nice and slow."

"If you think I'm moving anywhere quickly," Renard muttered, "you've never been properly hungover before."

Looking round, he saw that he was in his room in the inn, not Yselle's, which was probably a blessing. He didn't want her dragged into the middle of this. He didn't want him dragged into the middle of this, but that part didn't seem to be optional.

Instead of her, there were about a dozen of Lord Carrick's ... well, finest was probably too strong a word, but they were big, and they were tough.

"What's all this about, lads?" Renard said, trying for charm. It was amazing what charm could get you into, or out of. "I'm sure all this is some big misunderstanding."

"Oh, no misunderstanding," one of the guardsmen said. He lifted up Renard's coin purse, tipping out a wash of the stolen gold. "Just a mistake you shouldn't have made."

"Oh that," Renard said. "There was this man giving out coin last night, and who's going to say no to free coin? I mean, you wouldn't, right?"

Renard could only put the clumsiness of his attempt to bribe them down to his aching head. It wasn't improved when one of them hit him.

"If you do that again," he said, "there's a very good chance I'll throw up on you."

Right then, it was about the only threat he could muster. One, even two of them he could have fought clear of, but a dozen?

"You're the one who was giving out coin," one of the guards said. He beckoned and yet another guard came in, holding a familiar figure by the arm. Renard recognized the broad-faced farmer instantly.

"That's him," the man said, pointing. "That's the one who gave us those strange-looking coins. Just remember I'm the one who told you. I'm loyal."

Renard sighed. There was just no helping some people. Try to do a good thing for them, and they only found a way to turn it into trouble. Or maybe it was him; he'd always had a knack for finding trouble where there hadn't been any before.

"Oh, him," Renard said. "He's just jealous because I beat him in a card game and won all these coins off him. If you ask me, he's probably the one who stole them."

"You announced your theft to the entire inn," the peasant pointed out.

Ah, he'd done that, hadn't he? Exactly how drunk had he been last night?

"We've all the evidence we need," the guard said. "We have coins that could only have come from Lord Carrick's supply, and a witness who says you were the one who gave him them. I'm sure that when we put them to the question, the others in the inn will say the same too."

Put them to the question? For an instant, just an instant, Renard had an image of these men trying to force answers out of Yselle, maybe treating her like a co-conspirator. That thought was enough to send Renard surging forward, with all the force and fury of... well, that was the problem really. He was still too hungover to fight, and one of the guards simply stepped out of the way, hitting him behind the ear with the hilt of his sword. This time, he did throw up.

Strong hands grabbed him, pulling his arms behind his back and binding them.

"If it were up to me," the guard who seemed to be in charge said, "I'd take you out and hang you right away as an example, but you're lucky. His lordship wants to know how you found out about his treasure, and after that... well, maybe you aren't so lucky after all."

"I'm always lucky," Renard managed as the guards started to drag him away. "Can't you tell?"

He forced a smile, but only ended up spitting blood. This was bad, worse than even the time when... well, frankly, worse than all the times. Before, he'd always been able to fight his way out, or talk his way out, or just run away in an act of brazen cowardice that definitely didn't make it into his retellings of his deeds. Now though, he couldn't see how he was going to get away with this.

He was going to die.

CHAPTER THIRTY FOUR

Erin rode toward the village, not stopping, not able to stop. It was all very well the others saying that they should hang back and wait for more knights, but every moment that they waited was a moment in which the people in the village, the quiet men pretending to be villagers, might leave and get away with the things they'd done.

Erin couldn't allow that, whatever it might cost.

The possible cost flashed by her on either side as she rode in between the scarecrows they'd formed from the actual villagers. Erin thought about what it might be like to be tied there like that, left out for the scavengers, killed and abandoned. That only fueled her need to do this.

"Come back, you fool!" Til shouted behind her. Fenir was with him, the two galloping along in Erin's wake. Erin supposed that from the outside, they must have seemed like an arrow wedge of charging knights, rather than one charging princess and a couple of knights trying to catch up to her. She almost laughed at the thought, then remembered what she was charging into and stopped herself.

A couple of crossbow bolts flashed past as Erin charged, close enough that she felt the thrill of fear that came with the near miss. She gripped her short spear tight in an overhand grip, ready to strike down with it as she charged. The supposed "villagers" were drawing weapons now, ready to fight.

"Die!" Erin roared, striking down at the first of them as he was still trying to reload his crossbow. Almost obligingly, he did, her spear plunging deep into his throat and ripping clear again. Erin leapt from her moving horse and it slammed into a group of them, scattering them and crushing one man while Erin was still rolling back to her feet.

They came at her then. One cut with a curved blade and Erin blocked it with the haft of her spear. Another lunged forward with a long sword in two hands and Erin felt it scrape from her chain shirt as she swayed aside. She struck back with her spear, one blow, then another, trying to find a way through.

More of the soldiers disguised as villagers came forward then, trying to encircle her. There were men and women there, armed with a wider range of weapons than Erin had seen. Some had swords, others daggers or axes. One woman had a morning star, the head of which she twirled before swinging it at Erin to try to tangle her spear. Erin let the chain of the thing wrap round the haft of her weapon, then went in with it, launching a crunching head butt into the woman's face. She fell back and Erin stabbed her.

The others tried to close in around her, but Fenir and Til were there then, slamming into the enemy with all the skill and force of trained knights of the Spur. Til hacked downward from his perch on his horse, while Fenir dismounted on the run, advancing with sword and shield to batter at the nearest foes.

Erin didn't have time to watch them, though, because she had her own opponents to worry about. The one with the curved sword was coming at her again, with a wicked series of slashes that threatened to catch her out with the slightest misstep. Erin used the sheath for her spear head like a shield, deflecting the blows one by one, but then the one with the longsword was coming at her from the side, weapon raised.

In desperation, Erin threw herself into a ducking roll, thrusting upward with her spear as she came out of it. She felt the head of it slide upward into flesh, and the man gasped, his longsword clattering to the ground before he fell.

Erin tried to pull her spear out of him, and for a moment, it stuck. She felt something slash across her leg and she cried out in pain; then she set her foot on the dead man's chest and wrenched the spear clear. She turned in time to parry another slashing blow of the sword, then cut back with a swipe of her own weapon at throat height. She tore through the soldier's throat, and this time, she didn't pause, but plunged back into the fight.

She could see Til fighting on foot now, his horse down. There was an arrow sticking from his shoulder, but it didn't seem to be slowing him. Erin saw one of the enemy coming up behind him with a dagger, and there was no time to get there. Erin hefted her spear and then threw it, the weapon plunging into the man's chest to bring him down.

It left Erin facing her last foe, a woman armed with an axe, armed with only the staff-like sheath of her weapon. She parried the first swing, catching the head of the weapon on the stave, and then the two of them were pressed in close to one another, striking and pushing, trying to find an angle for the next blow. Erin tried to get to her belt knife, but in the tightness of the battle, it was hard to do even that.

Erin felt her foot catch on something, had a moment to register the corpse of the first opponent she'd killed, and then she was tumbling backward to the ground. The woman with the axe was standing over her, her armor shining out now beneath the tears in her peasant's garb.

"Should have stayed away, girl," she said, in an accent that was clearly from the south. She lifted the axe, and in that moment Erin knew there was no way to dodge it in time, certainly no way to parry it without a weapon. If she'd still had her spear, she might have been able to strike back, but like this… she was going to die.

Erin found herself thinking of her family. She missed them in that moment. Missed her sisters, even her brothers. She wished they'd been able to understand that she wasn't like them. She wished… she wished so many things…

Then Fenir stepped in and cut the axe woman's head from her shoulders, cutting short all of those thoughts. He looked down at Erin.

"Shouldn't throw your weapon," he said, terse as always, before turning back to the rest of the fight.

Except that now, there was no fight, because Til was just finishing the last of their enemies, cutting him down with a wet, sticky sound. Erin forced herself back to her feet, gritting her teeth against the pain of the cut in her leg. She wasn't going to let the others see her weak. She hobbled over to the body with a short spear sticking from it and dragged it out. Cleaning it meant that she had something to do to take her mind from the post-battle shakes that were starting through her, threatening to take over her whole body.

"Should bind that wound," Fenir said, nodding toward her leg. "Could get infected."

Beside him, Til was less generous. "What were you thinking?"

"What?" Erin countered. "We won, didn't we?"

They had won. The three of them against a dozen or more foes, and they'd won. It seemed that everything they'd said about the Knights of the Spur was true.

"And what if there had been more of them hiding in the buildings?" Til demanded. "What if there had been just one more, to distract Fenir while you were nearly dying?"

"Ease off," Fenir said. "She fought well."

Til shook his head. "She took stupid risks, almost died, and got herself wounded. More than that..." He returned his attention to Erin. "More than that, you ignored everything I said about the need to wait."

"What if they'd run?" Erin shot back. "What if they'd left while we were waiting? What if they'd gotten away with it?"

Til must have heard the fury in her voice at that thought, because he took half a step back.

"Do you think I wanted them to get away with what they'd done?" he asked, softly. "I'm as glad they're dead as you are, but we have to think bigger than that. We have to think about saving the people who are still alive."

"Well, we've stopped them from killing anyone else too," Erin said.

Fenir spoke then. "Not about that. These are Quiet Men."

"Which means what?" Erin asked. Maybe it was the pain in her leg, but she didn't have time for his terseness right then.

"Which means," Til explained, "that there's something bigger going on. The Quiet Men are the spies and advanced forces of the southerners. King Ravin sends them out to do specific tasks, or he sends them out like here, as scouts."

"Scouts?" Erin said. "You mean—"

"I mean that they took this village so they would have somewhere safe to bring more men," Til said. "There's nothing special here, nothing valuable, so it's the only thing that makes sense. They were preparing the ground, opening the way. And if we'd died trying to stop them, no one else would have known. Do you understand?"

Erin understood. If these were scouts, it meant that the rest of an army wouldn't be far behind. There was an invasion coming from the south, and she'd just experienced the first touch of it.

CHAPTER THIRTY FIVE

Nerra went to the woods, because she didn't know where else to go. She could feel the tears falling from her eyes as she walked, but they just blended in with the damp and the strangeness of the forest. Her hands trailed over the trees around her, identifying the plants there by touch: fungus and trailing leaves, flowers and bark.

Her dress was torn, because her bleary eyes hadn't allowed her to move with her usual fluidity through the trees. Nerra didn't care: fancy dresses were Lenore's obsession, not hers. No, that wasn't fair, not when her sister was one of those who had tried to stand up to their father. She and Rodry had done it when their other brothers had stood by, even though it risked their father's wrath, and that of the nobles around.

That had been part of why Nerra had carried herself away to the forest. If she'd stayed, her siblings would have kept trying to push the issue, and would only have found themselves in trouble for it. Those helping the ones with the scale sickness were reckoned almost as bad as the sick themselves.

"I'll not see them hurt," Nerra said. She didn't want anyone hurt over her. She didn't want anyone hurt at all. The threats the southerners had made of war seemed worse than anything that could happen to her; bad enough that she knew she shouldn't be worrying about being cast out like this. What did that matter that she was cast out, when there was something happening that could threaten everyone?

"I don't matter," Nerra said, although it still hurt, still felt worse than anything in her life had.

The hardest part of it was the sense of betrayal. All through her life, her father had been there for her. He'd known that she was sick, had known about her sickness. Hadn't he been the one to ask Master Grey about it? To send for the best doctors that the House of Scholars could find? Yet in the hall, he'd acted as though he had never seen her arms before, as if it were all some great shock to him.

"He had to," Nerra tried to tell herself, but it was hard to convince herself, so hard. She couldn't believe that a father would just cast out a daughter like that, would refuse to listen.

What was so bad about the scale sickness, anyway? Nerra looked down at her arm, realized that her sleeve was still loose, and ripped it away completely. What did it matter, now that people already knew? She stared down at the black, scale-like lines that traced over her arm, more solid now than they had been, palpably different from the rest of her skin. They were as much a part of her as anything else, so what was so wrong about them?

No one had ever answered that question for her, or even come close to it. The doctors her father had found had looked as though they hadn't even considered that question, and certainly didn't know the answer. Master Grey... well, who knew what the sorcerer really thought about anything? He spoke little at all, and about this, he'd said nothing to her, only offered her a poultice that had taken away some of the itching that came with the scales' growth.

"There has to be some reason why people are cast out," Nerra said, as she continued her way through the forest. People wouldn't do it for no reason, would they? Or would they? It was hard to fathom half the things that people did. She didn't understand the way Vars treated people, or why Rodry felt the need to fight all the time. Maybe it was just because she was different, or maybe it was just the fear of ending up like her, turned into something larger.

It didn't matter now, of course. The reason for her banishment didn't matter so much as the simple fact that she was banished. Anyone who saw her would be entitled to try to kill her, or do whatever else they wanted, and she would have no protection from the law. It was a terrifying thought.

"You're safe here," she told herself, leaning against one of the trees and feeling the solidity of it. She knew the forest better than anyone, knew every twist and turn of it. She could survive here, could even thrive here...

...and she had her secret here.

Nerra realized that even without thinking about it, she'd been heading in the direction of the cave where she'd hidden the dragon. She wanted to find it, wanted to see it again. She had been looking after it, and now it was likely to be the only companion she would have. They could live in the forest together, hunting down food, staying safe from the view of men.

It was a nice thought, but it was also one that was interrupted. Nerra knew this feeling; knew the dizziness and the sense of sickness. On another day, she would have retired to her rooms so that no one could see her like this, maybe sent for hot drinks as if it were just an ordinary kind of sickness. Now she had no rooms to go to. There was only the thought of the dragon, somewhere ahead of her.

Nerra kept walking, ignoring the unsteadiness. She would feel better soon, because she always did. She would feel better once she found her dragon, because at least some of this was the pain of loneliness and separation; it had to be. Maybe if she found something to eat.

Back home, she would have sent for a servant, but out here Nerra knew she would have to find her own food. She knew what she was doing, at least, knew which fungi and plants were edible, and which were poisons. She took a handful of berries, eating them one by one even though her dizziness made them taste like ash in her mouth.

It didn't help, so Nerra found herself looking around for leaves that she could make into a tincture to slow down the feelings of weakness that were making her limbs start to shake with every step. The effort of looking, though, made it seem as though she was wading through the depths of the great river that divided the kingdom, every step an effort.

"Maybe I'll sit for a while until it passes," Nerra said. She found a solid-looking oak to sit against, setting her back against it as she sat there and waiting for the feelings of weakness and dizziness to pass. They always had in the past.

She sat there and tried to think of all the things she might do with her life. All that she had lost hurt so much, but Nerra was determined to think about all the things she might still do, all the things that might still happen for her. She'd hated court life, had always wanted to be out in the forest, had always wanted to spend her time apart from people, only offering help where people needed it. Maybe this was her chance.

Maybe, except that even those thoughts didn't encourage the feelings of sickness to pass. Nerra felt it in the dizziness that threatened to consume her, in a tingling in her mouth, in a pulsing in her arm from where the scale patterns felt as though they were about to burst from her skin.

"Help," she called out weakly, but there was no one to help her out there. Even if someone had come, they'd have seen her arm, and killed her for it. At the very least, they would have shied away from her, leaving her to the mercy of the shivering and the weakness and ...

Somewhere in the course of it, Nerra realized that she had fallen over to her side, her cheek scraping against the leaves and twigs of the forest floor. Her breathing was shallow now, and the world felt as though it was coming from behind a veil that meant Nerra could barely see it. Her eyes flickered open and closed, and this felt different from all the other times she'd felt unwell, different, and worse.

There was a pressure building in Nerra's skull now, as if a whole world was there inside it, fighting to get out. She screamed, then realized that no sound had come out; she was just twitching there on the ground, staring up at the canopy of the forest, sure that she would die there alone and unheralded. Would someone find her there, or would her body simply stay there to be scavenged by the animals? Would she even be dead before that happened?

Suddenly, Nerra felt very afraid. She found herself thinking of her brothers and sisters, of the dragon abandoned in the cave. She wished that any of them were here, that someone were here.

"Help," she called again, and to her shock, there was someone there now.

There were several people, gathered around in the woodland and staring down at her. The largest of them was at the front, bald and tattooed, muscled like a bear and looking at her like he'd just walked into a room full of treasure.

"Princess," he said. "I've been waiting for you."

CHAPTER THIRTY SIX

Greave lay in bed, panting, and, for almost the first time in his life, truly happy. Sunlight spilled in through the window, shining down on the sleeping form of Aurelle Hardacre. She looked perfect lying there, but then, she looked perfect everywhere.

Greave's mind flashed back to how she'd looked before, in the moments when they'd been making love. It had been an experience that had been beyond anything he could have imagined, beautiful and wondrous, pleasure filled and somehow complete in a way that almost nothing else ever seemed. Greave could see now why men wrote poetry about such things, and sang songs about the beauty of love.

She had grabbed him almost the moment he had left his father's chambers.

"You're angry, my love," she had whispered.

"I…" He hadn't had the words for how upset he was. "I need to find a way to make this right, to make this *better*."

"I can't help with that," Aurelle had said. She had pulled him back in the direction of his rooms. "But there's one thing I *can* do."

Now she lay beside him, breathing softly in her sleep.

"Aurelle, my love," he whispered. "Are you awake?"

There was no answer, and Greave did not wish to wake her now. He stared at Aurelle as she lay there, feeling luckier than any man had a right to be that she had simply walked into his life like that. Previously, women had always thought his features too effeminate, or his personality too dour. Aurelle had seen something in him that had lifted Greave to more than that, made his heart sing in a way that he hadn't known was even possible.

He thought about waking her with a kiss, but slipped from the bed instead, dressing in silence. He'd been so caught up with Aurelle in the last few days that he hadn't done even the one thing that he'd promised himself he would do. Now, with the reminder of his sister being sent away, and the argument with his father, he needed to do it.

Greave slipped from his rooms and headed through the castle in the direction of the library. Now that the last of the feasting was done with, it was a quiet place, almost an empty one. Greave could feel some of that emptiness inside him, at the thought that one of his sisters had been cast out, while another was missing. Greave could help with one of those, though, if he could only find what he was looking for.

He stepped into the chaos of the library, which looked even more out of order than when he'd left it. Had servants been in trying to find things, or maybe a noble bored from the feasting? It didn't matter, so long as he could still find the book he wanted.

What had it been called? For a moment, Greave thought perhaps he might have forgotten the title, and he had an instant of panic at that thought. What if he couldn't remember? What if the chance to find out what his stepmother was involved in had slipped from him through simple thoughtlessness?

No, he remembered it: *On the Body*. There, it seemed that a mind used to remembering vast tracts of poetry and plays had its uses. Idly, Greave wondered what his father might make of that thought.

He couldn't tell him, of course, couldn't tell anyone. Until such time as he found a cure that might save his sister, then just by telling people that he was looking, Greave would place them all in danger.

"No," he said. "I need to find the cure first."

That meant finding the book, and that was easier said than done in a library like this. Greave started to search the shelves.

It took what seemed like forever, with book after book tossed aside. Observations on philosophy went the way of *Fauna of the Third*

Land and *Notes on River Navigation*. On another day, maybe Greave would have glanced at them, reasoning that all knowledge was worth having, but not today.

On another day, of course, he would have given up by now, his efforts washed away in the sense that all was worthless. If there had been one thing Aurelle's arrival in his life had shown him, though, it was that some things were worth the effort. Greave kept digging through the library.

And then, it happened.

He froze.

Greave caught sight of the book he wanted almost by accident, buried behind a collection of works on the architecture of the king-dom back in the days when it had been unified.

With trembling hands, he reached out and took it.

It was so frail in his fingers.

On the Body was a slender volume, so old that Greave barely dared to open it. He did so with trembling fingers and started to read.

What he read there made no sense to him. He had read many books in his time, but here there were notes on dissections and the chemical processes of the body. There was a whole section on the scale sickness, detailing the process of the transformation, and the damage to the body that it could do, tearing people asun-der as it sought to reshape them into … into …

… things. Greave stared at the pages, unable to believe the hor-ror of some of the things there. Would his sister become one of these? No, not if he could do anything to stop it.

But despite all the horrors of the disease, a cure exists. The process for producing it is complex, but …

It ended there.

"NO!" Greave shouted. "IT CAN'T BE!"

Greave roared with frustration. Someone a long time ago had torn pages from the book.

Who? Why?

No, as crucial as that question was, it wasn't the one that mat-tered right then. The thing that mattered was finding out the contents of those missing pages. Finding who had taken them could come later.

First though, he had to find the cure. How could he do it when this was all he had to go on? Greave read the book again, and there seemed no more clues, until his eyes fell on a small, crabbed note at the front.

Based on notes at GLA.

GLA, Greave wondered. *GLA* .....

Then it came to him: *the Great Library of Astare.*

Greave had heard of the library. It was a place in the northeast of the Northern Kingdom. It was closer to the dead, volcanic lands of the far north than it was to Royalsport, and would represent many days of travel. Even then, Greave didn't know if he would be able to get in, because it was a place belonging to the House of Knowledge, and none but their number were supposedly allowed within. Even a prince might find himself refused for not being one of them, especially asking about something as sensitive as this.

Greave knew though that he had to go anyway. The contents of the book told a story that would have shaken most people, but to him, they were crucial to saving his sister. If a cure existed, then he had to find it, whatever the difficulties or the dangers. He knew then what he was going to have to do.

He would risk his life if he had to. He was riding to Astare.

CHAPTER THIRTY SEVEN

Vars had planned to get Rodry to take over the duty of leading his half-sister's guards. He had *planned* to listen to whatever nonsense his brother wanted to spout about him shirking his duties, then head off to the warmth of one of the House of Sighs' establishments while his brother trudged through the rain after Lenore's carriage.

Instead, something had gone wrong. Nerra had been sent away, not that Vars cared. Rodry had gone away on a hunt or something, at Lenore's insistence. Now *he* found himself riding at the head of a marching column of men, all willing, even eager to protect his half-sister on her wedding harvest. Vars suppressed a sneer as he looked back at them. There must have been a hundred men there, and for what? To protect a sister who didn't even *matter* as far as the succession went? Would they spring to his defense with such eagerness?

Vars really didn't understand why he was being placed at risk for a task like this. His father could send the men if he had to, but to send Vars, the second in line, to the throne? It was madness. If there was trouble, he was the one who would be at risk, while his half-sister sat safe behind all the soldiers there. Vars shook his head, took a swig from a wineskin, and kept going.

Ahead, he could see a fork in the road. There had been a sign there once, but it had clearly blown down in a storm, so that it was impossible to tell which way was which. Riding up to it, Vars brought the column of men to a halt, giving them brief leave to sit and rest, readying themselves for the rest of the march. To his irritation, they didn't break ranks while they did it, which put his own near slump from the saddle to shame. If a few had started dicing or drinking spirits, Vars would have felt a lot more at home.

"Which way, your highness?" the sergeant at arms who was supposedly second in command of the men asked.

"I'll check," Vars said. He got out the map, checking it and the route, wanting to make sure he knew where he was. The route stood out as a red ribbon leading around the kingdom; around far more of it than Vars cared for, through long sections that were nothing but villages, probably without a decent inn between them. Oh, Rodry was supposed to come help, but that just meant having to put up with his insufferable comments about how little Vars did that was brave or good.

If only there were some way to get out of this nonsense.

"Do you require assistance, your highness?" the sergeant asked.

"No, I do not," Vars snapped back, realizing that the man probably assumed he was going to make a mistake about the route. He paused for a moment, thinking about that. He was the only one who had seen the map, after all, and the sign was down, so there was no way for the men to truly know...

"This way!" he said, pointing to the left hand fork with all the confidence that he could muster.

"Your highness..." the sergeant began, in a tone that was clearly about to question Vars. "Are you certain that's the way? I thought that we were due to go through Neddis, and that's—"

"Well, you thought wrong," Vars said. "The route we are to follow is clearly marked. We are to go to the left and continue until we meet my sister. Now, stop questioning your prince and have the men ready to march, before I decide that you would be better off back in the ranks."

"Yes, your highness," the man said.

Vars smiled to himself. Manage this right, and he could take a tour of all the best places to drink before he headed back. Lenore would be fine; after all, she had that fool Rodry coming to protect her.

❧ ❧ ❧

"A little to the left, Hershel," Rodry called out to one of his companions. "You'll never hit what you're aiming for at this rate!"

He pretended joviality, although right then, he could only think of Nerra, and what he could be doing that was more useful.

"I bet that's what the last woman you were with said," the young nobleman called back, and nocked another arrow, firing it off in the direction of the pheasant that had just eluded him.

"Are all your hunts like this?" Finnal said, sitting atop his horse so primly and so calmly that he might have been riding in a courtyard and not across open fields.

"Like what?" Rodry demanded.

"So raucous?" he asked, and not for the first time that day, Rodry had to remind himself that this was the man his sister planned to marry, and that they would need to get along. He had promised Lenore.

"It's not that raucous," Rodry said. To be fair, it was quite raucous. Of the Knights of the Spur who had been co-opted into this, Halfin and Ursus seemed to be arguing about whether strength or speed was better on a hunt, Sir Twell was disagreeing vehemently and saying that they should set traps, while the younger noblemen seemed to be riding and shooting, or practicing sword blows with one another while looking on and hoping that the older knights would notice them.

"Okay," Rodry admitted. "It's a little raucous."

"Just a little," Finnal said. He held out a hand to an attendant, who passed him a loaded crossbow, since it was clearly too much work for him to draw it himself. Rodry saw him track a bird as it rose, then pull the trigger. There was a squawk as the quarrel struck home.

"A fine shot!" Rodry said. He would give his future brother-in-law that much.

"I suppose so," Finnal said, apparently uninterested. He looked out over the knights and the noblemen. "So, is this what your companions do with their days? They ride and they hunt?"

"What would you have them do?" Rodry asked.

Finnal shrugged. "I don't know. I just thought there would be...more. Lenore has spoken of your heroism."

Rodry smiled at that. "Let me guess, she was trying to get you to be better friends with me?"

Finnal paused for a moment, and then nodded. "Though I have no wish to be your enemy, and there is no need. After all, your sister is to be my wife. She is the love of my life."

Rodry wished he could believe it; that he hadn't heard the rumors that had been brought from the House of Sighs.

"So long as you treat her well," Rodry said. "So long as you *mean* what you say about loving her."

"Why would I mean anything else?" Finnal countered. "Lenore is the most beautiful of women, and the daughter of a king. Any man would be lucky to be marrying her."

That was true, but Rodry still couldn't escape the feeling that Duke Viris's son wasn't being quite sincere. Right then, he would rather have had someone else marrying his sister; someone *worthy*.

"Maybe we should go to find Lenore," Rodry said. He wasn't due to start accompanying her yet, but at least it would mean that he wasn't stuck alone with Finnal any longer.

Finnal shook his head. "It is considered bad luck for the groom to accompany the bride on any part of the wedding harvest."

"Probably because people might think that he's counting up all the gold she brings in before deciding whether to marry her," Rodry said, unable to keep a trace of bitterness from his voice. He knew he should have liked Finnal. He was clever, elegant, a good shot, a better horseman. He was the son of a duke, handsome and not boorish. Yet there was something about him that Rodry mistrusted, something that made him certain that the rumors weren't just rumors, and that he couldn't truly be trusted with his sister's heart.

"You don't like me, do you?" Finnal asked.

Rodry paused, and then shook his head. "You think I haven't heard the rumors about you? About the House of Sighs?"

"Rumors mean nothing," Finnal said.

"They do if they're true," Rodry shot back.

"And why have you decided that these are true?" Finnal asked. "I'm the son of a duke; I attract my share of jealousy."

"A duke who stood with those who saw my sister banished," Rodry said. He had to work to contain his anger now.

"I had no part in that," Finnal said. "And my father... I suspect he was standing for the laws. Would your family overthrow them?"

"I wouldn't see my sisters hurt!" Rodry all but snarled at him.

"I wouldn't want that either," Finnal said. He looked at Rodry levelly. "What will it take to convince you that I mean to do the right thing by Lenore? That I have no intention of hurting her?"

That was the problem; Rodry didn't know. He couldn't think of anything that would take away his suspicions, or that would make him see past all that he had heard about this man. He looked around, hoping for some distraction that would at least mean he didn't have to answer. In the distance, he spied an inn; just a simple place, and probably the sort of establishment Finnal would never have set foot in. Suddenly, Rodry found himself needing a drink.

"Come have an ale with me," he said, pointing to it. He called out to his companions, because he had no intention of that being an ale alone with Finnal. They might have to actually talk if they were alone. "I spy a tavern, men! I think we've hunted enough for one day, so let us celebrate our successes!"

He rode for it, wishing he could be riding to his sister's side instead, but she'd asked him to take the time to get to know Finnal, and he was going to do that, even if he had to down a tavern's worth of ale to manage it. She would be fine out on her journey. After all, she had Vars's men to guard her.

CHAPTER THIRTY EIGHT

Lenore found herself looking around for her brother as her carriage trundled down to the crossroads and past it. The roads were muddy here, paved only in places and with clumps of vegetation on either side.

"Vars was supposed to meet us somewhere here, wasn't he?" she called out to one of the half-dozen guards with her.

"I'm sure the prince will meet us in due course," the man replied, although he sounded as surprised as Lenore felt that Vars had not done so already.

"Should we stop and wait for him?" Lenore asked. Probably, though, as the princess, she should have been giving the orders. The soldier seemed to think so too.

"If it pleases you, your highness," he said.

"We've still a long way to go today," one of her maids pointed out. She gave a disgusted look out of the carriage window. "And if we wait here, we'll be doing it in the mud. We could at least wait for the prince at the next comfortable inn."

Lenore sighed. Her maid had a point. More to the point, it was likely that Vars was there already. Probably he'd decided that he had no more interest than the maid in waiting out in the mud, and the thought of beer or wine had drawn him on.

Then there was the thought of the cargo they carried. They only had the gifts from Royalsport and the nearest villages so far, but even so, it seemed like too much to be sitting out in the open with. Better to press on and wait surrounded by whatever walls the inn had.

"We'll keep going," Lenore called to the driver.

The carriage continued to bump its way down the road, while Lenore looked out and tried to find something different in the landscape. Probably Nerra could have told her the name of every tree, pointing out the differences as they went, but she wasn't here. Lenore hoped her sister was all right, and that Rodry had been able to find her.

She hoped a lot of things, because if there was one thing a lengthy carriage ride had time for, it was hopes and dreams. Lenore found herself hoping that the rest of the ride would be smoother, and that the people on the rest of the journey would love her as much as the ones before had. One of those hopes seemed more achievable than the other, given the way the carriage was jolting. She hoped Nerra would be found soon, and Erin, and that their father would forgive them both. She hoped her marriage to Finnal would be the perfect dream that the feasting with him had been, although why did that have to be a hope, when she couldn't imagine it any other way?

"Almost at an inn, your highness," the driver called out. Lenore looked out of the carriage, seeing the building ahead. It was a structure of painted wood and stone, with a thatched roof and a sign in front that had no words, only a picture of a celandine flower. A small stable stood next to the main building, obviously there to receive travelers, although there was no sign of the body of men that her brother was supposed to be bringing.

"We'll stop here," Lenore declared. Vars would find her more easily here than out on the open road if he'd missed her, and they would all be safer behind walls than in the open. Lenore could see the guards around her relaxing slightly at the news.

The driver pulled the carriage in front of the inn for Lenore to alight with her maids, and it struck her just how quiet the place was. Weren't inns normally bustling places, filled with the sounds of raucous celebration? Maybe she had that wrong; after all, Lenore spent far less time in such places than the likes of Vars or Rodry.

"I'll take the carriage to the stables, your highness," the driver said, a couple of the guards going with him to protect the goods they'd been given.

She walked in, surrounded by her maids and the remaining guards who had come with her, and immediately knew that something was wrong. There were people there, sitting in place, but they were far too still as other figures moved among them wearing steel and leather. Lenore hadn't seen enough of the stillness of death to know it by sight, but she could see the cut throats of the men there, the stab wounds and the marks of strangulation. Against the silence, she could hear the whimpers and cries of a woman from somewhere upstairs, and she knew that what was happening there was every bit as bad.

The living figures turned to her, and Lenore saw the marks of King Ravin's army emblazoned on the armor of men and women. They had a variety of weapons with them, from swords to strange, many bladed daggers, and they moved with a quiet coordination that terrified Lenore almost as much as the blades.

"Princess," one of the men said, "we had expected more men with you."

"Still, it makes it easy," one of the women said. "Means we don't have to poison a regiment."

"There is that," the man said.

"Who are you?" Lenore demanded, trying to sound braver than she felt, trying to buy time, or find a way to talk clear of this, or just understand. "How are you here?"

They shouldn't have been there; Southern soldiers shouldn't have been able to cross the bridges.

"Oh, we're the ones King Ravin has been putting in place for a while," the man said. "His best. One by one, over the bridges, in with the merchants. Men and women, because no one thinks a married pair will be killers." He smiled over at one of the women. "Isn't that right, dear?"

"Absolutely," she said. She looked at Lenore with a gaze that promised awful things. "Can I cut her?"

"You know the king's orders for her," the man said. "Suitably broken, suitably used before she's brought to him, but intact. I don't think that includes your games, Syrelle. You can have one of the others."

"Oh, I suppose so, Eoris. They all scream well enough in the end."

The man nodded, and that nod seemed to be a signal, because the others surged forward.

"Back, Princess!" one of the guards with her called, stepping forward to try to slow them, to give Lenore space in which to run.

He died.

He died so quickly that it didn't even count as a fight. Lenore had heard stories of heroic combats and seen her brother Rodry practicing with swords. This was nothing like that. There was no back and forth flash of blades, no witty talk, no chance for the guard. He was simply hacked down by a sword stroke so fast that Lenore barely saw it, while the rest of the southerners leapt at the other guards, thrusting blades into chests, dragging them across throats.

Lenore knew that her only hope was to run. She turned to do so, and saw one of her maids dragged to the floor by one of the soldiers, pinned there while she fought to get away. She saw a guard cut down, and in it all, Lenore wanted to help, but she couldn't; she couldn't persuade her body to do anything but run.

She ran, pushing her way clear of the inn, bursting out into the open sunlight with a scream that she hoped would attract the attention of any help nearby.

"We're under attack!" Lenore cried out, racing for the stables. There were still two more guards in the stables, along with the driver. She just had to pray that he hadn't unhitched the horses from the carriage yet, because right then the only hope was to flee. There was no hope to fight, not against foes like these. She sprinted for the stables, hoping she would be in time, hoping she would keep ahead...

Lenore reached the stables and saw the bodies there. The two guards lay on the ground where they had fallen, clearly cut down in seconds. The driver swung from a noose, legs still kicking as he died. Even as Lenore stared in horror, a man stepped from the shadows, dangling another length of rope

"Hmm, Eoris said that you might come this way," he said. "But I thought he was mistaken. Tell me, are you going to fight?"

"Please," Lenore begged, but all the time she was doing it, her hand was creeping down to her eating knife. "Please, I'll do whatever you—"

She lunged with it, hoping the element of surprise would make up for what she lacked in skill and strength. Instead, she found her opponent twisting aside, and that rope tangling with her hand, wrenching tight and ripping the knife from it. In another second, he'd somehow caught her other wrist, tying the two together behind her.

"Yes," he said. "You will. And then what all the others want, too. King Ravin was quite clear."

"Please," Lenore begged. As he threw her down to the stable floor, she found herself hoping, praying, that one of her brothers would arrive just in time to save her like something out of a song. It always happened like that, didn't it? They would be there, and they would save her, and …

Suddenly, a rope wrapped around her neck, forcing her to look up at the man who scowled down at her with pure hatred.

"Good," the man said. "Let's begin."

CHAPTER THIRTY NINE

Aurelle stretched out in the prince's bed, waiting to see if he would return to it, and to her. When it became clear that he wouldn't, she stood and dressed before heading down quietly through the castle. With the feast done, there weren't as many people to see where she went, but it also meant that there weren't as many to mask her comings and goings.

At least the guards in the castle were used to her now. They'd seen her on Prince Greave's arm, and that seemed to be enough to grant her license to leave without questions. She assumed it would get her back in when she needed to as well.

"Everything is fine," she told herself, but she looked behind her for the possibility of anyone following, just to be sure.

Her first stop was the alley where she'd hidden a cloak and a change of clothes: a plainer dress that wouldn't catch the eye, and shoes that were anything but delicate. There was a dagger there too, just in case she needed it. Aurelle dressed quickly, making sure no one was coming, then set off again, still checking for anyone following. Past a certain point, paranoia was simply a sensible precaution.

Out through the city she went, into the entertainment district, heading in the direction of the looming House of Sighs. It was the sort of place where someone who came and went normally could do so without attracting unwanted questions, without the risks that would come from a neighborhood filled with thugs and cutpurses. Aurelle would hate to have to kill someone; it would draw far too much attention.

She walked along, feeling the changing shapes of the cobbles of the streets as she went, making her way to a side door of the

House, one of those reserved for quiet entrances and exits. The House of Sighs was good at discretion. It made it such a perfect meeting place. She went in, heading for the usual room, a surprisingly simple one given the wealth of her... benefactor.

The arrangement of ribbons left on the door would have seemed like simple decoration to anyone else, but to Aurelle it was a sign carefully left, saying all was as it should be. The House of Sighs taught more than simply how to give oneself to those who paid, after all, at least for those with the talent for it.

Aurelle reached out and opened the door, stepping inside elegantly. Her employer was sitting on the bed, waiting for her, sharp eyes scanning her, lingering as they always lingered. Those hawk-like features lent a predatory edge to the movement.

Duke Viris stood, and Aurelle curtseyed elegantly. She knew he liked that.

"There is wine, if you wish it," Duke Viris said, gesturing to a bottle and two glasses. He took one, rolling it between his fingers. Aurelle took the other, sniffing it carefully. As far as she knew, the duke had no reason to poison her, but that was the problem—she would only know afterward.

"So," the duke said. "Is all going as I require?"

Aurelle nodded. "The prince is suitably distracted from thoughts of a cure. Your men were able to search the library while I kept him... busy, although they made a clumsy job of it."

"I'm sure your own efforts were far less clumsy," he said. "Did you have any problems with Greave?"

Aurelle laughed at that thought. "Hardly. Poor Prince Greave has been so starved of affection that he all but threw himself at me, even if he didn't know he was doing it."

"Good," Duke Viris said. "Is the prince suitably enamored of you?"

"All that and more," Aurelle said with a faint laugh. "You should see him: poor, sad Prince Greave, running around after me like an eager puppy."

"Just remember who gives the commands," Duke Viris said.

Aurelle nodded carefully. "Yes, my lord. You employ me."

"I do," the duke said. "Remember, the youngest son cannot be allowed to find a cure. The princess's illness, and all that King Godwin has done out of his love for her, will continue to drive a wedge between him and the nobles. With my son married to his daughter, when things reach the point that they are looking for a new king, my family will be in a position to take its place."

"As you say, my lord," Aurelle said. She filed away the reasoning, because it was knowledge worth having.

"You do not think it will work?" Duke Viris said.

Aurelle spread her hands. "I am sure that you have considered every possibility."

"I have. The king will be too tainted for having hidden his daughter's illness. Prince Rodry will no doubt do something rash. Prince Vars is sufficiently hated that none will side with him. You will act as I say against Prince Greave. Princess Lenore will be controlled by Finnal. Princess Nerra is banished. Princess Erin is off doing the kinds of dangerous things where she could easily meet an accident..."

"No doubt an arranged one," Aurelle said.

The duke flashed her a hard look and Aurelle instantly made her expression one of contrition.

"You play your part well," the duke said.

Her part: Aurelle Hardacre, sweet, innocent flower of a noble house, who had fallen instantly in love with her handsome prince and could barely bear to be parted from him. That Aurelle was the kind of figure the real Aurelle would have had nothing but contempt for, simpering and sheltered, with no understanding of the realities of the world.

"The House of Sighs did well, sending you to me," the duke said. She saw his glance across to the bed in the corner of the room. Most of the rooms in the House of Sighs had a bed.

"Thank you, my lord. I live to serve."

"And since you are paid for ..."

He drew her to him and kissed her, then pushed her back in the direction of the bed. Aurelle didn't tense at it. She could play this part as well as any other.

At least, until it became more advantageous to play a better one.

CHAPTER FORTY

Devin heard a dragon roaring, the sound of it filling the world around him. He was standing in a place where volcanoes filled the skyline, and winged shapes flew around them. He could see other things there, things that weren't human, things that were twisted out of shape and strange, things that could only exist in one place...

Sarras.

As if the thought had summoned it, his mind's eye conjured a map of the place, moving in and out so that he could see the jungles and the wastelands, the glassy spaces burned by dragon fire and the ash. Then the map became lines on an arm, a tattoo...

Devin was looking at a younger version of his father now, and there was another man with him, wrapped in a cloak. He was looking up at them, as if he were very small, and Devin had the feeling that this was more than some imagining; it was a memory.

"Take him, raise him. If I find any harm has come to him..."

"None will, my lord."

"The boy is special, born on the dragon moon, in that place. None can be allowed to know..."

Devin woke.

His head hurt, and the whole of the inside of his mouth felt like it was covered in fur. He looked around for the dragon, for the forest, for the youth who had spoken, because it had seemed so real that for a moment he had expected that they would still be there. Instead, he saw the interior of Sir Halfin's rooms, where he seemed to be wrapped up in furs in front of the fire.

There was a note there, left by the knight. *Gone hunting with the prince. Stay as long as you wish. Maybe learn to hold your drink better.*

Devin smiled at the knight's idea of a joke, and even that made his head ache. He rose, knowing he couldn't just wait here for the knights and the prince to return. For one thing, there was too much he still needed to do.

He hadn't managed to speak to Master Grey yet, and he suspected he wouldn't until the sorcerer was ready. Then there was the dream. It nagged at him, and Devin knew it wasn't just a dream. He'd been remembering, remembering things that had actually happened to him. If that was true though…that meant he wasn't who he had thought he was. He was someone else entirely.

He needed to talk to his parents.

Devin set off through the castle, seeing that while the servants were up, many of the nobles and commoners were still rising in the wake of the prematurely finished festivities. The servants were tidying away all the mess the feasting had created, which meant that Devin was able to slip out unremarked. He spared a glance for the tower belonging to Master Grey, knowing that he would have to return there soon. For now though, the only answers he wanted were at home.

Royalsport was starting to wake up around him, so Devin found himself hurrying, wanting to get home before his father left for work. He passed an apple cart and brushed it accidentally, sending one of the apples within to the ground. "Sorry," Devin called, and tossed the man one of his few coins.

"That's all right, milord," the man said, and it was only then that Devin realized what he must look like, still dressed in Halfin's spare clothes. He hurried on quickly. He was getting closer to home, crossing the bridges from one district to the next, moving from cobbled streets to stones and dirt, having to watch more carefully around him to make sure the spaces between the wattle and daub houses contained no cutpurses.

There were signs of activity when he reached the small house his family called home: smoke from the chimney and sounds of people moving around within. Devin opened the door and went inside to find his parents at the dinner table, almost as he had left them. It seemed strange to him that everything should just be a normal morning then, especially when he hadn't been home for ... well, days now.

His mother turned, and in that moment, Devin could see no real concern, only annoyance.

"Where have you been? Why are you dressed like one of the rich folk?"

His father stood up. "Well? Where have you been?"

"I've been up at the castle," Devin said. "They wanted me to work some special metal for them." He could have left it at that, but the dream demanded more. "I was traveling with Rodry and the knights."

"You were *what*?" his father said. "Who are you to go talking about your betters like that?"

"I don't know," Devin said, the words almost seeming to slip out. "Who *am* I?"

The words stopped his parents short. At least, the people he'd always thought of as his parents. In that moment though, he could see what was obvious: there was no resemblance there with him. There had certainly never been any love.

"What do you mean, who are you?" his mother demanded. "You're our son."

"Then why can I do magic?" Devin asked. "Why do I have dreams of being given to you? What happened on Sarras?"

His father stared at him then, his expression darkening. "I told them. I *told* them when they brought you to me that you were too dangerous, that you'd find out..."

He stepped forward, and instinctively, Devin flinched. How many times had his father lashed out when he was drunk? How many bruises had Devin suffered?

"Well, now that we know you're something twisted," his supposed father said, "at least I don't have to hold back anymore."

He lifted one meaty hand, fist closed, and Devin reacted on instinct. He knew the feeling of power rising up in him now, and once more the world around him seemed to slow as he saw it, understood it, saw all the things that he could do in it. He lifted one hand, feeling the power pulse up inside him, and it took all his control not to fling all of it the way he had with the wolves. Even so, it was enough to send his father flying back, tumbling into his chair and then over it, to lie looking up at Devin from the floor.

"Get out!" he yelled. "Get out, you monster!"

Devin left, mind still reeling from what had happened, barely able to comprehend how quickly he'd gone from asking questions to not having a home. Yet in another way, it *wasn't* quick, because it felt as though this had always been coming, as if everything had been heading this way Devin's whole life.

It didn't make anything feel any better, and he rushed out into the street, not knowing where he was going or what he was doing. And yet he did feel driven by something pulling him this way. What, he was not sure.

He was so caught up in the shock of the last few seconds that at first he barely noticed the fog that had swept up, surrounding him until he couldn't see the buildings on either side, and the world became a thing of shadows and echoes.

The city around him faded, so that Devin barely knew which way he was going. He could hear the sounds of it at first, but now even those started to be swallowed by the fog. Mists were common enough in a city intersected by so many river branches, but this … this felt like something different.

How long he walked, Devin didn't know. In a space like this, it seemed that time itself stood still, so that he walked forever between one heartbeat and the next. He thought again of his dream. And he felt that force pull and pull him.

And then he spotted something ahead where the mist thinned. It seemed to summon him.

He started toward it and eventually came out into a clearing. It stood in the midst of thick sections of what seemed to be a forest, far from any spot most people would find, and there seemed to be a cave entrance there. Someone had pushed rocks in front of that entrance, rock after rock until it was tightly sealed.

Devin could hear sounds coming from within, and he guessed that they must be those of an animal, except that they were like no animal he had heard before. There was snuffling and roaring and scraping there, as if something was trying to get out.

Except... he *had* heard those sounds before. He'd heard them in dreams. It sounded primal.

Dangerous.

He knew, with complete certainty, that he had to help the creature that was in there.

Devin started to pull away some of the cave's covering, and it was anything but easy. There were plant fronds covering it, and those were easy enough to remove, but the rocks there were larger and harder to shift. Devin had to squat to wrap his arms around them, and then shove them to the side one by one. He got several of them clear, and then something came out to swipe more out of the way: a claw.

Devin leapt back, and the dragon came out through the mouth of the cave. It looked almost exactly as it had been in his dreams. It was huge, but somehow Devin knew that it wasn't yet full grown. It towered over him, wings folded against its back, blue scales flickering with iridescent rainbow colors. The dragon was large enough that Devin half suspected it wouldn't be able to free itself from the cave, its body scraping against the side as it pulled itself clear. Devin heard the crack of shifting rock, and several rocks tumbled down around the dragon as it exited the cave.

More than that, it was growing larger. With every second that Devin watched, it seemed to be growing, and Devin's eyes shifted, letting him see the clouds of light and power flowing into it. He didn't know much about magic yet, but he knew that was what was fueling the growth of the dragon, making it bigger, turning it into something impossibly huge.

He could only stare at it as it towered over him, rearing up on its hind legs, with its wings stretching out, bat-like, in the sun. Its neck stretched up sinuously into the sky, and then came down, so that its head wove in front of Devin like a snake's before its prey. Its mouth opened wide, revealing teeth that would be able to bite through him without any effort at all, while its hind claws left gouges in the dirt as it moved. It roared at him then, in a sound that all but deafened Devin as he stood there.

The dragon stared down at Devin as if trying to work out exactly what he was. Huge, reptilian eyes stared down at him, flicking back and forth. A snakelike tongue flickered out as if tasting the air around Devin, then scraped across his skin. The dragon blinked, as if not quite understanding, then paused, as if listening to something that only it could hear.

It roared again, and those great wings beat at the air, producing a rush of wind that almost knocked Devin from his feet. He had to brace to keep standing as the dragon's wings beat again in great swings of leathery flesh. The first couple of wing beats seemed to be as if the creature were testing what it could do, but the next ones were more serious.

Devin saw the dragon's muscles bunch, and then it leapt into the air, taking off and soaring above the trees.

Devin stared after it, trying to make sense of it. He didn't know where the dragon had come from, or what it signified, but right here, right now, that wasn't what mattered.

What mattered was where it was going.

That he, Devin, had a role to play in whatever happened next.

That, somehow, he had unleashed it.

CHAPTER FORTY ONE

Nerra was held up only by the tree against which Bern was pinning her, holding her in place with one hand while the other was raised to strike.

"Where is the dragon?" he demanded.

Nerra shook her head. She wouldn't say, she *mustn't* say.

He struck her, and Nerra's ears rang, as it left her tasting blood.

"Won't be able to ransom her back if she's hurt too much," one of the others said.

"Think this is about ransom?" Bern shot back. "Try to do that with a princess, there's a rope waiting for your neck, or worse. We kill this one and lose the body when we're done, that's what we do. The *dragon* is the important thing."

All the more reason for Nerra to say nothing. They were going to kill her anyway, so it was better to hold on, to say nothing, and hope...

Hope what? That her father's men would rush in to save her? Given her sentence, her illness, they would probably kill her just as quickly even if they found her. She could hope that the growing weakness in her limbs claimed her before she could talk, but that was *all* she could hope.

Nerra could feel herself transforming, feel herself dying. Her body wasn't strong enough for this.

She found herself thinking of her siblings: Rodry, who was so quick to act, and Vars, who only acted when it was to his advantage. Greave, who had tried to help her, and Lenore, who would never really understand what it was like to be the younger sister of someone so perfect. Nerra half wished that Erin were here with that little spear of hers, ready to take on the world...

None of them were there though, and she was dying.

Her thoughts turned to the dragon, back in its cave. It was so tiny, so young. Would it be able to leave the cave? Nerra had done a good job of stopping the entrance, so if she died... *when* she died, it would be trapped, starving in the dark. That thought made her cling to life.

She stared up past Bern's shoulder, and that meant that she was the first to see the shadow flying above the forest's canopy.

At first, Nerra assumed she must be dreaming, because it was impossible.

But then the creature banked, and dove, and *landed.*

Men cried out as the dragon rose up over them, a baby still, yet flashing fierce yellow eyes.

The men of Bern's gang clustered together, some looking to their leader, others looking as though they might simply run.

That great, reptilian mouth opened wide, and then fire poured from it, white hot and sudden, flashing over the men without mercy, without hesitation. They screamed, but the heat was so great that it claimed even their screams. In just seconds, there was nothing left but ash.

Bern grabbed Nerra, dragging her in front of him so that he was between her and the dragon.

"It will kill you before it gets near me," he said, and Nerra could hear the fear in his voice then.

"You should be afraid," she whispered. She looked up at the dragon, knowing it was the same one she had found, even though it seemed impossible that it should have already grown so much.

You're beautiful, she thought.

The dragon leaned forward, tongue flicking out to taste the air. That tongue scraped across Nerra's skin like a rasp, and she wondered if it could taste her fear, her wonder. Then the dragon's mouth opened and flame darted, focused and precise and *hot*, past her head. Nerra heard Bern scream, and his grip loosened as he tumbled back from her.

Nerra fell forward, collapsing to the ground. She didn't have the strength to rise. She could only look up at the dragon above her, thinking how beautiful it was. The dragon stood there, and in spite of its size, it mewled like the baby it had been such a short time ago, nudging her with its snout as if trying to get her to rise.

"I ... can't," Nerra managed. "I'm dying."

The dragon paused, and Nerra wondered if it understood any of her meaning. It didn't matter, because Nerra could feel the world fading around her.

She fell, eyes closing.

And then she felt it.

Huge, cold claws wrapped themselves around her.

She felt herself being lifted, back arched, higher and higher.

A flap of wings, a rush of cold air.

She was flying.

Nerra managed to open her eyes, and she looked down to see the world rushing by beneath her. They flew just over the treetops, laced with fog, and it was the most beautiful thing she had ever seen. For a moment, just a brief moment, she had a flicker of hope.

And then her world was darkness.

Now Available for Pre-Order!

THRONE OF DRAGONS
(Age of the Sorcerers—Book Two)

"Has all the ingredients for an instant success: plots, counterplots, mystery, valiant knights, and blossoming relationships replete with broken hearts, deception and betrayal. It will keep you entertained for hours, and will satisfy all ages. Recommended for the permanent library of all fantasy readers."
—Books and Movie Reviews, Roberto Mattos (re *The Sorcerer's Ring*)

"The beginnings of something remarkable are there."
—San Francisco Book Review (re *A Quest of Heroes*)

From #1 bestseller Morgan Rice, author of *A Quest of Heroes* (over 1,300 five star reviews) comes the debut of a startlingly new fantasy series.

THRONE OF DRAGONS (Age of the Sorcerers—Book Two) tells the story of the epic coming of age of one very special 16 year old boy, a blacksmith's son from a poor family who is offered no chance of proving his fighting skills and breaking into the ranks of the nobles. Yet he holds a power he cannot deny, and a fate he must follow.

It tells the story of a 17 year old princess on the eve of her wedding, destined for greatness—and of her younger sister, rejected by her family and dying of plague.

It tells the tale of their three brothers, three princes who could not be more different from each other—all of them vying for power.

It tells the story of a kingdom on the verge of change, of invasion, the story of the dying dragon race, falling daily from the sky.

It tells the tale of two rival kingdoms, of the rapids dividing them, of a landscape dotted with dormant volcanoes, and of a capital accessible only with the tides. It is a story of love, passion, of hate and sibling rivalry; of rogues and hidden treasure; of monks and secret warriors; of honor and glory, and of betrayal and deception.

It is the story of Dragonfell, a story of honor and valor, of sorcerers, magic, fate and destiny. It is a tale you will not put down until the early hours, one that will transport you to another world and have you fall in in love with characters you will never forget. It appeals to all ages and genders.

Book three (BORN OF DRAGONS) is now available for pre-order.

"A spirited fantasy....Only the beginning of what promises to be an epic young adult series."
—Midwest Book Review (re *A Quest of Heroes*)

"Action-packed .... Rice's writing is solid and the premise intriguing."
—Publishers Weekly (re *A Quest of Heroes*)

THRONE OF DRAGONS
(Age of the Sorcerers—Book Two)

Did you know that I've written multiple series? If you haven't read all my series, click the image below to download a series starter!